# The Guardian
# Blood in the Sand

# MJ Kobernus

NORDLAND

www.nordlandpublishing.com

# COPYRIGHT

Published by Nordland Publishing 2015

ISBN Print:    978-82-8331-007-8
ISBN E-book: 978-82-8331-008-5

# ACKNOWLEDGMENTS

I would like to thank the many people that helped me along the way. From my family, who had to suffer endless nights of my ignoring everything around me, to my friends and colleagues who had to suffer endless days of my ignoring everything around me (or worse, actually talking about writing) and to those strangers that I would insist on telling all about my work, if they had the misfortune to ask me any question, or even, in some cases, to only acknowledge my presence.

To Katie Metcalfe, thank you for your input and guidance in the early stages of this book.

And especially to Chris Hegan, thank you for your persistence, and support in guiding the manuscript towards its final draft, for going the extra mile, and for helping me sound smarter than I am.

The following is not an exhaustive list by any means. But to the many people that helped catch the little, and not so little things, thanks to PamelaS., MarkN., AileenY., Hugh B.Long, ElenaS., PiaT., SimonB., CarolynW., Paul O., and of course the many people on Facebook that had to endure endless requests for liking this, or liking that. In addition, my thanks to T. Amundsen for taking the time, helping me to elevate the writing just that little bit.

And finally, thank you to Ashrash E. Shalaby, who did an amazing job on the book cover.

MJ Kobernus

# DEDICATION

*To my wife and family. Without whom I have nothing...*

# CONTENTS

MJ Kobernus

# Prologue

Elizabeth Sandwell sprang silently from the shadows, her naked form moving fast over the rough planking of the attic floor. By the time Philip Entwhistle saw her it was too late and she crooked an arm around his neck, pressing a knife against his throat. He froze, held rigid by fear as Sandwell chuckled with delight.

She positioned herself behind him, pulling him tight against her body while the cold steel cut into his flesh. She started to hum, a tune grotesquely familiar, while one hand caressed his face in time with the melody. The words came unbidden. *Mary, Mary, quite contrary.*

Still humming, she pulled his head back, exposing his throat. A flick of her right hand and warm blood trickled down his neck. He let out an involuntary groan, in equal parts pain and fear at the realization that the knife was no empty threat. Sandwell meant him harm. Right here, right now.

Dozens of gnarled tallow candles littered the floor, their feeble glow illuminating nothing. The pervasive chill sucked both heat and light from the room and a shiver coursed through Philip. Shadows moved, growing deeper. He felt certain there were things in them. Bad things.

Sandwell stopped humming, jerking his head to one side, her control of him total. He was her puppet. Out of the corner of his eye, he could see an iron spike had been placed over the old clay bowl. It sat in the center of an ornate pattern on the floor. An honest-to-God pentacle! The circle and star glowed, pulsing pale gold, its gentle rhythm like a heartbeat.

The absurdity of it all. His only concern lately had been a promotion, and now he was about to be killed by a twenty-first century witch. He made a sound halfway between a nervous snort and a laugh. Sandwell yanked his hair.

1

"Is it funny, Philip? Is this?" She pressed the blade harder. Another flash of pain as it sliced into him and the warm trickle became a stream.

"No!"

He tried to alleviate the pressure, pressing himself back against Sandwell's breasts; a parody of an embrace, his empty hands clenching impotently at his sides. She renewed her grip on his hair, jerking his head savagely. He had never felt so powerless.

She leaned in close. He could feel her hot breath, then, incredibly, her probing tongue in his ear. He recoiled in disgust and a line of fire lanced across his throat. Now it was Sandwell's turn to laugh. Blood flowed in a hot, steady stream, collecting in the hollow of his collarbone, soaking into his shirt. She was getting off on this, making him squirm. He stopped struggling. He would deny her the satisfaction.

"It's good to see you, Philip," she said. "I've waited a long time for this."

"Liz, I don't know what you're trying to do here," he tried to sound confident and failed, voice cracking with fear. "But if it's what I think, then I can't let you."

She laughed again, this time husky and low. He could feel her breath on his ear again, her voice almost a whisper.

"Let me? I don't see how you can stop me. I take what I want, when I want. You should know that by now."

He flinched. What she had done to him that night came back in a rush and he almost gagged. She laughed in delight at his reaction.

"Please, Elizabeth," he gasped, lips barely moving. "You don't need to do this."

"No," she said. "No. You're right, of course."

She pulled back and relief flooded through him. Then the hand in his hair tightened and her body pressed hard against his.

"But I want to."

He could hear the smile in her voice as she drew back the blade.

# For every start, there is an end

## 1

Be happy for this moment, for it is your life.
*—The Rubaiyat of Omar Khayyam*

Five weeks previously . . .

It was the third day and he had nothing. Philip Entwhistle picked up another book from the pile on the reading desk, decades of dust threatening to bring on another round of sneezing.

For three years he had been working on a biography of Sir James Francis, the renowned linguist, explorer, occasional spy and, if the accounts were true, notorious womanizer. However, after countless dead-ends, the explorer's fate remained a mystery. Philip was close to giving up. Whatever eventual end Sir James had encountered would probably never be known.

Philip sighed, exhaustion etched into his features as he rubbed his temples against an incipient headache. It didn't help and he carried on reading. He was astute enough to know that his obsession with Sir James was in part because the man was everything he was not: capable, confident, daring, his life an adventure. His disappearance in the Sudan in the 1920s exerted a hold over Philip's imagination. In his gut, he was certain Sir James had not died there, and he was going to prove it. Time. He needed time. He would just have to hope he had bought enough of it.

The previous day, the Head of Department had called him in for a meeting. Philip had found Sam Evans reading undergrad applications in his office.

"Hello, Philip. Come in, take a seat."

Evans dropped the papers into a pile teetering on the edge of his ancient oak desk. Philip always felt as if he were stepping back in time when visiting Sam in his den. The walls were lined with leather bound volumes, including a first edition of Gibbon's *Rise and Fall of the Roman Empire* and Pope's translation of *The Odyssey*. Apart from the sheer value of the collection, history was somehow more *focused* in Sam's room.

Philip settled into the only guest chair, a maroon leather chesterfield. Sam smiled, ran a hand through thinning hair and adjusted the spectacles perched on the end of his nose. He gestured to a bottle of sherry and cluster of small glasses on a nearby bookcase.

"Drink?"

"No thanks," replied Philip. "But don't let me stop you."

The older man nodded. "I never do, dear boy. I never do."

It had scarcely gone eleven but by the rosy glow on his cheeks, Philip suspected that Evans subscribed to the maxim that the sun was over the yardarm *somewhere* in the world.

"Alright then, to business. You know why I asked you here?"

"I assume it has something to do with the Associate Professorship."

Philip observed his boss carefully, suppressing the urge to fidget. It had been a while since he had published anything of note, so Evans' recommendation was critical if he was to have any chance of the promotion.

"Indeed. As you know, I'm on the selection committee. I'm afraid you're up against a strong candidate and, if I may be frank, you've been a bit spotty of late. I'm not sure I can, in good conscience, support you. I just don't want to see you waste your time or get your hopes up. The smart money is on that parawhatsit woman."

"Sandwell."

"Yes, that's right. You still have some, uh . . . bad blood there, I take it?"

That was one way of putting it. Somehow his work on Disraeli had gone missing—from inside a locked office. No evidence of a break-in, nothing else missing, but someone had taken all his research notes. And if that was not bad enough, there was also the computer virus that had eluded his usually meticulous defenses, wiping his hard disk clean and leaving him empty-handed. Then, weeks later, Sandwell published a paper on Disraeli's meeting with a Sufi mystic, a fact that Philip had discovered and shared with no one.

Against his better judgment he confronted her, asking about the 'startling coincidence.' She had just laughed in his face.

"You know I don't trust her, Sam, and frankly, nor should you."

"What exactly do you have against her?"

Philip shrugged. It was a question he had asked himself on more than one occasion. Without wanting to sound paranoid, he was of the opinion that it was Sandwell who had a grudge. When he had first arrived at the University, she had been cautious around him, as if wary of saying or doing something wrong. Even now, whenever they met, there was a distinct frostiness, both of them compensating by being overly polite.

"You know my suspicions regarding that paper. But, well . . . she seemed to have it in for me long before that."

"Hmm. Perhaps it's a case of the less said and so forth? Anyway, Sandwell is the strongest applicant. There is a third, but I don't give him much of a chance, really. Congreve-Symmonds, the linguist chappy. So, you might have to come to terms with Elizabeth Sandwell as a senior faculty member."

Philip snorted, but he was not going down without a fight. "Look Sam, I just need a little more time. Sir James Francis left Khartoum alive and I'm going to prove it. Cracking that little mystery and finishing his biography would put me back in the running, surely?"

Sam proffered a tight smile. With a slight shake of his head, as if he might regret his next words, he leaned forward. "Well, that would be something, *if* you can prove it."

He reached for the sherry bottle and a glass and poured himself a liberal dose. "Francis disappeared without trace, correct?"

Philip nodded. Sam continued to regard his protégé, then gave him a slow nod.

"Okay. Find some solid support for your theory and I'll back you. You're a fine researcher with a good track record and you write well, if a trifle dramatically for my taste. Of course, if you want to sell a book these days, you need to give them what they want. Panem et circenses, eh?"

*Bread and circuses.* Both men smiled at the quip, then Evans knocked his drink back in one swift swallow.

"What you need is a Hail Mary, as they say in the colonies," he said, cheeks flushing. "It had better be damned convincing, or . . ." Sam shrugged.

Philip knew exactly what he meant. As things stood, Sandwell was a virtual shoo-in. With nothing else on the horizon, the Francis biography was his only shot at the professorship, and once that was his, whatever the reason for Sandwell's silent vendetta against him, he would at least be secure in his position in the department.

So he was down to digging through the stacks. He had long ago exhausted all the likely primary documents. Letters, legal records, even ship manifests. Now, with nothing left but dogged determination, he was praying for a clue in a secondary source – translations of epistolary collections and journals, anything. Many of the originals were Arabic, translated as an academic exercise but never read. Even if they had been, perhaps the connection between a white man who spoke fluent Arabic and Sir James had been missed. After all, he could blend in like no other European.

Philip put another book on the discard pile. Hundreds of such translations had piled up in the archives over the years, too low on the list of priorities for digitizing. He wiped his hands on his trousers, wrinkling his nose at the pungent smell of mildew and vanilla from the dusty books.

Sighing, he picked up yet another translation. Flipping open the cover, he ran his eye down the publisher's information.

An Account of the Extraordinary Events Leading to the
Failed Rebellion of the Saharan Nations
Translated from the Arabic, with copious notes, by
REGINALD FORTESCUE
A NEW IMPRESSION IN THREE VOLUMES
Vol. I

The failed rebellion, an attempt to unite the North African tribes and oust the Europeans. He opened a page at the back, relieved to find an index. He scanned it quickly, looking for the name *Francis*. Yet again, the familiar sense of disappointment. Then something caught his eye. A name: Pasha Ibn Musaafir, Damascus. The hair on his neck prickled. Could it be? Francis had often traveled in disguise and one of his many personae was as a Pashazada from Damascus. This was not a name he had used before, but still, it was something. Quickly finding the referenced page, he began to read the entry.

*One of the scouts returned, reporting he had met a lone traveler. By account, a Pasha from Damascus on a personal haj. He had been robbed in the desert and left for dead. This would not be of any interest, except the scout reported that the Pasha wrote in a small book. He said the script was peculiar, being neither Arabic nor Ottoman. According to the scout, the Pasha spoke Arabic and understood the Berber tongue well, for all that he claimed he had been learning it only a matter of months. The scout also said his eyes were blue and I have a suspicion he could be French, and have given orders to have him located and brought in for questioning.*

As he read, Philip's heart beat faster and his exhaustion fell away. The report was in a letter sent to the commander of the rebel forces in the Atlas Mountains. An account of a man who spoke Arabic as well as the Berber tongue, and most crucially had been *learning it for only a matter of months*. James Francis was a renowned linguist. A gifted polyglot. Could he have been in the Sahara? Philip checked the year the report was written, hardly daring to hope: August, 1922. But the account said his eyes were blue and that did not match. Sir James Francis had brown eyes. He would need to verify that.

And yet it fit. The dates were right, the description was plausible, there was the mention of linguistic ability, and the clincher was the man wrote in a non-Arabic script. He was keeping a journal! Another facet of Francis' character was that he kept copious notes on his travels and wrote a great many letters. One of the methods used to pinpoint his location was the franking on the letters he had sent over the years. Sir James, an erudite man, kept up correspondence with a surprisingly diverse group of people. As a result, his thoughts and observations from his travels had been preserved, throwing light on a great many topics, particularly his views on colonialism.

However, the letters stopped abruptly in March 1922. He simply vanished. It was inconceivable that a man like Sir James Francis could just disappear, unless he wanted to. Yet no contemporary sources indicated anything after Khartoum. Until perhaps *now*.

Philip smiled as he read the entry again. If this was indeed Sir James, then he was the first to know the man's whereabouts in nearly a century. This was his Hail Mary!

The sudden click-clacking of high heels on a wooden floor startled him and he looked up from the book, frowning. He had thought the place empty but those footsteps were a sound he knew all too well. Thrusting his prize into his satchel, he hurriedly started to pack his notebook and pens.

The footsteps grew louder. Now he could hear humming; a children's song or rhyme. Elizabeth Sandwell turned the corner of the shelf unit nearest his desk. She smiled broadly at discovering him, her even, white teeth bright in the shadowed hall. She had pulled her copper hair back into a ponytail and her clear skin and pale eyes contrasted with her dark designer jacket. Philip met her gaze briefly and countered with the barest of nods.

"Hello, Dr. Entwhistle," she said. "What are you doing here?"

He didn't look at her as he tied the straps on his satchel and began tidying the books on the table. "Oh, hello, Dr. Sandwell. Just reading some of the more obscure North African stuff."

For a parapsychologist she seemed to have an inordinate amount of interest in certain historical figures and had cornered him more than once to question him about his research.

"I see," she said. "Anything interesting?"

She glanced at the books on the table, moving in closer to get a better look. Not that they would mean much to her, but so much the better if she wasted half her day combing through them. He took a step back as she brushed past, the smell of chamomile and strangely, caraway, enveloping him.

"No. Not really. I'm done for the day, so the table is yours. I'll put the books on the trolley and be out of your way."

"No, that's okay. Leave them," she said with a sniff. "One of the staff will take care of them."

He edged away from her, clearing his throat of her cloying perfume. A line from a poem by Kipling popped into his mind: *More deadly than the male.*

She closed in on him and he backed up further, the smile she proffered now more artificial than the first. It's the eyes, he thought. They don't smile, even when her mouth does. There was something more than a little odd in the timing too, her turning up just as he found something.

Was she watching him? He stepped past her, plastering on a false smile of his own.

"Well, I have a class starting soon, so I have to run."

"Of course, Philip. I have a lecture too. No time for chit chat."

He walked quickly towards the exit from the hall. Before he turned the corner at the end of the final row of shelves, he glanced back. Sandwell may not have time to chit chat, but she had time to read the titles of all the books he had left. He turned, making his way to the front desk where he stopped to talk to the librarian. It would have been easier if he had walked out with the book. There were no electronic tags on anything from the stacks but the thought never occurred to him. Books were sacrosanct.

"Hello," he said. "Do you think that I can borrow this? Just for a day or two." He took out the *Failed Rebellion* and passed it to the tall raven-haired woman behind the counter. She must be new, he had never seen her before.

She was his height and slim, her long hair tied back. A scar that pulled her upper lip into a semi-sneer on one side failed to detract from her good looks. He briefly met her gray-blue eyes then looked away.

"This is from the stacks," she said. Her voice had an unusual lilt. Was she Welsh?

"Yes," he replied.

"You can't borrow those. They're research only."

"I know, I know. But I need it. I think it might contain valuable material requiring independent verification. I can't do that here." He gave her a hopeful look and proffered his University ID. She took it, examined it briefly, smiled and shook her head.

"No, I'm sorry, but . . ."

"What if I get my department head to make a request for the book to be reassigned to the reading library," he said in a rush.

She looked at him levelly for a moment, then a slight smile tugged at her lip.

"Of course, that would be fine. I could hold it for you until then."

"I don't have time to wait for the paperwork," he said. "Let's just work on the premise that the book will be transferred to general reading. But I need to take it now. When I return it, the paperwork will be in order, and no one will be any the wiser."

"No, I don't think so."

"I understand your position," he said, looking her in the eye, "but could you make an exception? It would mean a lot . . ." He trailed off, wilting before her raised eyebrow. He tried one last gambit. "Perhaps I could make a photocopy then? Just a couple of the pages."

Embarrassed, he stared down at the desk already accepting defeat.

"Alright, Dr. Entwhistle. I'll make a rare exception. You can have it for two weeks. Not a day longer. Don't make me come after you. We know where you live, you know."

He looked up in rank surprise. "Thanks! Fern, is it?" he said, glancing at the ID on the chain around her neck. "You're the best!"

"Yes, I am. But you still have to sign it out." She quickly wrote the details on a slip of paper from a drawer.

Philip signed with a flourish, gave her a shy glance, and was rewarded with a dazzling smile in return.

He left the hall with a spring in his step, descending the great staircase and out onto the campus, one hand firmly on his satchel and the precious volume within. Squinting in the bright sunlight, he made straight for the faculty parking. He did not have a class but Sandwell would not know that. Fishing his keys from his pocket he made a beeline for what was unquestionably the oldest and rustiest car in the parking lot, his mid-seventies Vauxhall Viva. He prayed it would start. There was someone he needed to talk to; the one person who might know if the Pashazada in the report might possibly be Sir James. Unfortunately it was someone who had previously refused every request for an interview.

But it seemed as if this was his lucky day. Maybe it would hold. Philip turned the key. The engine groaned but did not start. So much for luck.

"Come on, don't do this to me now!"

He tried again, and this time the engine caught, firing up with a rattle and a pop.

"Good girl!" With a smile, Philip pulled out of the car park.


Elizabeth Sandwell entered the auditorium behind a group of students. She loved this room. She almost felt happy when she addressed a full auditorium, with all eyes upon her.

Students continued to trickle in. Two dozen at most, sitting in sporadic groups of twos and threes with the usual loners occupying single spaces. Her lecture would be far from full today, it seemed.

Sandwell crossed to the lectern and gazed out at the students. Her course on primitive belief systems always started out popular. The prospectus indicated fieldwork, frequently taken to mean wild parties in the woods, but students who took that approach failed. She demanded diligence and a good understanding of comparative beliefs, encouraging the undergrads to take Professor Litmore's class on the Anthropology of Religion alongside her own on Shamanism and Animism. She demanded a lot and those expecting an easy credit met disappointment.

She needed neither notes nor laptop, as this was a lecture she had given many times. Looking out at the faces, she caught the eye of one or two students in the closer rows.

"Good afternoon, everyone. So glad you could make it. We seem to have lost a few of our number to the sun but never mind, we shall just have to make do."

Her lectures promised an interesting and unique perspective on pop culture. Although devoid of lurid fantasy, her expositions of the underlying beliefs and superstitions popularized on television and in the movies, guaranteed high enrollment in her classes. However, few anticipated the serious effort required and by midterm there was a marked drop-off in attendance.

"OK, let's get started. You should all have read Kendall, chapters nine through twelve. Are we all up to speed?" Most nodded, pulling the text from their bags. She spotted one young man frowning as he turned to mutter to his companion.

"Brent Ellis, isn't it?" she said, addressing him. He shifted in his chair, trying not to meet her gaze.

"Uh, yeah?"

"I take it from your demeanor, that you have not, in fact, prepared for this lecture."

"Uh, no," he said. "I didn't have time."

"Yeah, too busy getting laid," his friend chimed in.

Sandwell's gaze did not flicker. "Mr. Ellis, if you are not prepared to do the work then please do not waste your time or mine."

That would have been that as far as she was concerned. But then Ellis muttered to his friend again, who sniggered quietly. Sandwell's eyes narrowed at the obvious affront.

"Mr. Ellis, if this *Ice Queen*, as you so charmingly referred to me, did indeed defrost, then believe me, you are the last person on earth I would let 'do' me."

The young man's face went slack from shock. He squirmed in his seat, looking around to his friend who suddenly found the ceiling to be of profound interest. Many of his fellow students laughed as Ellis flushed a violent red. He whispered something else to his friend, too dim to realize that Sandwell could lip-read. She may have let the first comment slide but the second was beyond the pale. She would teach him some manners, but not with every eye upon her. First the lecture, *then* the lesson. She looked to her audience.

"Anyone not prepared to do the work, kindly do yourselves and me a favor and leave now."

Forty minutes later, a scattering of applause greeted the conclusion of her lecture, much to her pleasure. Not from Mr. Ellis or friend, she noted. As the students began to file out, Ellis threw one last look in her direction. His eyes narrowed, mouth forming a word that needed no lip-reading skills. Her own eyes narrowed in turn. With a practiced hand she traced a pattern on the lectern, chanting almost silently, her eyes fixed on the boy's back as he climbed the steps. He had almost reached the top when her index finger inscribed a small circle in the air. She clenched her fist hard to complete the ritual. Immediately a subtle smell, like ozone, told her energies were in play.

Brent Ellis tripped and fell, cascading down the stairs. Students jumped out of the way as he tumbled past. Then his foot caught in a chair, bringing his descent to an abrupt stop with a sound like the snapping of a dry branch. He screamed.

"My leg. Oh my God, I think it's broken!" His face was ashen, the words coming between gasps of pain.

Sandwell joined the milling, gabbling crowd of students that quickly surrounded him, herself the picture of calm. The lecturer picked a girl and snapped her fingers in front of her face.

"You. Go find the nurse. And hurry."

Another student had removed his phone and was busy filming Ellis. He was concentrating on holding his makeshift camera steady, while slowly panning to take in the entirety of the scene, including her. That would not do. Sandwell gave him a look and he sheepishly put the phone back in his pocket. As the girl ran off, Sandwell leaned down to the wailing boy. His hands clenched around his leg above the shard of white bone jutting through skin. She whispered in his ear, too low for anyone to hear but him.

"Who's the bitch now, Mr. Ellis?"

Then she stood and turned to the boy with the phone. "Call an ambulance," before proceeding up the steps, a slight smile on her lips.

The candle flared to life under Fern Aasheim's hand. She did not use a match. That was not necessary for a witch of her ability. As offerings went, the flame was tiny, but like most things it was the intent that counted.

She turned to her guests. Two women, one a few years older than herself, the other almost twice her age. Her sisters, her circle. She was the Maiden, Alicia the Mother and Tessa the Crone. She smiled as she sank gracefully to the floor, facing them, assuming the lotus position with practiced ease. The smell of fresh baked bread permeated the tiny apartment and both her guests glanced to her small kitchenette with more than idle curiosity.

"What is that spice," Alicia asked, sniffing the air. "It's cinnamon and . . ."

"Pecan," supplied Fern.

"Interesting," said Tessa. "I assume it's for us."

Fern chuckled. "It is. But business first. Something happened at the University today. I didn't think it should wait until the next meeting."

Fern's voice had a distinct musical quality. Her English was fluent but clearly not her mother tongue. She adjusted her hand-knit sweater of undyed, gray wool, tugging it to cover her bare feet.

Alicia and Tessa both sat on a small, beige couch; a foldaway sofa bed that managed to be equally uncomfortable whatever its guise. It was also practically the only furniture in the small room, apart from an overflowing bookcase filled with books about magic. There was a tall lamp and a number of cushions which did double duty as chairs. Alicia was a slight woman, with brown hair, cut short. Her tiny size belied her strength of will however, a fact to which her two young boys could attest. She stared down at Fern intently, her habitual good humored smile disappearing as she waited for Fern's news.

The other woman was Tessa Richards – fifty something, stout, graying hair in a tight bun – she had been both Maiden and Mother in her time. Now she looked like someone's grandmother. Someone's *stylish* grandmother. Regardless of her role in the circle as the Crone, that did not mean she couldn't look good. Although Tessa was often taciturn, she had a warm heart and would do anything for friend and stranger alike.

But she could maintain her equanimity for only so long. She leaned forward, eager. "The meddler?" she said. "Are you saying you succeeded?" Succeeded where she had failed went unspoken. There was no animosity or resentment in her voice. The circle had no room for ego.

Fern nodded. "I felt her today, stronger than ever. She is definitely in the University. You were right about that, Tess."

"I knew it," replied the older woman. She leaned back on the sofa, a look of vindication on her face. "I don't have your sensitivity, but I knew."

There had been some clues, things that only another witch would see. But they formed a pattern, one that suggested that someone was practicing the black arts.

That was why Fern had taken the job at the library. Even though she was a recent adept in the circle, placing her talent inside the campus was inspired. Since Tessa Richards was head of Human Resources, it was no problem. Fern would find the rogue practitioner; the coven would do the rest.

"Very good, Fern," said Alicia. "Now, put a name to her. We might need to take . . . *measures.*"

Fern blinked. Measures? Yes, of course. The meddler was a danger to herself and others. She took a deep breath.

"I'll find her. Now that I've felt her energy I can do it again. Soon, I'll be able to see her and that will be that."

"And she you," said Tessa. "We don't know anything about this woman, or what she's capable of, so be careful."

Fern was keen to show the coven her dedication, prove her value. She would do whatever was needful. But another matter required attention.

"Actually, there's something else. I need to move house now, so that complicates things for me."

Tessa raised an eyebrow and looked around the small one room apartment. "Oh, how come?"

"My landlord has split with his wife. He needs the place back for himself. I've been here almost a year but we agreed it was only temporary. Anyway, something closer to campus will make it easier to track the hedge witch, after hours."

Tessa frowned, pursing her lips. "You're sure she is a hedge witch? That she's acting alone?"

"Definitely. Isolated energy. Certainly not a coven."

Tessa nodded. "Good. That should certainly simplify matters."

Simplify matters if they have to take measures, thought Fern. She shivered, her arms coming up with goose bumps. Her coven were good people but they could not condone the use of the black arts. Should this rogue witch prove to be . . . difficult, their *measures* would not all be pleasant.

"Just be careful, Fern," said Alicia. "This is not someone dabbling. If she's doing what we think then she won't hesitate to harm you."

Fern nodded and breathed calm into her rapidly beating heart. She was no novice and knew how to protect herself from malign energies. Even so, she said a quick prayer to the Goddess. She was Fern Aasheim, *the hunter*. She just needed to make sure she didn't become the prey.

"Right," said Alicia, "now how about that bread?"

# For every hope or dream we rend

## 2

My story is of such marvel that if it were written
with a needle on the corner of an eye,
it would serve as a lesson to those who seek wisdom.

*—The Arabian Nights*

As a result of his single, tenuous clue, Philip had called the last living descendant of the Francis line, an old man who lived only an hour from the city. At first the conversation had gone badly and it was clear he was going to be shot down, until Philip explained why he needed to solve the mystery surrounding the man's illustrious ancestor.

"You're simply my last chance, Mr. Francis. If I don't finish the work not only will I have wasted three years of my life, but I'm going to be passed over for a promotion that I really want. I can't tell you how much."

"Why not," came the reedy voice of Mr. Francis. "Let me hear your reasons."

"Why I need to finish the biography?"

"Why you want that promotion."

Philip had been surprised at the request. Nonetheless he spoke of his relationship with his colleague, and how she seemed to have a running vendetta against him. Mr. Francis remained unimpressed.

"I don't see how that should matter to me," he said.

Philip could feel the conversation slipping away from him. If he could not get an interview and validate his hypothesis, then his position at the University would be more tenuous than ever. Sandwell would get the promotion and that would be that. He sighed.

"Look," Philip said. "Cards on the table. Without your help, Dr. Sandwell will get the professorship. As much as that galls me, I just want to know what happened to Sir James. I am certain he left Khartoum."

"Sandwell? Did you say Sandwell?"

"Yes."

"Why don't you come by for tea? Shall we say three O'clock?"


Never look a gift horse in the mouth, thought Philip as he arrived at what he hoped was the right address. Mr. Francis had seemed to recognize Sandwell's name. Philip was in no doubt that mentioning her was the reason for the invitation. He parked in the quiet country lane and locked his car. Although older than him, it did not have the cachet of being a vintage collectible. Still, he'd kept it on the road and running when most people would probably have scrapped it. Philip felt oddly proud of that, as if he were saving a piece of the past. Besides, he could not afford anything newer.

The drive out of the city was very pleasant, invoking memories from his childhood. Philip had grown up in a small town, surrounded by green fields. He missed the open spaces. City life was fine, but his spirit was not there.

Now he found himself in the heart of the country – working farms, a small village and the occasional cottage peppered the landscape. A large barn a mile back had caught his attention. It looked to be hundreds of years old. If so, it was in surprisingly good condition, with the irregular planks freshly painted and great wrought-iron hinges still black and shiny as if newly oiled.

Horses roamed freely in a nearby paddock. One wandered over, curious at the interloper. Philip smiled. This was what the countryside was all about, fresh air and mind where you step. He smoothed his jacket, straightened his already-straight tie, set his shoulders and crossed the lane.

He had pulled off the road opposite the only house in sight, an old whitewashed stone cottage. A Constable painting come to life, it even had an old cartwheel leaning against a wall.

He took in the well-ordered garden, the trimmed hedges and knife-edged lawn borders. Gravid fruit trees, bursting with apples and pears added color, and the serried rows of the gray thatch on the roof gave the cottage an air of ancient continuity, as if it had always been there, a part of the landscape.

Philip took a deep breath to calm his nerves. He hoisted his leather satchel over his shoulder and fished a folded piece of paper from a pocket. He glanced at the smudged address, barely legible under the stains and brown rings from the tea spilt on it the previous night. Reassured, he strode up the path to the great red door. The numbers three and two shone in brass, prominent above an ornate bronze knocker.

Even without the address, he would have guessed this was the house. Although green and black with age, under the grime and verdigris of the doorknocker, he made out the finely cast face of a fiercely bearded, turbaned man with a hooked nose. The whiskers of the mustache and beard flowed down into a loop under the chin, creating a handle. This was a puzzle. Distinctly Arabic in origin, intricately cast – but a human face, a representation of Allah's creation, strictly forbidden by the Quran.

He raised the knocker and let it fall. No sound within. Tried again, this time harder. A full half minute went by before he could hear shuffling. A moment later, with a clatter of locks and deadbolts, the great door opened. A pair of piercing, clear blue eyes looked up at him from an old man's face, crazed and deeply lined as if someone had written his life in his features with a heavy pen. Another disconcerting puzzle – those eyes, shining with a vitality that belied their years belonged in a much younger face.

The old man opened the door wider, revealing a collarless shirt, several sizes too big, and slacks held up by braces. A pendant hung from a silver chain around his neck, an ensemble of little triangles, each joined to the next creating a shape suggesting a cross, or perhaps an ankh. The old man fingered it idly while peering up at his visitor.

"Hello. Mr. Francis? My name is Philip Entwhistle. We spoke on the phone."

The old man gave no sign of recognition but carried on regarding him with an expression of shrewd interest, like an owl staring at a vole. Then, as if a light were switched on, his face cracked into a beaming smile.

"Oh yes, the historian. Come in, come in."

With a gesture that seemed to mean enter he turned and shuffled slowly back along the narrow, murky passage, past a gallery of portraits in ornate gilt frames. Philip followed, after first wrestling the heavy door closed. Yet the old man, bent and frail as he was, had seemed to handle it without effort.

Philip admired the oils hanging from the walls. Heavily bearded men in stovepipe hats, women with pinched waists and enormous bell-shaped dresses; figures from a forgotten world.

One portrait stopped him, the face immediately familiar. The heavy moustache, drooping at the ends, the fierce, predatory gaze. The eyes though, were wrong, deeply blue, although this was certainly Sir James himself, posing beside a fine black horse, with a flintlock pistol of all things tucked into the wide crimson sash tied around his waist.

But those eyes. Artistic license, possibly, but the eyes were blue. The book in his satchel had also reported blue eyes, yet all the other sources were clear: Sir James had brown eyes. It was very strange.

Philip leaned in to examine the painting in detail, finding more incongruities. The pistol, with intricate, swirling patterns picked out in mother-of-pearl on the long handle was a good hundred and fifty years out of place. And then there was the horse. Growing up in the countryside, one learned something of horses. The horse was small and fine-boned, with the characteristic flare at the nostrils that meant it had to be an Arab thoroughbred, prized for its speed. When and where was this painted?

Oddities apart, something nagged. A detail out of place perhaps, that he could not put his finger on. He squinted, peered, then shook his head.

The sound of running water pulled him back to the present, drawing him to the kitchen where he found his host setting out cups and saucers on the slab-like pine table.

"How about a cup of tea, Mr. Entwhistle. And while the kettle boils you can fill me in on your project."

He set an old, dented copper kettle on the stove. Like much in the house it had seen better days, an ill-fitting newer steam whistle jammed onto its blunt spout. Philip nodded, hung his satchel from the back of the plain pine chair and sat.

"Certainly, Mr. Francis. My pleasure."

While his host readied cups and saucers, Philip steepled his fingers and began. "As I mentioned I am writing a book about your great-uncle, Sir James."

Francis nodded, spooning fine black tea leaves into an ornate teapot.

Philip paused for a breath. It was now or never. "Your great-uncle's life is well documented. Very well – until Khartoum, that is. After that, nothing. But I have just come upon a reference to an unnamed man who could fit his description. It was near the Atlas Mountains in 1922. August to be more precise."

As he warmed to his subject he grew more confident, his voice smoother, more assured.

"I have written several articles about his life and times. It's my specialty. Biographies from the eighteenth- and nineteenth-century. I published a rather well-received bio of Saad Zaghloul last year. Perhaps you know it?"

The old man shook his head. Philip continued.

"Well, Sir James has always fascinated me. You know he met with Zaghloul in Egypt, just before they declared independence?"

"Yes. Yes, I know. It is in his letters. At one of Princess Nazli's infamous soirées."

Francis smiled, his eyes distant. Philip nodded, silently concurring with the old man's characterization of the Princess; infamous. A perfect foil for Sir James and certainly a character, a friend even of Kitchener's, another of Philip's historical interests. Several worthies of the time recorded their impression of his attendance at the Princess' party in Cairo in 1920. Sir James wrote of it himself in a letter to his cousin, now in the British Museum along with most of his other correspondence: Philip's primary sources, exhaustively researched. Not one contained a word, a hint, of his eventual fate. The hundreds of academics who had plumbed their depths over the years were in agreement. Sir James had vanished, literally without trace.

"Well, I came across a report by rebels in the Atlas Mountains which referred to a man writing in a non-Arabic script. A journal, perhaps, or a diary? If it was Sir James, what was he doing there? I want to know. I want to publish the first account of his Saharan adventures. Of course, to date, there has been no evidence of what he did, where he went or whom he met. It's all a mystery. This report contains the only reference to him for almost half a year, if it *was* him. The record stops in Khartoum with his disappearance. It is generally assumed he died around March, 1922. If he didn't, I want to know where he went and why. End all the supposition."

He took the book from his bag and laid it on the table, opening it to the page with the scout's report. The kettle's soft whistle rose to a squeal and Francis whisked it off the range, poured the steaming water into a teapot and returned the kettle to the stove. A sleek black cat appeared in the doorway, evidently used to the routine of tea and biscuits, which possibly meant milk for her.

Philip smiled to himself. A classically-conditioned cat, like one of Pavlov's dogs. The cat stalked into the kitchen and eyed him with disdain as if it could sense his thoughts, then contented itself by winding around its owner's legs.

"So," said Mr. Francis. "What he was doing in his last months? Is that it? What makes you think I would know?" He took an old clay bowl down from the windowsill and placed it on the floor, then scratched the cat, absentmindedly.

"To be honest I'm just out of ideas. I hoped you might have some suggestions on where to look next. I've exhausted every source I have access to. There is simply nothing left. Now I've found something that *might* be relevant," he tapped the book on the table, "but it's obscure, to say the least. So I hoped you might know something, anything."

Francis placed a fine china cup and saucer before Philip, then sat, holding his guest's gaze, blue eyes boring into green. Then, what seemed a decision. He gave a brief nod.

"I have to say, he was an interesting man. When did you say?"

"It would be 1922. Four months after he left Khartoum."

"I see. His last trip then. I suppose you must be thinking of his travels with the Tuareg."

Philip leaned forward eagerly. "The Tuareg?"

"Oh yes. I heard about that, as a boy. There was even a diary, you know. Papa mentioned it once. He called it uncle's great secret. He rarely talked about it. I'm sure it's long gone."

His mind seemed to drift, searching for a long-lost memory. He frowned in concentration as he tried to grasp at his distant childhood.

"He said . . . he said it was full of blood and sand. That was it. No, blood *in* the sand. And *her* of course."

Francis' words electrified Philip, the hint of a sensational story was exactly what he wanted. He willed the old man to continue, hands gripping the table, knuckles white.

"That's all I can remember. I really am sorry I can't be of more help."

Picking up the teapot, he poured for them both. "Milk and sugar?"

Philip leaned back in his chair, deflated. He sighed. So close. Then realization dawned. Sir James did *not* die. He went north! Now there was something to go on. There must be more clues somewhere. "Just milk, please."

They sat in silence, neither able to add anything after the anti-climax of the failed revelation. The cat continued to rub itself against the old man's legs. He stroked its arching back as it stretched, then pushed it away when it tried to climb into his lap.

"Not now, Jinny," he said, his tone one of amused tolerance.

"Blood in the sand," Philip muttered. An excellent title for the biography. Shame his host could not remember more. He tried a different tack.

"Who is the 'her' you mentioned?"

"His wife, of course."

"He was married?" Philip could barely keep the surprise from his voice. Sir James, incorrigible in his pursuit of the opposite sex –married? No source even mentioned a wife. Surely everyone could not have missed that? But first things first. "The diary. Do you know what happened to it?"

"Well, papa used to keep it hidden away in his study. I never knew where. I did see it once though. I came in without knocking and surprised him reading it at his desk. He flared up and sent me packing. A second later he called me back and it was gone. I nagged him for days, and he finally gave in and told me about Sir James' journal. He showed it to me once. Just a plain old notebook. Nothing special in appearance."

It could have been scratched on tree bark for all Philip cared. "But that's amazing!"

"I never did see it again and when papa died it was not with his things."

"Ah . . . but Mr. Francis, this was your father's house, wasn't it?"

"Oh yes, indeed. It has been in my family for over two hundred and fifty years. Sir James grew up here you know."

"So the study was here?"

"Of course. Where else?"

"Would you mind awfully if we took a look around. Who knows, maybe it's still there somewhere."

"Oh, I am sure it's not. I've looked, of course. Papa would never let anyone in there, and it's just as he left it. Truly there's nothing to see."

The old man got up slowly, with effort. "But I have no objection to a quick look. If we are careful. Just don't go getting your hopes up. I hate to think you came all this way for nothing, but in forty years of dusting, I've never found it."

Francis poured a little tea from his cup into the cat's bowl and the cat immediately set to lapping greedily, finally rewarded for its patience. Then he led his guest along the hall past the portraits to the last room on the left, before the front door. He proceeded to unlock the study with a large iron key. From the location, Philip knew it would look out over the beautifully manicured front garden, and the lane and fields beyond.

"Papa kept it locked. I do it now as a sort of tribute, I suppose."

Philip, trembling in his eagerness, forced himself to hold back. Francis shuffled inside with Phillip close behind.

Expecting wood paneling, ancient armchairs of cracked leather and mahogany bookshelves crammed with gilt-edged classics he found an ordinary room with the same rather drab wallpaper as the rest of the house. A simple wooden desk held nothing but an old rotary phone. An oak swivel chair, a lamp and a metal filing cabinet completed the inventory.

"This is it?"

"Yes. I told you there was nothing here."

Philip felt his hopes fade. But the desk must surely be the key. He got down on his knees and peered underneath. Nothing.

"Is it okay if I have a poke about?"

"Oh yes. By all means. Just don't break anything. Papa would not like that!"

There was a sudden mewling from the cat, which had followed them.

"Jinny wants more tea. Have a look around, Mr. Entwhistle, but please leave it as you found it."

Mr. Francis turned and left the room, making his way back to the kitchen.

"Of course. I'll be careful," Philip said to the old man's slowly receding back. His first thought was a secret compartment built into the desk. Where else to hide something of value in a room so spartan? But no amount of poking, tapping and feeling for hidden catches revealed anything. He turned his attention to the filing cabinet. Each of the heavy boxlike drawers pulled out easily: empty. He considered removing the drawers from the cabinet but remembered how Mr. Francis' father has hidden it quickly. No. Somewhere handy.

Looking around the small room, he shook his head. Hopeless. He sank into the chair, arms on the desk, imagining he was Francis senior, whisking it out of sight in seconds. Nowhere obvious, for sure.

Philip turned his eyes to the only object within arms' reach, the old phone. He put the handset to his ear. No tone. There was not even a wire running into it from the wall. But he had talked with the old man, just the day before. He must have another phone hidden somewhere, as he was certainly not using this one. He returned the handset to the cradle. A phone unplugged was no phone at all. This thought made him stop. Scarcely daring to breathe, Philip picked up the phone, turning it over to examine the base, seeing a large metal plate fastened by two obviously loose screws. They turned easily between his fingers. The plate shifted. A small black notebook fell onto the table. He stared at it, not moving. The diary.

Dr. Elizabeth Sandwell sat quiet and alone in her almost compulsively tidy office. The books on the shelves were all aligned, pens organized in a neat row on her desk, and the silver bowl she used for spying on her colleagues burnished to a bright shine.

At her desk, she peered intently into the shallow bowl, its contents still as a mirror and black as night. However, unlike a mirror there was no reflection. The bowl seemed to suck light into itself with nothing coming out. But in Sandwell's violet eyes, her pupils tiny dots, images danced and weaved. Oh yes, there *was* something to be seen, and it made her smile.

Hydromancy – the least of her talents. Seeing in the dark water what was, what is, and what may be. A cheap trick to an ambitious woman who wanted far more than this, or the mere casting of illusions. It was nothing to *charm* someone. People did it all the time without even knowing. After all, every interaction between two people involved some attempt to influence, in one way or another.

Her work at the University positioned her ideally in open pursuit of the esoteric and occult. A form of maskirovka, where she hid her true desire in plain sight, publishing papers on ritual belief and tribal shamanism while she conducted experimental rituals of her own, pushing her powers and abilities further and further. Recognized for her expertise and knowledge, she'd gained a degree of acceptance in the academic world. This brought some small rewards, but nothing that would satisfy her hunger. She had a burning need, not just to be held in high regard and respected, but to be worshipped. She wanted the power to command millions and let them die for her. She craved adoration without love, fear without respect and power above all things.

A poster for a symposium on the paranormal completely covered the window in her office door. A guest speaking engagement for her, in fact. The poster showed a woman with one hand on a crystal ball, the other on a computer screen, displaying the legend *The Future of Fortune Telling*.

No one questioned why she chose the transparent glass of her door and not the perfectly unadorned wall outside her office. Anyone knocking and trying to enter would find the door locked. Not so unusual, hardly worthy of comment. But what she was doing would most certainly have raised eyebrows. Whether any witness would understand or believe did not matter. The occult, meaning simply *hidden*, was a perfect definition for her activities. She could not afford to be found out. Not that anything terrible would happen, but she needed to be careful to maintain her scientific credibility. The University provided the perfect cover and in order to continue working there, exploiting the endless supply of wide-eyed innocents, she needed to remain . . . hidden.

But now she was taking a small chance. She needed to cast a scrying, and it was far easier when physically close to her target. That would not matter one day. One day, she would be more powerful than anyone had ever been. She would be like a god and people would worship her. She would be God. This caused her a momentary thrill, a sensation almost sexual in its intensity. When she came into her power, things would be different. She would not hide herself or her true nature. And those who had looked down on her, who had derided or resisted her, they would suffer.

In the dark water, a vision of the past formed. Philip Entwhistle, hunched over a book. Elizabeth could not make out the text but could sense his energy, his mounting excitement. She smiled at the look of alarm in his eyes when he heard the sound of her approaching footsteps. She saw him place the book in his satchel and their brief conversation. She knew what followed from there, so she dipped a finger in the water and stirred, causing ripples to form and shatter the vision. She'd seen what she needed.

He had found something he did not want her to know about. And whatever Philip Entwhistle was trying to hide was of interest to her. She did not yet know how, but he was a threat to her. Her Master was clear on that. If she was to attain her ascendency, then she needed to make sure Entwhistle failed. The only problem was, her Master was not forthcoming on *how* the historian could be a threat to her. If Entwhistle was going to do something in the future that would harm her, then all she had to do was stop him before he got started. She needed to get that book. This would require a *hands-on* approach.

She took her mobile from her handbag and scrolled through the directory until she came to the name she wanted. While the phone rang she stared at the still rippling water, imagining it was Entwhistle's life stream, the currents of his fate within her power to alter. Well, soon enough.

A voice answered roughly. "What?"

"Hello Paul. This is Lizzy. I want you to do something for me."

"Oh, hi. Yeah, sure. Whatever you need, Liz. Just say the word."

Paul Sumpter was an ugly, shaven-headed dullard. She shook her head in distaste, recalling how she had followed the ill-mannered skinhead to a squalid pub. Paul was not chosen randomly. He was a weak man looking for a powerful, dominating woman. No spells or charms were required, but, ever careful, she had seduced the dolt to seal his loyalty.

Now he served. A *familiar*, her little pet. An unquestioning creature to command. Not a servant, more like a . . . lapdog, one with a valuable extra feature – his address.

"I want you to do me a little favor, Paul. There's something I want from one of your neighbors."


Philip stared at the diary, heart pounding in his chest. With trembling hands he picked up the grimy, tattered notebook and carefully opened it at a random page, instantly recognizing the tiny, close-packed letters, the neat hand. *Sir James.* Clearly the journal from the report and surely the only account of his life after his disappearance. He looked to the door, then flipped back to the first page and started to read.

*June 10. With luck the merchant will mail the other journal on, but I have my misgivings. I start a new notebook, and as always savor the inimitable pleasure of the very first entry.*

*The days pass and we make progress. We arrived at the oasis early in the morning. Notwithstanding my worries for Taj, I was rather taken with the place. The dawn bathed the castles of sand in a glorious golden light. It is everything I had hoped after the journey through as-Sahra al-Kubra. As we flee for our lives it seems we are cast back into a fairytale. The oasis rises from the endless dunes like the mirage I first took it for. I cannot help but compare it with one of the tales from Hazar Afsan. But it is no story. I wish it were, as the fairytale princess would be hale. Yet Taj is weaker than ever. Tajeddigt, my little flower. I lament the necessity of our flight. My dragoman has gone ahead to negotiate with the villagers while we take our ease in the shade of a date palm. He tells me the horses are done. I have to agree. Brave creatures, they have earned their final rest.*

*June 12. Izem and I will purchase camels today. We shall need four sturdy beasts if we are to lose Ibrahim again. For a surety he still dogs our heels. We shall make for the Atlas Mountains where my friends may negotiate a truce. I practiced my Berber while Izem was off on his own. Taj has been teaching me these last months. The local tongue is so different to hers and closer, it seems, to the dialects I've heard further west, in the mountains of Nafusa. I am determined to acquire every Berber dialect but for now I am better perceived merely as a visiting Pasha. A touch of arrogance is expected of such a one. It would cause no end of trouble to be exposed as an infidel and worse to have Taj's identity known. But already I make progress with their language and if the people think it odd that a grand Pasha wishes to speak like them, what would they think to discover I am fluent in fourteen African tongues? Izem continues to amaze me. I found him in the market waging a terrific row with one of the camel drovers. Finishing, they laughed and clapped each other's backs like old friends. Negotiations are colorful, to say the least, and they proceed apace. I bought some honeyed dates for Taj. Her favorite.*

*June 13. The camels will be delivered on the morrow. We must obtain sufficient protection for the journey. I would hire locals, but Izem thinks that a mistake. I trust his judgment in this matter. Perhaps better we go it alone? I have cleaned the Westley-Richards. Sand gets everywhere . . .*

Startled by a noise, Philip looked up from the diary, his heart racing, breath catching in his throat. Only the cat. The feline was sitting in the doorway, its head cocked to one side, regarding him as it might a mouse. Philip shook his head in admonition for the disturbance. It hissed its reply and disappeared into the dark of the corridor, leaving a strange smell in the room, naggingly familiar. A memory surfaced from his childhood. After a lightning storm. Ozone, his father had said. Damned cat.

He forgot the animal immediately. The rush of adrenaline from finding the diary lingered in his veins. He felt like jumping, shouting, and could not suppress the foolish grin on his face. He could not have dared to hope for such a bounty. An actual, first-hand account by Sir James, hidden for more than sixty years. It would have historic significance. It might even give a clue to the final resting place of Sir James himself! Philip's head reeled. It came to him that he had Francis' permission to find the diary, not to read it. He laid it on the table and took a deep breath to settle his nerves. There was only one acceptable outcome. He would have to persuade the old man to let him take the journal with him, at least to make a copy. The notebook required close study. He longed for its secrets so badly he physically ached, his belly clenching painfully. He must have it. It would make his career. What a book he would write.

He could not resist the temptation to read on, just a bit. His mind racing, teeming with the possibilities, he opened the journal and resumed where he had left off.

*Perhaps better we go it alone? I have cleaned the Westley-Richards. Sand gets everywhere and causes no end of bother. Both Izem and I can give a good accounting of ourselves but raiders are not uncommon and I have to think of Taj. She is not well enough to ride hard. A rich Pasha from Damascus would be a juicy plum indeed. Perhaps stealth is the wiser choice?*

*June 14. I have had Izem drop clues that we intend to head east. It will not fool the most determined but we may well throw off a couple of the more opportunistic fellows.*

*June 16. We have wined and dined Berber style. The headman of the oasis invited us to feast, with much singing and gift giving. I gave him a dagger of fine Damascus steel and he presented me with his grandfather's pistol. A single-shot flintlock, a gift bestowing great honor. Proudly, he showed me that it still worked. Old it may be, but it will still kill a man, of that I have no doubt. I have enough black powder for half a dozen shots, and wadding and lead for same.*

*June 17. We left quietly before dawn, heading due east. We design to swing around, skirt the oasis far to the south, and resume our course after nightfall. We shall lose a full day and more, but it cannot be helped. Taj is in good spirits. She ate well, and seems more rested than I have seen her in weeks. She was strong enough to converse and we practiced my conjugations.*

*June 18. Now heading west again. It is reassuring to finally make progress on our journey. The camels seem sturdy and we have enough food, although water is a concern, as always in the desert. The little detour cost us. I have little faith in it, but we must make every effort. Izem constantly fingers his rifle. I keep my Westley-Richards close to hand too. Should Ibrahim catch up we shall give a good accounting. Taj has taken the old flintlock and carries it, loaded, as one might carry a baby, cradled in* her arms. *Not a bad idea, I suppose. She refused a revolver, which I do not understand as she is willing to use the single-shot. But she has her own will in this, as in all things.*

*June 21. The expected attack came last night. We had seen sign of someone following – buzzards, which track men in the desert. We made a fire of dried camel dung and went to sleep like good little lambs to the slaughter. As they approached, all stealth, I let go with the Westley-Richards and took the head clean off the first man. Izem took out two with his pistol. I was forced to defend myself in close combat with my shotgun, which now bears a large nick from a scimitar of all things. Superficial, but it was a lovely weapon and now it is marred. The same model as the* Maharaja of Alwar's. *Very lovely. Still,* rather the gun *than one of us. Tajeddigt put a lead ball through the man's shoulder and I had to finish him with my knife. A low thing, killing a defenseless man, but alive he would have come again, with others. Izzy and I took anything of use and buried the bodies. The horses we let go, minus all the water skins. They will find their way home but I doubt anyone will locate our camp or their master's graves. The desert will swallow us all.*

"Mr. Entwhistle, how are you getting on?" The voice came from the hallway. Mr. Francis was coming back.

Philip had been holding his breath and he gasped, drawing in deep draughts of air. He had completely forgotten he was still in the Francis house, still sitting at the desk belonging to the old man's father. The journal had Philip spellbound. He momentarily considered stealing it. He had never stolen anything in his life, but these were exceptional circumstances and he had to have it. After all, sometimes the end justified the means, didn't it? Simply conceal the discovery, make an excuse and leave.

No. It was beyond him. Mr. Francis had invited him, as a guest. It was not in him to take advantage of an old man in his home and he flushed with shame to have entertained the thought. Decision made, he called out.

"Mr. Francis, I have it. I found the diary."

The thin, reedy voice came back, closer this time. "Really? Oh well done, Mr. Entwhistle. Well done indeed!"

He sounded happy, excited and Philip found that he was pleased to bring a little joy to the old man's life. Soon Francis and Jinny entered the room together, the cat weaving in and out of his legs, almost tripping her master who clung to the support of the doorframe, letting the cat continue its play.

"And you are sure it is *the* diary?"

"Yes. No doubt. None at all. It's exactly as your father said. Blood in the sand."

"Oh my. That is most interesting. And you've taken a look?" He shushed the cat away and came into the study, his face beaming at the sight of the journal on the table.

"Well, a couple of the entries. I just wanted to make sure it was the real thing."

"Where on earth did you find it?"

"It was here all along, in the telephone." Philip lifted the phone and turned it over, showing the old man the bottom plate, the loose screws.

"Well, I never. How many times have I walked past that in the last forty years?" He chuckled. "I never really expected to see it again. Very well. So now you wish to write about him?"

Philip nodded. "With your permission, yes. Now we can set the record straight. Maybe tell the whole story. And I will do it well, you can be assured of that. I have already completed a great deal of work on Sir James, and this . . . well, this will tie up the rest, I am certain."

Francis nodded. "Very well Mr. Entwhistle. Why don't we go back to the kitchen and you can tell me your plans. I have some," he paused, "conditions."

Philip nodded, face lit by an uncontrollable smile. He could not help himself. Conditions? It did not matter. He would meet them and gladly.

Francis, the cat, and then Philip made a slow progression to the kitchen. The table was now laid with a selection of biscuits on a cracked plate, a small cake and the ubiquitous teacups and teapot.

"Let's have another cup of tea. Then we can talk," said Francis, offering a piece of cake that Philip took from politeness. "Do sit down, please." He waved Philip to a chair.

Francis sat on one side of the table, Philip the other. Fortescue's 'Failed Rebellion' was still there, lying between them. The book that had led him here. It had done its job, but Philip felt it deserved more than being relegated to the stacks. He would see to it. He would make sure it was placed in the main library. The old man passed Philip a cup and saucer.

"Mr. Francis, please. I am eager to hear your conditions."

"Very well. They are simple enough."

Whatever they are is fine, thought Philip. He waited impatiently, repressing an urge to fidget while the old man took a sip of tea, smacked his lips and sighed in satisfaction. He looked at Philip and spoke, his voice firm, authoritative.

"You will write your book here, in the cottage. You may come every day, whenever you wish. You are welcome to use the study. I think it quite fitting that the final chapter of my great-uncle's life be written in his own study, don't you?"

Philip did. He could not imagine a more suitable location. With a smile and a nod, he sipped his tea as Francis continued.

"You may not copy the diary. Nor may you take it from the cottage. You will have access to it only while working here. You will tell no one what you are working on. You will most especially not mention the diary. When you are finished, provided you have met my requirements satisfactorily, you will have my permission to publish."

With the exception of the secrecy, with which he foresaw problems, Philip was ready to agree. "That all sounds perfectly acceptable, Mr. Francis. I cannot tell you how grateful I am for the opportunity. Of course, the diary needs to be authenticated. There will be considerable interest in it, I am sure."

The old man nodded as he put down his teacup and fixed Phillip with a stare that nailed him to his chair. His voice was stronger now, more resonant.

"Meet my conditions and you may have the diary to do with as you deem best. One final thing, Mr. Entwhistle. Like all the other demands, it is non-negotiable. You must finish within five weeks. After that you may depart and go back to your normal routine. Except, you *must* take Jinny with you."

"Uh, pardon? The cat?"

"Yes, Mr. Entwhistle, the cat. Writing the final chapter of Sir James' life hangs on your agreeing to all of my requirements, including, and especially, this final one."

My entire future could hang on this, thought Philip. But in truth, the conditions were hardly onerous even if he did end up having to keep the animal.

"Well, alright. I have to be honest, I've always been more of a dog than a cat person, but if that's what you want, then I agree."

Francis' lined eyes crinkled even further as he smiled and said, "Well, there is no accounting for taste. Eh, Mr. Entwhistle?"

Philip found himself grinning back, excited by the prospect of the work ahead. Then the smile slipped a little.

"I don't live in the country though. So long as it's okay for Jinny to be a house cat, I don't see a problem. I do have just one question, if I may. Why five weeks exactly? Is something going to happen?"

"Yes, you could say that. You must be finished with your study of the diary, because in five weeks I shall be dead."

Philip froze, astonished.

"Wh . . . what? Are you sick?"

"No, not sick. Just quite, quite certain. Call it intuition, if you like. Well, Mr. Entwhistle? Do we have a deal?"

Philip had had few dealings with people of Francis' clearly advanced age and wondered if the old man might have a mental condition. Not Alzheimer's, but you never knew. A touch of senility? It didn't matter. He had to read, had to know.

"Yes, Mr. Francis, we have a deal." He stood and held out his hand. The old man reached across the table to shake. Philip found himself grinning again.

"Well, now," said Francis as he leaned back again in his chair, "I believe this deserves a little celebration. More tea, Mr. Entwhistle?"

Philip shook his head. He reached down and scratched the cat, which responded by rolling onto its back, exposing its belly.

"No. No thanks. I can't tell you how pleased I am. Thrilled. Why don't I come back tomorrow then, so I can get started?"

"Of course, by all means. And I wish you a merry rest of your day."

Francis stood awkwardly as Philip gathered up his book and shoulder bag, giddy with exhilaration. Blood in the sand!

Philip drove, barely noticing the road. Had he not seen it for himself, he would never have believed so much could result, in such a short time, from deciding to dig a little deeper in the library. It must be fate. No, that's just foolish nonsense. It was his methodical research and persistence. The book would be a sensation. All he had to do was write it. And fast. Bound over to secrecy while working, free to publish when finished. Hopefully before the committee made its appointment. He needed a first draft at least, or it would be Associate Professor Sandwell. That must not happen.

It was not that he disliked her. He simply did not trust the woman. Plus there were the whispers. He did not put much stock in them himself, having learned to his cost that not all rumors are true. In his first year of teaching, one young woman had become infatuated with him, and it had led to some uncomfortable moments. More than once he had heard one or more of his colleagues say his name then fall silent as he approached. But if Sandwell was having inappropriate relationships with some of her more ardent postgrads, it would come back to bite her in the end. But he would give her the benefit of the doubt. Sometimes there *is* smoke without fire.

But when it came to her willingness to take his ideas as her own there was fire alright. If only he could prove it. He would be careful this time. He would not leave his notes or laptop unattended, that was for sure. Nor would he use the University phone system. Philip suspected that Sandwell was able to monitor calls from the internal phones. How this was possible, he did not know, and not wanting to sound paranoid, he had kept his suspicions to himself. But sometimes she appeared to know things she just shouldn't.

Philip turned the old car into the narrow street where he lived, and began the task of finding a parking space. The whole estate was built back in the Victorian era, and no provision had been made for the permanent presence of automobiles. Now that many families had two cars, it was always difficult to find a free spot. Vehicles of all types lined both sides of the road, almost bumper to bumper, but miraculously there was a space directly outside his own building, a three-story redbrick house that had once belonged to a single family, but now boasted six residences. With a delighted smile that his luck was holding out, Philip pulled into the space and shut off the engine. A perfect end to a perfect day.

As he got out of the car, the front door to the building swung open violently. One of the neighbors, a heavyset man with a shaved head and a lit cigarette, came running out, waving his arms.

"Oi! You can't park there, mate."

Philip grabbed his satchel, and slung it from his shoulder as he locked the car.

"Why not?"

MJ Kobernus

"Traci's just popped out to get some fags, and she'll be back in a minute. That's *our* space."

Taking a deep drag on his cigarette he blew the smoke into Philip's face. Philip took a step back.

"What? This is general parking. Anyone can park here."

"You ain't hearing me, mate. That's OUR space, and if you don't want a fat lip, you'll move your fucking car."

"Paul, right? Paul Sumpter?"

The skinhead glanced away. "Might be."

"Look, Paul, I came home and I found a space. When I don't find one, I don't complain. I just drive around until I do. It's all just luck."

"I don't give a damn about your luck, mate. Either you move that car or you can drive yourself to the emergency room. Either way is fine by me."

Philip was not the most physical type. He liked to run, kept himself fit, but that was it. Not like the burly skinhead now flexing bulging arm muscles. And although it had happened on more than one occasion, Philip did not like being pushed around. Perhaps it was the natural high from the excitement of his day, but uncharacteristically, he stood his ground.

"Well, it's not fine by me. I'm not moving."

The fist to the nose that knocked Philip down should have been expected; Sumpter had a reputation. As he tried to sit up, the skinhead made a grab for his satchel. Philip held on, wondering in his daze if he was being mugged. The arrival of onlookers foiled Sumpter's attempted theft. Mrs. Hardy came storming out of the apartment block.

"Stop being an asshole, Sumpter! Go pick on someone your own size," she shouted, arms akimbo, eyes blazing.

'Go fuck yourself, you old bag," muttered Sumpter, as he went back inside.

A bystander helped Philip to his feet as a torrent of blood streamed down his chin and dripped onto his shirt. Mrs. Hardy had a son he tutored occasionally and they usually chatted when they met, but he would not have expected her to come to his aid.

"You ought to give him a smack, Mr. Entwhistle. It's all his type understands."

Philip was angry, embarrassed and ashamed. He tipped his head back in an effort to lessen the flow of blood. His eyes watered heavily, and he blinked to clear them.

"I'm not going to resort to violence over a parking space. I mean, come on! Shouldn't we be a bit more civilized than that?"

Mrs. Hardy gave him a look that spoke volumes of her opinion on that subject but gave him her handkerchief. Philip staunched the dripping blood and thanked her.

"Looks like he broke your nose," she said, gently.

Every touch of the handkerchief hurt but the bleeding was easing.

As Mrs. Hardy, all sympathy, took him by the arm and guided him inside her face lit up with a grin.

"Oh, you didn't hear yet, did you?"

"Hear what?"

"He's only been and got himself evicted, is all. Didn't pay his rent."

So there was a little justice in the world after all. It was not that he wished ill on the man, but Sumpter had made life unpleasant for everyone. However, this was the first time things had become violent.

"Good. Couldn't happen to a nicer bloke," he replied. Mrs. Hardy nodded emphatically in agreement.

"Thanks for the handkerchief" he said. He turned to go, then stopped.

"Mrs. Hardy, You've been here for a while, right?"

She nodded, pausing by her open front door.

"Have you ever read the tenancy rules? Do they say anything about pets? Cats specifically?"

# Accept the world we cannot see

## 3

There are more things in heaven and earth, Horatio,
Than are dreamt of in your philosophy.
*–Shakespeare, Hamlet Act I, scene V*

The next day, Philip arrived at the cottage ready to start working. He entered the narrow country lane just after nine, the sun already bright in the sky. His nose hurt and a dark bruise shadowed his puffy eyes.

He felt eager, undaunted by the five-week deadline, buoyed by the new life in his long-dormant project. Five weeks on the diary, and that alone.

As soon as the bleeding stopped from his broken nose, Philip had sent Sam Evans an email. Evans was not just a boss, he was a friend and deserved more than the cursory explanation Philip was forced to give. He simply said something had come up and he needed to take a sabbatical, at least a month.

Philip expected some sort of censure. It could not be helped; his undergrads would just have to manage. His current course was basic stuff; anyone qualified could fill in. The lack of notice would be resented but Sanjay, his assistant, would welcome the opportunity to take center stage, something he had been wanting for a while. This would be the young man's chance to shine.

Philip parked and got out of his car, grabbing his satchel from the passenger seat. The strap caught on the door handle and the bulging bag slipped from his shoulder, spilling the contents. With a panicked yelp, he caught the laptop inches from the ground.

With a sigh he began gathering text books and dictionaries, shaking his head at each mud stain.

It was a full minute before Francis opened the big red door a sliver, peering up at the historian with eyes narrowed, brows furrowed in puzzlement, even suspicion. Did the old man not remember why he had come? One eyebrow on the wrinkled visage raised in mute question, as if demanding an explanation. But then the craggy face cracked into a wide smile and Francis stepped back from the door. Philip, getting the distinct impression he was being toyed with, suppressed a smile of his own.

"Good morning, Mr. Francis. Not too early I hope?"

"Not at all. And good morning to you, Mr. Entwhistle. No, you're not too early. At my age one needs little sleep. I was up before dawn. Come in, come in. We shall have a cup of tea and then you can get started."

The old man shuffled to the kitchen where Philip found the tea already laid out. He was expected. Francis' performance at the door had been a joke. Philip smiled, quietly pleased to see their relationship starting with gentle humor.

In place of yesterday's fine porcelain cups and saucers was a single white mug with a thick handle, the sort of cup you would offer a plumber. Philip smiled at his downgrade from honored guest to tradesman. Perfectly right. He was there for a job of work. Good.

"You can take it through to the study," Francis said with a nod towards the front of the house. "Papa called it the only place where he could think."

"Perfect, thank you," Philip replied, thrilled to think he would be sitting in the same chair, or at least in the same room where Sir James had penned some of his own letters.

Francis screwed his brow in concern. "Have you been in a fight?"

Philip laughed. "Not exactly. At least, I wouldn't call it a fight. A misunderstanding with a neighbor."

"I see. Well, why don't you go and get settled then. You have one of those computer things, I suppose."

"Yes, indeed," Philip said, patting his shoulder bag, inwardly wincing at how close he had come to breaking it only minutes ago. Since the Disraeli affair it was always with him but that did him little good if he dropped the damned thing.

"Jolly good. You run along then. The diary is on the desk. I have some odd jobs to take care of outside. Just call if you need me."

And with a half wave of his hand, Francis shuffled to the open door to the back garden and slowly made his way across the lawn to a wheelbarrow containing a collection of shears, forks and spades of various sizes.

Philip made his way back to the study, past the gallery of portraits, once again stopping before the painting of Sir James. He noted the superb detail, the painting of the thirty-five or forty-year old man impressively lifelike. The background and clothing suggested Egypt. It all looked very Romantic, even Byronesque. Again Philip noted the pistol tucked into the crimson belt. Obviously Arabic with its elongated, curved handle, and mother-of-pearl inlays. Of course. That must be the gift mentioned in the diary, from the headsman at the oasis. But that would place it after . . . Philip struggled to make sense of what he was seeing.

In his previous examination he had felt something was missing. Or someone. The feeling returned, stronger than ever, like a strange kind of déjà vu. He let his eyes wander over the canvas . . . nothing. With a shake of his head he continued to the study.

He opened the laptop and settled into the chair. The diary was there, as Francis had said. Entwhistle took out a new legal pad and pens, dropping them carelessly on the desk. He added a few textbooks providing background on the Sahara region, including material on the Berbers. Finally, the book that had started it all, Fortescue's 'Extraordinary Events'. Philip opened the diary and flipped to the start. Reading the first lines again drew him straight back under their spell.

*The days are passing, and we make progress. We arrived at the oasis, early in the morning. Notwithstanding my own worries for Taj, I was rather taken with the place. The dawn bathed the castles of sand in a glorious golden light. It is everything I had hoped after the journey through as-Sahra al-Kubra.*

The last was surely a reference to the Sahara, quickly confirmed in his Arabic primer. As-Sahra al-Kubra: 'The Great Desert.' So they crossed some part of the Sahara, arriving at an oasis on June 10.

He already had a suspicion where Sir James was on June 10. The next clue, in the entry for June 12, confirmed it.

*I practiced my Berber while Izem was off on his own. Taj has been teaching me these last months. My mastery of her dialect leaves much to be desired, but it is only distantly related to the local tongue. The local tongue is so different to hers and closer, it seems, to the dialects I've heard further west, in the mountains of Nafusa.*

Berber. He was in the Northern part of the Sahara, and in an area where Berber was spoken. A dialect similar to the Nafusa. The answer came to him.

The castles of sand. Not a metaphor for dunes, but literal. Castles made from sand. Siwa oasis, in western Egypt, where they still build with mud bricks the same color as the surrounding desert. Some of the buildings there would be sizeable, especially then. Sir James was literally talking about castles.

Philip smiled. The first challenge met and answered. On June 10, 1922, Sir James Francis and party were in the Western Desert, near what is now the border between Egypt and Libya. He paused to savor the thrill: the first person in nearly a century to know this for fact. He began to make notes, including a reminder to himself to confirm the construction practices in Siwa from that era.

What records were there for Siwa in 1922? Not much, he was sure, but it was another possible avenue that he could investigate. But something in the first entry had him puzzled. Using his mobile as a modem he searched the name, confirming his hunch. A female name from Northern Africa, Berber in origin. Specifically, "flower" in Tamazight, explaining the reference:

*Taj is weaker than ever. Tajeddigt, my little flower.*

Clearly Tajeddigt was a woman with whom Sir James was involved. The wife that Francis had mentioned? Or, more likely, someone else's? Sir James had the reputation of a rake. In the words of one early twentieth-century commentator, he had "whored his way around the world."

Several of his high-profile love affairs had landed him in trouble, including banishment, duels and even, on one occasion, a fatwa. "Infamous" would be an understatement and a love affair while on his travels was true to type.

Sir James was evidently travelling in disguise. Dressed as a Pasha, a civil servant, most likely out of Damascus, he would be able to blend in anywhere in the Arabic world. The language would be no problem. The talented linguist was known to speak at least twenty-five languages, including Arabic and Farsi.

The entry for June 12 was also revealing. *Izem and I intend to purchase camels today. We shall need four sturdy beasts if we are to lose Ibrahim again. I know he still dogs our heels.*

The Atlas Mountains were located in northwestern Africa. To get there by camel they would have to cross sixteen hundred kilometers of one of the harshest landscapes on Earth. It would take months. But who was this Ibrahim?

Philip continued to calculate the distances. They had traveled east for one day before rounding back west, no doubt in the night, sacrificing sleep to make up lost distance. Camels can travel thirty or more miles a day. If they went east, then turned to walk west for three days, that would put the attack described in the entry for June 21 somewhere in the deep desert of central Libya. He pulled up a map on the Web. They would need to get water where ever possible – the most likely spot stood approximately ten kilometers south of Al Jaghbub. A water source where there was little likelihood of encountering others. Most travelers would follow the string of small watering holes and oases running in a northwesterly line. To avoid being seen they would need to keep south of that line.

*That* is where where Francis blew a man's head off with a shotgun, then fought another in hand-to-hand combat before cutting his throat. Philip added a few notes to his legal pad and tapped his teeth idly with his pen. Noticing his cup of tea he took a sip. Cold. How long had he been at it? His watch said three hours. He would have guessed one, or less. With a mental shrug he continued.

The next entry in the diary was dated three days later, one that made him suspect that perhaps Sir James was not just running away from something, but on a mission of a more clandestine nature. He seemed to be using code words and he was well known to have worked as a spy on occasion. But what could possibly have taken him to the middle of the desert in 1922?


The red-blazered estate agent opened the door to the ground-floor apartment for Fern. The hallway was narrow but led to a spacious kitchen looking out over a small garden. One bedroom and a small living room. All in all, twice as big as Fern's current place.

"It's available for immediate occupancy," said the agent. "Three months rent in advance, and a minimum of twelve months on the lease."

Fern glanced about, then closed her eyes for a few seconds as she felt the energy in the room.

"Yes, that's fine." She took a deep breath and entered the kitchen. Through the somewhat grimy window, not too far in the distance, she could see the university clock tower. It chimed at that moment, ringing the half hour.

This would work, a good base for her to hunt the hedge witch. Close enough to campus that even at home she could sense any unusual disturbances emanating from the University.

Of course, the deposit was a problem. It was far more than she had available. Her part-time work in the library paid little, her real, more dangerous job paid nothing at all. She would need to ask Tessa to cover it from the

University's discretionary funds. She was confident that her mentor would agree. In truth, a fact few would ever know, it was a good deal for the University. Fern would earn every penny and then some.

"This will do nicely," she said. "I can move in the day after tomorrow."

Philip Entwhistle looked up from the cramped, tiny lettering of the diary. He stared out of the window, eyes glazed, not really seeing the trees and fields beyond. He rubbed his temples with the fingers of one hand and sighed. The reading, the fact checking, the writing were quietly exhausting. Not that he begrudged a moment. However, this last thing, this was too much. He was surely misunderstanding something. He read through again, just to be sure.

*June 24. Since the incident we have seen no sign of followers. Trouble now will be just bad luck. Izem is worried for one of the camels. Seems she has an infection. Her great pad of a foot is too tender to carry her load, most of which we have transferred to the others, but Taj's slight and ever-dropping weight does not trouble her. The days are insufferable, but suffer we must. At night, with our tiny fire blazing and the stars to entertain us we become elemental creatures. One with the universe. Worldly concerns depart in this most peaceful place on Earth. His right royal nibs should come out here one day and see for himself. Old George would probably love it.*

*June 27. A rather curious incident last night. We had settled in for an evening of stargazing, with Taj and myself sharing a blanket and Izzy on his own, as usual. It was still relatively early, when a Bedouin walked into the camp. Of course, we invited him to join us. They take hospitality seriously here and we laid it on thick. I made our guest tea, and Izzy gave him his blanket.*

*Taj even managed to get up the strength to make a little bread with honey. A toothless old man but a merry one. He had come to the deep desert to die. Not the worst way to go, I have to say. We made a fuss over him and he seemed to enjoy our attentions. He smiled a lot and told us we were blessed. He asked us if we were believers, which of course, we claimed to be; true, of course, in Izem's case. Tajeddigt is a Berber and they have their own version of things. The Bedouin wagged his finger at me as if he knew I were dissembling. I asked him how he knew he was dying, to which he replied that he was blessed too. He claimed to have known for a long time when he was going to leave (I assume he meant the Earth). From this, I took him to be a fakir, like those I had seen in Damascus, but he said not. What he said next gave me pause. He told us that a djinn was with him, and he knew much that was hidden. I know what a djinn is, but I was not expecting to run into one. Izem was most disconcerted but Taj took it in her stride.*

Philip shook his head. Ridiculous. In his mind, the words repeated themselves, tumbling over each other. Djinn. Arabic. Meaning Genie in modern English. Djinn. Preposterous.

It had to be some kind of code word. The previous entry was clue enough, with a reference to King George the Fifth. *His royal nibs.* What did he know about him? The first monarch of the house of Windsor. Not particularly political, but still. Egypt was granted independence from Great Britain just three months prior. Could there be some link there? With a look in his Arabic primer, Entwhistle quickly discovered that "djinn" could also mean "to hide" or "be hidden."

Perhaps Sir James *was* on an assignment. Espionage in 1922, in the Atlas Mountains. Travelling in secret. To what end? Although nothing of significance was mentioned in any of the contemporary sources, something, it seemed, called for a super-spy to be sent more than sixteen hundred kilometers across deadly desert. Certainly nothing which could have been of interest to the monarchy. But was the king meant as a proxy reference to the British Empire? Between the end of the Great War and 1922 the British had expanded their hegemony to rule over one fifth of humanity, building the greatest empire in history.

The hair on the back of Philip's neck stood up at the possibility that he had uncovered a previously unknown clandestine operation of one of history's most disreputable figures. If he could even credibly suggest that the British Government had been operating secretly in Libya at that time, he could publish something of historical significance. However, before his flights of fancy got out of control he would have to check every fact carefully. It did not pay to make quick assumptions.

He glanced again at the text of the diary, but his eyes refused to focus. He needed a break. He would ask Mr. Francis about this. Perhaps, some family story? Decision made, he got up and stretched to get the kinks out of his back, mildly alarmed to feel vertebrae popping.

The old man could not be too far. Although not necessarily housebound, Mr. Francis was clearly infirm, so was unlikely to be out on long walks in the adjoining forest.

The kitchen seemed to be his host's favorite place in the house. It was empty, but the back door stood open. Philip saw the old man absorbed in pulling weeds. It was Philip's first foray into the garden. An earlier glimpse through the kitchen window had not revealed what he now saw to be a delight of planning and care. He basked momentarily in the warmth of the sun, taking in a myriad of scents from flowers and bushes, none of which he could name. The scene confronted him with the fact that for an erudite man, he was quite ignorant of the varieties of flora and fauna; he resolved to remedy the deficiency.

Mr. Francis was clearly dedicated to his garden. This brought to mind Philip's own grandmother, who had loved her roses and cared for them assiduously. He had never quite understood her passion but looking around he began to see the beauty of a lifetime of service to something other than oneself.

He walked through a tall trellis of wrought iron, proud as the triumphal arch of an emperor, and entered the lawn and the colorful flowerbeds.

Mr. Francis was on his knees, bent over double, weeding amongst the flowers and turning the soil with a hand fork.

"It's lovely," Philip said, gesturing to take in the whole garden.

"Oh, Mr. Entwhistle," he said, startled. "There you are."

With obvious difficulty Mr. Francis sat up. "It is my pride and joy. I find my peace here."

As Philip considered the enormous dedication and perseverance needed to maintain the exquisite landscape he smiled, recollecting Napoleon's dismissal of the English as "a nation of shopkeepers." Wrong, monsieur. We are a nation of *gardeners.*

"Mr. Francis. About your great-uncle. Something in the diary makes me suspect he was on a secret mission. You know he was an occasional spy. Do you remember any stories, perhaps as a child, regarding the Atlas Mountains?"

The old man struggled, in pain, to climb to his feet. In two strides Philip was at his side, giving him his arm. Once up, Francis turned to him. "Well, I don't know. What did the entry say?"

"That a Bedouin walked into their camp during the night and mentioned what I *think* is a code word. Djinn. A genie. A previous entry mentioned George the Fifth. So I wonder if there was a connection. Perhaps he was on some business for the crown?"

"Well, as you said, he was a spy. However not, I think, this time."

They walked back to the house, through the trellis with its intertwining rods of hand-forged twisted iron. Entwhistle took a moment to admire it, well in keeping with the rustic cottage. An oddity in the working caught his eye. Several strands of metal flowed together on the side of the great gate, combining in a way that suggested a rotund face. A fat, Buddha-like visage, staring sightlessly, mouth open in a silent howl. The back of his neck prickled, as if he were being secretly watched. He hurried after the old man.

In the kitchen, Francis was busy with the copper kettle. Tea is the essence of being English thought Philip with a slight smile. Like most of his countrymen he thrived on it. As a teenager he had tried to learn to like coffee but found it harsh and bitter, though he did love the smell of freshly roasted beans.

"Please, take a seat, Mr. Entwhistle."

Philip sat in the same chair he had used the day before. Jinny's previous antipathy towards him had vanished, indeed she now found his legs to be of extreme interest, brushing against him with long, sinuous movements. Gratified at the creature's acceptance he stroked her head.

Francis smiled at the sight. "So what do you think that he meant by the word djinn?"

"A code, I think. A trigger word perhaps. Put certain words together in a specific order for a pre-agreed meaning. Whoever the message was meant for would understand."

"How do you know it did not mean just what it said? Sometimes a cigar is just a cigar, after all."

"And a good cigar is a smoke, I know." They smiled together, Francis' appreciation of Kipling a safe bet. "Well, yes. But he said djinn. Obviously it's not meant to be taken literally."

"Why not?"

Philip's eyebrows made a spirited attempt to out-climb each other. He shook his head. Was the old man being obtuse deliberately? "Because they don't exist of course."

Francis stopped spooning tea into the pot and regarded at the historian, a stern look on his face. "Mr. Entwhistle. Have you no faith? No belief in a higher order?"

Philip gaped at the question. "What has faith to do with it? Or religion for that matter?"

"Everything, my dear Mr. Entwhistle, everything. Have you never read the Quran?"

Entwhistle looked away, embarrassed. "Unfortunately not. Never found the time."

"Well perhaps you should. There is a whole chapter, a sura, for the djinn. They are one of the orders of life that includes mankind, djinn and angels. It is entirely natural for a Bedouin to believe in djinn and even to talk of them."

Entwhistle raised an eyebrow in tribute to his host. He had not known of the place of djinn in the Islamic faith and was grateful for the information. Perhaps there was no secret code after all. However, if that were so, why would Sir James accept it on face value? He did not believe in God, or angels. He was not a Muslim, that much was certain. In fact, he was on record as being an atheist, yet from the tone of the diary he appeared to believe in the djinn.

"I don't know what to think now," Philip said, confusion plain on his face. "As a historian, I try to deal with facts. We offer interpretations, try to understand motives, but generally facts are our bread and butter. So this business with the genies has me puzzled."

"Not genies. Djinn."

"What's the difference? Aren't they the same?"

"Not to a djinn," Francis said, face crinkling with laughter.

Philip persisted. "Well, I don't believe in a 'higher order.' Not in angels, genies, djinn or anything. I deal with the known. Facts. Dates. Places. The real world."

Francis laughed, then gave Philip a mock stern look. "My dear young man, you cannot possibly live in such an impoverished state!" He finally finished making the tea and poured for them both into a pair of large cups.

"Without the spiritual you cannot have the physical, and vice versa. There is a balance in the universe. Oh, I know that organized religion has perverted much, but all worship is ultimately the same. Man is genetically designed to seek the divine. Even if it doesn't exist. Make of *that* what you will! What I am saying is that you have to accept that you cannot always know. That you cannot always see, and that there are mysteries in the world and they should stay that way. Empirical science is not the be all and end all, believe me." Francis passed Philip a mug then settled into his chair. He sipped his tea, looked at the young man and shrugged. "The only true wisdom is knowing that you know nothing. A wise man once said the most beautiful thing we can experience is the mysterious."

This was the most he had ever heard Mr. Francis speak and Philip was amazed at the passion in his voice. Even if some of what he was saying was rehashed philosophy from a couple of millennia ago, Philip saw this was something that the old man believed. Mr. Francis was not quite done though.

"But what if you *could* see?" he continued. "What if you were to understand the hidden, to know the mysterious? Would you want that?"

Wouldn't that be empirical then? Not faith at all? Philip thought. He was brought to mind of a book he had read in his teens which had used logic to refute God's existence. In the book, God agreed that the logic was correct and then promptly disappeared. Philip smiled at the memory.

"Yes, of course. That is a logical proposition, no question. We researchers, we're a peculiar breed. We must have facts before faith."

"Ah, but you should be careful, Mr. Entwhistle. Not everything is quite as it seems you know. And knowledge always comes at a price."

"Well, if it's something worth knowing, then it must be worth paying for, right?"

"Yes, it is worth it. But still, care is needed. Est autem fides credere quod nondum vides."

Entwhistle recognized the quote. *Faith is to believe what you do not see.* He dredged his memory and in Latin considerably less polished and precise than the old man's, replied. "Cujus fidei merces est videre quod credis. The reward of this faith is to see what you believe." He clapped his hands and grinned. "Augustine's sermons. Although I have not read them in a very long while."

"Yes. Augustine. I still read him from time to time. Trying to stop my Latin from rusting into uselessness."

"But the diary was not referring to the djinn as an object of *belief*, but as real. I must say, Mr. Francis, I did not expect you to believe in genies. I mean, they can't be real, can they?"

"No," he agreed. "Genies are not real. They are a misunderstanding. A perversion if you will. Genie is a term etymologically derived from Latin and then French. It is related to the Roman belief in inspirational spirits. Everything had them. People, places, things. But a djinn is not a genie. The Western word for djinn is genie, only because someone thought they sounded similar. But in terms of what they represent they are distinct. According to the noble Quran, in the seventy-second sura, there is Man, Djinn and Angels. You should look it up. A genie, on the other hand, is the part of the spirit or soul where man's rational powers and abilities dwelled. The natural genius. Which, incidentally, is where we get the word *genius* from."

Philip was fascinated. He was not much of a linguist, but he was intrigued at the origin of the word. Something else he would have to look into. He sipped his tea and they sat in companionable silence. This had been a good day. He'd done a lot but it was already mid-afternoon. Now he should go home, write up his notes and perhaps do some research on the political situation in the countries around the Atlas Mountains. Tomorrow he would return to the diary and wrestle with more of its clues. He put down his cup.

"Well, Mr. Francis, thank you for today. I believe we are off to a good start. I think I'll head home."

"Very well Mr. Entwhistle. Will I see you tomorrow?"

"Yes, of course. The same time okay?"

"That would be fine. But don't worry about keeping to a schedule. Just get here when you get here."

Philip nodded, rose and went back to the study to gather his things. Francis followed and fussed about, putting the diary in a desk drawer and locking it, straightening the chair and the disconnected phone, making everything neat and tidy. Entwhistle looked at the phone with a feeling of affection, wondering if it had ever worked, or was it there only to hide the diary.

Philip thanked the old man again as he was walked to his car. Francis smiled in delight when he saw what Philip was driving.

"I had one of these. Endless trouble with the windscreen wipers," He patted the car on the hood nostalgically. "It was a bugger to start in the winter too."

Philip unlocked it, slung in his satchel and slid behind the wheel. Francis leaned over him through the open door.

"Well, sweet dreams, Mr. Entwhistle," he said, with a cheery grin. Philip started the engine, shut the door and pulled out into the lane.

Philip's drive home and arrival was uneventful, for which he was grateful. Once inside, he checked his answering system. No calls. At least, no messages. Plugging in his laptop, he logged into his University email account. Prepared for an unappreciative response from Evans to the news of his sudden absence, he was unpleasantly surprised to find an uncritical, almost casual acceptance. As if they would not miss him in the least, and he could take all the time he needed. Would he even have a job to go back to after his work on Sir James?

Accepting that there was nothing he could do about it, Philip attended to his hunger, making a sandwich from some cheese and suspect ham from the fridge. That and a bottle of cold beer rounded out his bachelor's meal.

Sitting at his desk he looked over his day's notes, flipping through page after page before pulling his laptop into position to begin the real work; transforming his scribblings into something of value. He opened the file containing the abandoned Francis biography, then created a new file.

He paused, savoring the moment. This was it then. He was about to start writing the book he confidently expected would make his name and garner him the title of professor.

Without hesitation he typed just four words. *Blood in the Sand.* Bold, provocative, they laid the foundation for the book that was to come. He stared at them, motionless, hands poised above the keyboard. Blood in the sand.

Images from the diary took fire in Philip's imagination and the words began to blur, swimming together. All his ideas for the introduction, carefully planned on the drive home, slipped away. A sudden, deep weariness came over him. The day's sustained excitement had wiped him out. His hands fell to his lap as he stared at the screen.

His eyelids grew heavy, drooped and finally closed. The room disappeared, a gray fog swirling in his mind, then a strange vertigo as if he were in two places at once. His head dropped and he tumbled into a dream, echoes of a time before coursing through his mind . . . a rank animal smell, a relentless sun, limitless sand.


The sun beats down with merciless precision. No part of my exposed body escapes. I do not sweat, all superfluous fluid gone. Neither Izem nor Taj fare any better, despite their heritage. Izem drifts close to a state of collapse; Taj appears asleep. My travels in the Orient and the Sudan have been scant preparation for this, but needs must when the Devil drives.

Izem seems to think that we are near the next watering hole. I most assuredly hope he is right. The camels are doing well enough, but our withered husks need more than a little nourishment to recover. We are not built for such feats of endurance yet endure we must. It is approaching late afternoon and the heat has gone from tolerable, beyond intolerable into the unthinkable and now we are in uncharted environs from which few, I fear, have ever returned.

A strange sight looms before us. A great, angular gray shell protruding from the sand. A vessel of some kind, I fancy. A boat, miraculously transported into the deep desert. But as we draw near I see I am mistaken. It is not a boat, but something with wheels. An armored vehicle, near the size of a trolley bus. I slow my camel and the others follow suit. Izem is staring curiously at the behemoth; Taj still slumbers.

"What is it, Sayyd?"

Izem's voice is as dusty as the air. My own is little better as I squint against the light.

"I think it is a tank, of sorts. Or an armored car." The stumpy muzzle of a light howitzer points to the sky. It lies almost on its side and partly buried.

"I am sure that I heard of something like these, in Cairo."

Taj starts to stir, the absence of the rocking motion of the camel evidently pushing her into wakefulness. She sees the great beast of a carriage and her brow furrows. "What is it, Jam-ez?" Taj always puts two syllables to my name.

"It is called a tank," I reply. "It must have been driven here. The Duke of Westminster's armored division took part in the Senussi campaign. What was it? Six years ago? But there shouldn't be anything here. We're too far south."

Neither Tajeddigt nor Izem have heard of the Senussi. Their interests in African politics begin and end with their own village, or, in Taj's case, family.

We walk our camels around the great metal whale and come to the driver's window. Inside, half covered in sand, a lolling skull stares sightlessly back at us. Izem lets out a small shriek and clutches at the chain around his neck from which hangs his protection against the evil eye. I am not so moved. That poor fellow is not going to curse anyone. He was probably injured when the vehicle pitched onto its side and, trapped, died of thirst. We are more alike than I would care to admit. I fear we may soon follow him to a sandy grave of our own.

Taj too, stares at the bleached bones without comment. She has seen her share of death. This is nothing new to her.

I examine the interior and recognize the design. A Rolls-Royce. I know something of these brutes. A modified Silver Ghost, I am sure. Not what I had expected to see here, or anywhere for that matter. Westminster's regiment had dozens. They did well in the desert, making possible the remarkable feat of liberating those two ships' crews. The Moorina and Tara, that's it. A remarkable story.

But now the vehicle is no more than a curiosity. A mausoleum to the wretch left to die in its carcass. We move slowly past the odd spectacle, more interested in the possibility of water than the unlikely sight of a ruined tank half buried by the desert.

I pull my scarf across my eyes to dull the inexorable onslaught of the sun. It provides a certain relief but I feel myself declining. Taj lies across her camel's back, even the effort of sitting upright now too much for her.

The goatskins are all as dry as that poor fellow's bones. I rue the lack of more skins, but it would have raised suspicion. Still, the ruse seems to have worked well enough. We turned in the night and looped back south of the oasis. Anyone keeping track of our whereabouts will think us fifty miles in the opposite direction. A necessary, albeit uncomfortable precaution with bandits everywhere.

Without noticing, I fall asleep, my body trained to maintain its position. It is hours later, the sun low in the sky when I hear a voice. It takes a while to process the words. It is no more than a whisper.

"Sayyd, look."

Izem is speaking, and I gather the strength to raise my head and see what has his attention.

"What is it?" My voice is a croak, the hot air burning my throat.

"Water, Sayyd. The camels."

He gasps the words as if they hurt. The camels have a spring in their step. They can smell water and know exactly where to go. I nod to Izem in recognition of his observation and assure myself that Taj has not fallen. She seems to be sleeping. I feel myself drift into a half-slumber too. Let the camels lead the way. They know what they are doing.

A remarkably short time later and we are smiling and laughing good-naturedly at each other's tomfoolery, reveling in the sweet taste of the muddy water. We drown ourselves in its cooling embrace and splash like children. Replete with a surfeit of the life-giving substance, we seek shade from the lingering afternoon sun, as the camels take their fill. Their need was not so great. They can survive for weeks, but for us it was a minor miracle of good fortune and timing.

Taj seems more observant than before. She looks around, taking in the vastness of the desert and the singularity of palm trees that spring from the sand.

"Izem," she asks. "Are we out of danger now? Do you think we are likely to run into more trouble?"

It has taken a while for Izem to become comfortable with Taj but now he seems to treat her like his honorary sister.

"This is as-Sahra al-Kubra. Trouble will follow us no matter what we do. I fear that we must be on our guard as much now as ever."

I nod in agreement. "As you say. And yet I could almost wish for trouble. Perhaps it is time to settle things with Ibrahim once and for all."

"Do not say that, Jam-ez!" Tajeddigt exclaims. "He will kill us all."

"I agree," said Izem. "Do not wish for that man to find us." He raises his hands, palms out, as if warding off the idea then clutches the talisman at this throat. "Come, Sayyd, we must prepare for the night. It will distract you from thoughts of that man."

I nod. Our preparations are simple enough. We hobble the camels and take from them our bedding. It is bitter cold in the deep desert at night. As cold as it is hot during the day. Can two more opposite states exist in any other single place?

We make a fire, which always cheers us. A little dried camel dung burns remarkably well. We have a wonderfully domestic routine, Izzy, Taj and I. We make tea, using my old copper kettle. I can still hardly credit that it has survived my wanderings, but it appears to be indestructible, although not quite so shiny as when I bought it at the souk in Damascus, all those years ago.

I take charge of the tea, while Izem digs out the remaining dried meat and cheese. There is even a little bread and honey and Taj musters the strength to prepare it. Can there be a better repast than a four-course meal in the desert? The great orange orb of the sun sinks down beyond the horizon, and takes with it the vicious heat. Night falls fast, as it always does here, and the temperature drops with it. For a while we experience the delicious sensation of not being hot, before the cold sets in and we start to shiver.

After the meal, Taj rests her head on my chest as we huddle within our blankets, more than comfortable. As harsh as the day can be, the night always makes it worth it. Not just the cooler temperature, which finally allows us to think, but also Nature's most wonderful entertainment. Before I ventured into the high sands I would not have believed a true description of the wonders of the sky at night, but here and now I can see further into the universe than I would have dared to imagine. The sky is ablaze with light.

We play our usual game of spotting falling stars and Izem, as usual, wins. His senses are more acute, a fact that has served us both well in the last months. In the last days even. The sad incident with the bandits being just the latest example. I push it from my mind as I grow melancholy when I think of the necessities forced upon me. They may have been simple opportunists. But then again, perhaps not.

Taj is sleeping, her face child-like in slumber. I have almost joined her when Izem nudges me with his foot. Instantly I am alert, my hand moving to my side. I carry one of Izem's pistols now, my beloved Westley-Richards too damaged to use. A shame. I can sense something, the hairs on my neck prickling. We glance to each other and I see Izem reach under his robe slowly.

A dark figure rises from the sand beyond the watering hole, keeping his distance. This is courtesy, showing he is not a threat. He shuffles forward, calling out a greeting, his right hand going to his heart.

"As-salamu alaykum."

I respond as any good Muslim would. "Wa alaykumu s-salam," my hand moving away from my pistol.

Taj wakens and stares about with wide eyes. I shush her and get up, gesturing for the man to approach our camp. He is Bedouin, and old. A toothless smile and a face like weathered mahogany is all his copious black robes reveal. Motionless, in the dark of the night, he is almost invisible. As he approaches, I scan the horizon for any sign of movement. Nothing. If he is not alone, his companions are not making themselves known. Yet, anyway.

So for now it seems we have a guest. I pour tea into a glass and Izem makes space for him by the fire. The man sits, taking his ease upon the blankets, his nod and hand on heart are thanks enough for us. The hand that takes the glass is brown and withered, gnarled by age, like the twisted roots of an ancient tree. But his eyes are a shocking blue. They are a young man's eyes and seem to take in everything around him.

"You are kind, my son," he says.

He speaks a language quite similar to the Tuareg tongue I have been learning. Though not yet fluent, I understand him well enough.

"You are welcome, father." My response is stilted, but he understands.

He smiles his toothless grin at me, sips his tea and sighs.

Tajeddigt sits up straighter, and straightens her robes, making herself presentable. "Where are you going, father?" she asks. "This is no place."

He does not answer but nods heavenward. I miss his meaning but Izem clearly does not. His look of concern is genuine.

"Is there anything that we can do for you, father?"

"No, but you have my thanks. It is good to rest a while amongst honorable folk."

"You are welcome to stay with us as long as you wish," Taj says. "We journey west. Will you join us?"

"No, my daughter. My journey will end here, insha'Allah."

Taj has spread some of the honey on the hard dry bread to soften it. She offers it to the old man.

"Then you will at least stay with us tonight?" I ask in my halting Berber.

He nods, and gravely accepts the bread. "Yes. You have my thanks."

I have heard how some of the desert people will walk out into the deep sand to meet their end when they feel their time has come. It has appeal, if I am honest. I can feel an attraction, pulling me towards the dunes. To be swallowed, perhaps to appear again in another thousand years, where archaeologists will puzzle over me as they do with the mummies of the ancient Pharaohs.

"Are you of the faith?" the old man asks.

The question startles me, given my train of thought, but Izem answers without hesitation.

"There is no God but Allah, and Mohammed is his prophet."

He prays, when he can. I do not. "Yes, father, we observe the five pillars."

The old man raises a finger and wags it in my face in admonishment, a knowing smile on his face. I wonder if he can tell I am not what I appear?

"You are walking into the desert, father?"

He knows what I am asking and nods. He sips his tea, still smiling, as if perfectly content with his world and his place within it.

"How do you know it is the time for your passing?" I ask.

"I have known for most of my life the hour of my leaving."

His answer provokes more questions in my mind but I merely nod. I have known men like this before. Fakirs, touched by something beyond understanding. They know things, see things. Understand what others cannot. Is he such a man? His gaze pierces me. Eyes so blue. He sees my thoughts and answers them.

"I am not one such," he said. "But I am blessed. I see what is hidden. But it is no power of mine. When young I was given a great gift. It is both a wonderful and terrible thing. A djinn has been with me since I was a small boy."

I had not expected this. I look to Izem to gauge his reaction and see his face has paled. He is glancing about, as if expecting a specter to jump out at him. I have heard the tales and read the stories. But here is a man who believes in a powerful being that is halfway between the worlds of the physical and the spiritual. I nearly laugh, thinking for a moment he is joking, but Izem's face could not be more serious.

Taj blinks rapidly, surprised by the revelation. But she seems to take it in stride. "An Ifrit?"

The old man shakes his head. No, not an evil spirit. Taj nods, satisfied, but Izem looks disconcerted.

Is there really something to it then? Surely not. But I cannot help but wonder what it would mean to have such a companion. The old man looks at me.

"It is a burden and a gift. What it will become is up to you, my son."

I do not like the way he looked at me when he said *you*. But he would not say more on the subject and we content ourselves with watching the stars and sipping tea. The moon is up now, its silver dollar face shining brightly.

A camel snorts, then groans an alarm. Something is disturbing them. We become alert, eyes searching in the gloom. The old man sees our agitation and shakes his head.

"It is nothing. There is no harm here tonight." He looks at Taj, then looks away, his expression carefully neutral, but for just a moment I thought I could detect an infinite sadness.

I suspect I know what has the camels spooked but believe him when he says there is no harm. The silence now is so profound that none wishes to break it. It is time to sleep. I put my arm around Taj and she nestles against me, as close to the fire as we dare. Sleep takes us swiftly, as it always does in the great desert. When we wake in the morning the old man is gone.

He left behind a gift to repay our hospitality. The only worldly thing remaining to him. A small clay bowl, inscribed with simple geometric patterns along its chipped and worn rim.

I take it and place it with great care in the pack on my camel. I do not know why, but I feel it is important and that I will need it. Both a burden and gift, I remind myself, and suddenly I know what it signifies and know, too, that I am strong enough to carry it. Izem sees me pack the bowl away and starts muttering to himself. He also understands, but is evidently much perturbed. I find myself intrigued and frightened in equal measure.

# And you'll believe in more than me

## 4

The function of prayer is not to influence God,
but rather to change the nature of the one who prays.
*—Søren Kierkegaard*

Philip awoke to find himself still at his desk. The sun shone brightly through the windows and he blinked groggily as he began to straighten, turning his head to work out the kinks in his neck. Then the dream came back in all its extraordinary detail. He gasped, shocked at the strength of the vision that had taken him into the deep desert. It was like no dream he'd ever had, as clear and real as if it were his own memory. More than a little dizzy, his heart pounding, he was overwhelmed. Nothing could have prepared him for this. He had not just seen the events described in the diary, he had lived them. He had seen with Sir James' eyes, felt what he felt, knew what he thought. Without the slightest understanding he was certain that what he had seen was real. It had happened exactly like that.

He took a deep, shuddering breath. Had he been drugged or hypnotized? Could Mr. Francis have worked some elaborate hoax? And if so, why? Philip knew that hypnosis subjects could be made to believe almost anything. Even easier when they wanted to believe, and who could want to see the past more? He shivered, frightened to discover he could be so influenced. To have someone else pulling the strings, manipulating what he saw. Perhaps even controlling what he believed and thought. It was appalling. He felt sick to his stomach.

He was still sitting at his desk in front of the laptop where he had written the title before he fell asleep. Four words. Then he nodded off and experienced the . . . the what? The dream? The vision? Ridiculous. And yet what else could he call it?

His eyes went to the screen, finding far more than four words. Page after page flowed before his eyes. He stared, dumbfounded at the word count in the lower menu bar. Seven thousand, three hundred twenty-two. He scrolled through in a frenzy, reading parts at random. It was his, what he had planned to write, including content from the abandoned manuscript. Over seven thousand words, and no idea how they got there.

Philip had read about something like this. A nineteenth-century text that described a phenomenon called automatic writing. A serious individual, he had dismissed it as unscientific hocus-pocus. Anyway, this was something else. The style. Distinctly his voice. Main points, some of them, structured exactly along the lines of his own thought. But try as he might he could not recall writing a word.

The old man, obviously, had done something to him. How? His last words from yesterday, the piercing blue eyes and the knowing smile, came back with a shock. Sweet dreams, Mr. Entwhistle. Philip clutched his head. Was he going mad? He dragged his eyes away from the screen to stare deliberately out the window, forcing himself to take in the tops of the houses opposite, the blue of the sky. Then, hesitantly, he turned back to the screen. Still there. This was impossible.

He would take a shower, a change of clothes, and go back to the cottage to confront the old man. Demand an explanation. Whatever had happened to him had been incredible. Yes, the text was good, solid work. But he was being messed about. He would put a stop to it. Could Francis have put something in his tea? Perhaps . . . LSD? No more of dear old Mr. Francis' tea, thank you very much.

Leaving his apartment, he ran into Mrs. Hardy in the lobby, a grander name than the common hallway deserved. She greeted him with a smile and, distracted as he was, he took the time to ask about her son. His exams would be coming up soon and Philip knew she was worried.

"Good of you to remember, Mr. Entwhistle. He just did Geography and English. Now it's just History and French left, and then it's off to the dole queue."

"Just let me know if he wants any help with his history revision. Always happy to lend a hand. Give me a chance to natter on about something that happened a hundred years ago and I'm in heaven."

"That's so kind of you, Mr. Entwhistle. I'll tell him to pop by. You can give him some pointers and whatnot."

"Do that. It would be my pleasure. Maybe sometime during the week? Doesn't matter when, I'll be working late, regardless."

"I'll let him know, Mr. Entwhistle."

Mrs. Hardy's son was an average student but he did try and wanted to succeed. Philip would help him if he could. It was not entirely selfless. The boy, like many of his generation, had a knack with computers and Philip had good reason to seek extra security. They could have something of a quid pro quo session, give the kid a few pointers, in exchange for setting up a firewall or whatever it was called.

On the drive out of the city he reviewed again and again the extraordinary dream. Playing back the emotions and the thoughts and feelings as if they were a reel of film. No, not quite. Not like a movie. Precisely as if they were his own memories. In spite of his discomfort, he was fascinated.

Arriving at the cottage he parked in what he had already begun to see as his spot, smiling grimly at what he imagined Paul Sumpter would have to say about that. He gave himself a few moments to contemplate the entirety of the last twelve hours. Did it matter if it was a hoax? It had given him so much more than he could have hoped for from the diary alone.

With a deep breath he made his decision. Yes. He wanted it. He wanted to do it again. No. More – he needed to do it again. Hypnotism, LSD or pixie dust, he simply did not care. As a historian, to be able to actually relive the past was the closest he could imagine to a religious experience.

Philip grabbed his satchel, climbed out of the car, slammed the door and strode up the path to the cottage. The great red portal stood ajar. Of course. The old magus would not have been in the slightest doubt of his return. With a last deep breath, he straightened his back and went inside the cottage.


Elizabeth Sandwell was in the Humanities building. A broad church, it was the home of literature studies, languages, history, psychology, anthropology and sociology. So many 'ologies,' including her own field: parapsychology, a label she regarded with cynical amusement. Psychology had nothing to do with it. If only they knew. The idiots.

She walked up to the third floor and took the left corridor to the offices of the history dons, knowing exactly where she was going. She looked around casually; just a stroll. With lectures in progress the place was deserted. Swiftly she pulled a key from her handbag and unlocked the third door to the right. The key had proven most useful this last year, a master key to every office in the entire University.

It had been a snip, telling the maintenance chief she had lost her own office key. A simple charm and she had the master key in her hand just long enough to pop into her office and get her bag. He had insisted on coming with her, as she fully intended. But what he did not know about, standing waiting for her to emerge, was the picture she had quickly taken of the master key using a special key copy application on her mobile phone. And now she had the run of the University with nobody the wiser.

The lock turned with a click and she slipped inside the room, pulling the door closed behind her. The black lettering on the door read *Dr. P. Entwhistle.*

Sandwell's lip curled at the sight of the mess, the chaos of the small office. Piles of books on the floor, everything in utter disorder and confusion. How could a man with a doctorate in history ever achieve anything working in such conditions? She fought down a powerful urge to tidy and straighten. There was something distasteful about a man who could not keep things in decent order.

She put down her bag, sat at his desk and tapped the computer mouse. The large screen lit up; the login page. Password required. With a smile she changed users to 'Administrator' and typed the credentials. With the master key in hand the admin password had been her first objective. The head of IT was hardly the genius he imagined. Finding his list of passwords on the corkboard under last year's Pirelli calendar took Sandwell all of ten seconds.

Logged in, she started to systematically check Entwhistle's files. Beginning with the most recently opened, she worked her way back, checking anything he might have accessed since she was last in his office.

Finding nothing of interest, she checked into his email account, scanning through subject lines. Still nothing, just the usual correspondence from staff and students. Nothing out of the ordinary. She toyed with the idea of sending something malicious from his account. No. The date stamp. He may be able to show he was not in his office when it was sent, and even the head of IT, that poor dweeb, would figure that out eventually. No. Better keep it simple.

Then she spotted something in his Sent folder. An email addressed to Sam . . . Sam? Yes, Dr. Evans, surely. Eagerly she ran through the content.

*Hi, Sam. I have had a bit of luck, found something that could be big. And I do mean big. Sorry to put you in a bit of a bind but I am going to need to take some time off, effective immediately. Don't worry, I am fine. I just need a month or so to research and write a new book. Once again, apologies for the abruptness of my request. Sanjay can cover for me, no problem. I'll send him my lecture notes, not that he needs them.*

She smiled, delighted. Well, well. This confirmed her scrying. He really did find something in the stacks. But what? No clue in the email. Delight gone, she ground her teeth in frustration. Could it be here? Most of the books were new, with shiny covers and barcodes. It must have been pre-war. It seemed even Entwhistle wasn't stupid enough to leave it lying in plain view in his office.

She logged out, leaving the mouse in the exact position she had found it, not that he would notice given his obviously chaotic nature. But she was careful. She was always careful. Frustrated, she had to do something, anything. Some small spite that could plausibly be overlooked or explained away.

On the desk she spied a pen, black, with a herringbone pattern etched in the body and a gold nib. It looked expensive. With a smile, she snatched it up and dropped it into her handbag. Opening the door a crack she peeked through. The corridor was empty. She was out and back in the main campus within minutes. But now, at least she had something. Whatever Entwhistle had found it warranted a month off. *Really big.* His own words.

She would have to keep a close eye on Entwhistle now. It would be easier if she could rely on someone other than Sumpter, but that was the cost of her solitary approach. Sandwell's mouth twisted into an ugly sneer as she thought of the covens, and Wiccans with their beauty charms and herbal remedies. Wretched pretenders. If there were other practitioners in England close to her in power, she had not sensed them. No, she would go it alone, just as she always had. Whatever Entwhistle was doing, she would find out eventually.

Philip entered the darkened hallway. All the doors were closed in the narrow passage, leaving little natural light, rendering it gloomy and claustrophobic. He called out, his voice sounding odd to his ears, as if it belonged to someone else.

"Hello? Mr. Francis?"

Getting no answer he strode down the hallway towards the bright light of the kitchen. He found Francis stirring milk in a saucepan on the stove. His face was somber, his typical urchin grin missing. If he knew anything he was not giving it away. Francis looked up from his task, his face only now cracking in a slight smile as he saw the younger man.

"Good morning, Mr. Entwhistle. Sleep well, I trust?"

"Yes, Mr. Francis. Very well. A most elucidating night."

The old man dropped the wooden spoon and turned quickly, his smile now merry and wide. "Oh, I am so glad. You know it is not everyone that can connect."

So Mr. Francis admitted responsibility for last night's experience. Rather than being angry to discover the architect of his vision, Philip was thrilled. If the old man had done it once, he could do it again.

"I dreamed of him, Mr. Francis," blurted Philip, grinning with excitement, his hands energetically punctuating each word. "I *was* him!"

The old man clapped his hands together, looking almost like a little boy at Christmas. "Oh, how wonderful. And what did you see? Tell me everything?"

Philip sat at the table while Francis poured warm milk into the cat's old clay bowl. Philip looked at it as if seeing it for the first time. An odd little thing, weathered and chipped, with a strange geometric pattern painted around the rim.

His heart did a flip. It was the gift from the old Bedouin. Francis placed it on the floor and Jinny began to lap hungrily.

"Come, come, Mr. Entwhistle, you must tell me everything."

From his usual chair across the kitchen table he looked at Philip searchingly, his eyes sparkling, almost glowing with an inner light.

As he related the events of the dream, Philip felt again the weight of Sir James' emotions. His fears, and needs. His fierce hunger for *her*.

From the dream, Philip now knew if not who she was, at least what she was. His lover. The woman who commanded his heart. Tajeddigt. Taj, he called her. Taj, his little flower.

"I have to know more, Mr. Francis. I neither know nor care how you did it, but I have to know more."

The old man nodded. "Rest assured that if you choose to do it again, you may. And soon. But if you continue there will be a price, which you must pay."

"Mr. Francis, I willingly agree to whatever terms you state."

The old man shook his head, one finger raised in warning. "They are not my terms, nor is it I who will collect the debt."

Philip shrugged his shoulders and nodded. Whatever the old man's meaning it did not matter. All that mattered was the work. The visions were the key to everything.

The old man's next words gave Philip a fleeting sense of finality, as if the die had been cast.

"Very well. So shall it be."

With that the old man got up slowly from his chair, picked up the cat's bowl and started to wash it in the sink. Philip marched smartly back along the hallway to the study. The diary was on the desk. He pulled his laptop from his bag and settled down to work. He turned the pages carefully until he found the entry for June 27. He read the line again. The line he had thought to contain a code word.

*He told us that the djinn was with him, and he knew much that was hidden.*

But the dream had destroyed Philip's initial theory. He had *been* Sir James and knew the Bedouin was no messenger. There was no secret code. The Bedouin was just what he appeared. A harmless, possibly crazy old man, walking to his death in the desert. He turned the page and began to read, pen poised over his legal pad.

Fern Aasheim lifted another heavy cardboard box and stacked it on top of an already teetering tower standing by the door to her tiny apartment. She had been packing all day and was finally getting down to the last bits and pieces. The room was almost bare now with just a chair in one corner, a floor lamp and a glass of white wine sitting next to her phone on the mantle above the fireplace. Around the room, a haphazard collection of bags and boxes, many labeled in hastily scrawled marker pen. Words like kjøkken, stue, bøker and klær.

She stepped back from the precarious pile and nudged one of the lower boxes with her knee, trying to align it more neatly, nearly toppling the entire stack.

A mere three steps and she was across the room reaching for her glass, sipping the sharply aromatic wine. With a shrug of her shoulders she tipped the glass back and emptied it, downing it in a couple of swallows. As she replaced the glass the phone began to ring.

She snatched it up and the screen came to life. "Hello?"

"Heisan Pernilla. Hvordan går det?"

She snorted. How many times had she asked him not to call her that?

"Jens, why can't you call me Fern?"

"Hah! Maybe I should just call you pot plant, eh?"

Her brother Jens was a year younger than her and a tease. At twenty-eight she was not above a little childish behavior herself, but her new name was not something to make fun of. Pernilla was common enough in Scandinavia, even if it had fallen out of fashion in recent years. Devoid of vanity, she had no particular problem with it but now she had found her true name, her craft name. "Please Jens. If you want an answer, call me Fern."

"Alright. Hello, Fern. How are you?"

"Busy. What do you want, Jens?"

"Well, things are a bit tight on the farm. Papa would never say so but he could use some help. If there is any chance that you could do anything it would be appreciated."

"Oh. I wish I could. But that's not going to be easy."

"Strapped for cash?"

"You could say that. But I'll do what I can."

Fern considered her position. Once the hedge witch was dealt with she could move on, maybe find a full-time job that paid better than the University.

"Maybe in a couple of months," she said. "I really wish I could help. Is the farm really in trouble?"

"From what I understand it's barely ticking over. One bad spring, and that could be it."

"Oh. Not good. Well, I promise I will do my best. Give my love to mama and papa."

"Sure, will do. Thanks Pernil . . . Fern."

She hung up. Calls from Norway to mobiles were still expensive. No point in wasting money neither of them had.

The farm was home. It worried her that her family might lose it. She had not been back for several years and wondered if it was time for a visit. Perhaps by now they may have gotten over their shock at her choices.

No. She must not be distracted, even by thoughts of home. Find the one abusing the natural order, that was paramount. More than once, while working in the library, she had felt a sense of unease and that nameless feeling came upon her again. Fern trusted her psyche to tell her what she needed, eventually. It would come out in a dream, washed onto the shore of her conscious mind like flotsam. But there was another way. A quicker way. She went to one of the boxes, opened it and removed a small silk-wrapped packet.

She pulled the layers apart, revealing a pack of brightly colored Tarot cards, sank to the floor and placed them before her. Briefly, she laid a hand on them and closed her eyes. After a moment, a little sigh of satisfaction. Ready.

The cards were special, the work of her own hands, painted over many months and quite literally the only thing of value she owned. At least, of value to her.

As well as the traditional figures with the greater and minor arcana she had added the sixteen characters of the Old Norse runic alphabet, one rune per card but with two for each of the final two arcana cards. The angular symbols of the older futhark, in combination with the Tarot cards, laid out two divinatory paths.

She shuffled the deck and split it into two roughly equal piles. Placing the pile to the right on top of the other she quickly peeled off three cards, laying them face down on the floor.

She turned over the center card: the energy of the present. Artemis, sitting on her throne. The card of wisdom, seeking knowledge that is hidden. This, Fern saw, was her search for the rogue witch. Now she flipped the first card: the energy of the past. A figure walking away from the seeker. A searcher for fulfillment. A card Fern saw often, representing her own search for knowledge and place in the world. Satisfied, she reached for the final card. As she turned it over her eyes widened, one eyebrow arching. This was most unexpected.

The Lovers. Relationships, choices, union, passion. A slight smile curved her lips. Well, well, well. I wonder who?

Still smiling, she stood, collected her glass and made for the tiny kitchen and the bottle of wine. She poured herself another drink and raised her glass in a silent salute; to herself, to the fates and to the future.


Philip read the next five entries with a mounting sense of skepticism. In the cold light of day the previous night's vision was fading from his mind, suppressed by his ingrained analytical and empirical view of the world. It could not be serious. There must be some kind of underlying meaning he was not getting. He went back and started to read them again.

*June 30. It came in the night. The djinn. Was it a dream? I know not. I believe it judged that I had reached my limit. It offered me water and wine. I refused of course. Izem is terrified. He wants me to cast it off. I cannot. He does not understand. The gift was given freely. It was accepted gladly. Every man to his fate. We need water badly but I will not be tempted by the djinn's promises. Taj suffers. We all suffer.*

*July 1. We are in the deepest desert now but too far south, I fear. Nevertheless, there is no going back. To return is to perish. Our only choice is to press on and hope for water, and it must be soon. One of the camels died in the night. We butchered the poor beast, draining its blood into the copper kettle. Taj and I drank. What we could both stomach, anyway. It is not the first time I have found myself in straits so dire. But it is no easy thing. Izem refused, of course, and I gave him the last of the water. I had to threaten to pour it into the sand before he would take it. We have one more day in us. We might make it. Just. Insha'Allah.*

*July 2. Again a visit from the djinn. This was no dream. No child of an idle brain, no fantasy. It spoke, beseeching me. Why? Why? I do not know what to tell it. I refuse every offer. What can it give me that I need? Water is nothing. Wine is nothing. What need have I for things of the body when it vies for so much more? I fear what any obligation to it will mean. Will it own me? Will it control me? I will be no puppet for some wraith's amusement. Besides, we will reach water soon enough. My only concern is Tajeddigt. During the night her breathing was so shallow I could hardly tell if she yet lived.*

*July 3. I dreamed of Taj during the night, just as she was when I first met her. It was heaven. When I awoke, I cradled her in my arms and wept like a child. She has become so frail. I do not believe she will survive this journey, and if she dies, so shall I. Izem says we are cursed. I laughed, but he is probably right.*

*July 4. We found water. The camels always know. The djinn says that it can help us, we just need to ask. So far, I have resisted all temptation and it grows impatient. But again I dreamt of Taj as she was. Young, healthy, beautiful. Each night, I would sleep longer. I would sleep forever, if I could always dream of her. And each day when I waken I find her diminished. She cannot speak now without slurring her words. She is delirious. If cutting out my heart would save her I would do it, but that is not in my power. I am helpless. She is leaving me behind and I will not have it. The djinn thinks it has found the chink in my armor. It knows my heart and what I would do to have her as she was. It whispers. It is always whispering. Its offers of water and wine mean nothing, but it knows it has found my only desire. It will give me Tajeddigt back again, just as she was. I only have to ask. God help me, I am tempted.*

What was all this nonsense, talking about a djinn as if it were real? It was certainly no metaphor, nor a code for some secret purpose. Grudgingly, Philip was forced to accept it for what it was. A true relating of Sir James Francis' thoughts and experiences in June and July of 1922. And the man clearly seemed to believe every word he wrote.

For the purposes of research, Philip knew he need not believe in fairytales, only accept that his subject apparently did, which disturbed him. From his research he knew Sir James for an absolute pragmatist with a keen intellect. One who drank the blood of a dead camel when there was no water to be had. What could be more pragmatic than that?

Of course, as a Muslim, Izem would refuse the blood, preferring to die of thirst. What did they call it? Philip looked up the word in his Arabic primer. Yes. Haram; any act repugnant to Allah. Drinking blood was most certainly haram. But if Sir James was dealing with the hardships of crossing the great desert in his usual practical manner, what had changed? Why was he acting so superstitiously? It was almost as if he was crazy. A suspicion began to form in Philip's mind. What if Sir James was experiencing hallucinations? They have no water! Can that cause someone to hallucinate?

But last night's dream defied logic. Accepting it, could he judge Sir James for his apparent belief in the supernatural? Philip brushed the thought away. He would find a logical explanation for everything. He would. Dehydration, that was it.

This was a lead worth pursuing. It would certainly explain the odd behavior. Sir James Francis believing in a djinn, of all things. But if Tajeddigt was seriously sick, possibly with malaria, was Sir James as well? They could have been infected years before, anywhere in Africa. He felt relieved. A reasonable hypothesis. Yes. He was reading the ravings of delirium, plausible and certainly preferable to the alternative fairy tale.

He made a note on his legal pad. *Dehydration. Side effects– hearing voices? Aural hallucinations?* He returned to the diary, sifting for subtle clues to location or motive.

Counting the days, assuming a reasonably constant speed of travel, he estimated that the source of the water they found on July fourth would be the Jalu oasis. A journey of approximately two hundred forty miles. An average of forty miles a day might be possible – thirty or more was commonplace – and Jalu seemed the only option. He made another note in his pad. *Search museums, any institute that might have records from the time, looking for mention of mysterious visitors.* Corroboration. A slim chance, he knew. Decision made, he jotted a few more notes, then came to a halt.

It was no good. The diary was gold but last night, that was the diamond. Few historical biographies truly brought their subject to life in the way that his dream offered. A dream that produced thousands of words. Incredible. To feel with Sir James's body, think with his mind, and wake to find the work done. However Mr. Francis did it, he had to do it again. The old man had talked of a price, suggesting some Faustian bargain. Well, let him name it. It would have to be high, very high, for Philip to refuse. He quivered with anticipation, then stood suddenly and began to pace around the small office. How should he broach the subject?

Almost as the question formed it was answered. He heard Francis shuffling in the hallway. He came into the study, clutching a tray and clearly struggling to suppress the trembling of age. On the tray, a mug of tea and a scattering of biscuits.

"I thought that you might like a break, Mr. Entwhistle."

Philip looked suspiciously at the tea. Had he been drugged the day before? Was this how he did it? So what? He wanted more, didn't he?

"Thank you, Mr. Francis," he said, relieving the old man of his burden and placing it on the desk. He took one of the biscuits and the mug. The cat made an appearance, gave him a look and disappeared again to wherever it is that cats go when they are not observed.

"Would you kindly give me a moment in the hallway, Mr. Entwhistle? I wish to tell you a little of my family."

Philip took a quick sip and followed the old man into the hallway, where Francis flicked a switch to turn on the ceiling lights, giving Philip his first clear view of the pictures.

"I am the last of the line, you know," he said. Philip nodded. What do you say to that?

Mr. Francis pointed to a picture of a young woman with curling, golden locks hanging to her shoulders. Dressed in a symphony of white, almost sheer lace, the contours of a woman's figure showed through the almost translucent material. Rather racy for its time.

"Mama. A famous beauty. She died young, not long after I was born, I am sorry to say."

"She was lovely," Philip said, meaning it.

Mr. Francis closed his eyes and bowed his head, scarcely breathing. When he opened his eyes a moment later they were wet with nascent tears, making Philip uncomfortable, unaccustomed to such feelings. Should he say something? Unable to find anything adequate he kept his silence. Francis turned to him and shook his head gently.

"It's fine, Mr. Entwhistle, really. I have had a long time to become accustomed to my life. You need not feel bad for me."

Philip looked down at his feet, avoiding Francis' gaze, then glanced up at the portraits.

"Mr. Francis, I'm puzzled." He took a few paces to stand before the portrait of Sir James. "When was this painted?"

Jinny had reappeared and wound between their legs, alternating between Philip's and her owner's. She looked up at them, head cocked quizzically.

"I don't know the exact date. Does it matter?"

"I'm not sure. It seems somehow . . . wrong. Incomplete. As if something is missing."

The old man shrugged. "You have seen much in the visions, yes?"

"Yes. I have to admit that they reveal more than I could possibly understand from the diary alone."

"Quite so, Mr. Entwhistle. There is much for you to understand. But not everything and not all at once. But the answer to your question is before you, I think. It is perhaps the quickest, certainly the surest way. I believe you are ready for more, yes?"

Before Philip could reply he felt Mr. Francis' oddly cold hand grip his own. A wrench, and he was sitting on the lurching back of a dromedary, a riding crop dangling limp in his hand, tongue swollen with thirst, gazing through Sir James' eyes at a vast desert. The sun burned but he refused to shut his eyes, risking blindness to defy the elements.


I must hang on. We shall make it. I refuse to die here. The camel plods remorselessly on, transporting our incipient corpses from one barren dune to another. Izem fares no better than I. He drank the last of the water, is it two days ago already? Taj and I are the better for drinking that wretched animal's blood. I will never eat blood sausage again should I live past this day.

*Hearken, Man. You can have cool water. Why thirst?*

The djinn is now my constant companion, like a shadow that flits ahead, then behind, never still, intent on securing my gratitude for some deed. I have no doubt it seeks to draw me into obligation. I am reminded of tales of the djinn and their three wishes. And if I wish for water, will it get my soul? The laugh comes out as a strangled cough.

Get thee behind me, djinn. I will see myself dead in the dust before I let you own me. I do not know what it needs but it offers nothing I am prepared to ask for. Not at its unknown price. Better to ignore it.

*Please. Just drink. I would help you!*

Perhaps. Perhaps it is just trying to help itself. I do not know. But my instincts tell me any bargain will not be in my favor. The longer I resist, the more strident its pleas. The day after the old Bedouin man blessed, or cursed me with the creature, I still had little idea what it was. I packed the bowl. I accepted it, thinking myself the stronger, but now I feel it probing my weakness. I fear an infernal enslavement. Death, rather.

Izem is falling from his mount again. I reach across and with all the strength at my command push him upright. He seems to come out of his trance and smiles a wan thank you.

"Sayyd. I do not think I can go on much longer." His tongue is thick, his voice slurred. His words are hard to understand, barely a mumble.

I have the same sentiment but it does not do to give up. I try to give him a smile but his eyes have glazed over. Tajeddigt lies motionless, preserving every scrap of energy while her tawny camel soldiers on. They are too dumb to just lie down and die. But when they finally collapse I will simply wrap my blanket around myself, and let their bones mark mine.

But wait. The camels are changing direction. The beast in the lead lets out a bellow and as one they all pick up speed, describing a slight tangent to our path. I am restored to hope.

"Izem, they smell water."

"Thanks be to Allah."

"Thanks indeed."

Even Tajeddigt raises her head and smiles. We are saved.

*Wine. You can have date wine, cooled in a river. Just ask it of me.*

We are close now to salvation, any temptation too late. The djinn knows, and falls silent. Silent, but not gone. I can feel it, hovering close. But I did not yield. I did not yield!

# But if by trick or subtle ruse

# 5

The undiscover'd country from whose bourn
No traveller returns,
*—Shakespeare, Hamlet Act III, scene V*

Philip returned with a start, reeling, his legs weak. He took a moment, breathing deep. Emotions stormed – loss, longing, anger, fear, all mingled. He rounded on the old man. "Hell and damnation! I have to know. What is this? How are you doing this to me?"

Mr. Francis looked up at him and shook his head, his eyes sad. "I suspect, young man, that you would not believe me. Not quite yet, anyway."

He turned back to the kitchen.

"No. This has gone on long enough. I demand to know the truth. You owe me that much."

The old man whirled around, his finger jabbing the historian in the chest.

"Owe you? Exactly how do I *owe* you anything?"

He was right. Philip sagged, helpless. With a sigh, Francis regarded the younger man for a moment, his features set, then shrugged and gave a low chuckle.

"Very well. You need to know. I understand. But first, you must see."

Bending down to pick up the cat, the old man held it in his arms and said a single word. "Hawk."

Francis stepped back and the world started spinning, twisting. Philip Entwhistle was falling, the dark corridor growing brighter. Impossibly bright.

"Izem, a hawk!" I point skyward and Izem looks, his head swiveling as he searches for the tell-tale black dot of the hovering raptor. His gaze, normally so much keener than mine, has failed him this time and it is I who reap the kudos of discovery. He shades his eyes with a hand and sees it, as it circles, searching the ground far below.

"Very good Sayyd. It is a buzzard, I think."

I have won a small victory and it helps to break the monotony. Our simple game, the first to spot a living creature in this wasteland, normally goes in my dragoman's favor with Tajeddigt a close second, both versed in desert life and lore. But Izem's mind is on other things. On *It*, I am quite sure.

I now see the small creatures long before he does, including the rather deadly scorpion that he almost put his hand on this morning. Our positions have reversed; it is now I who care for him. But we still play our game and he does not mind in the least to see me finally winning. He believes I am simply becoming used to the environment. Perhaps so. But is it something else altogether giving me the advantage?

We need the game. Any game. Any distraction to keep us from falling into a stupor. The majesty of our surroundings has not paled, but grandeur enchants for only so long. Fill a vessel and continue to pour, nothing more goes in. I am the proverbial vase, filled to the brim with rolling sand and steep dunes and an eternal, blue sky.

The camel and I have become old friends and I have grown quite accustomed to her peculiar, rocking gait. Her method of settling still has me clutching the pommel of my saddle as she folds her legs but I have learned to anticipate the sudden lurch preceding the descent.

Regardless of our tentative friendship, the most one can expect of these beasts, she will still chance an opportunistic bite. A sharp whack on the nose is usually sufficient to curb her more recalcitrant nature. As fond as I am of the creature, I dream of flying over the dunes by horse. However, I am forced to admit that, fine as Arab steeds are, they would be dead by now, and us with them. Camels it must be and Izem chose well.

But today we have an easy travel. A mere twenty-five miles before we can drink our fill and replenish our supply of brackish water and unripe dates. As meager as it sounds I look forward to it greatly.

*Hearken to me. I can bring you food. A lamb or a goat. Just ask!*

I believe that I have started to understand something of the nature of the djinn. First seeking to enforce its will upon me, I have stoutly resisted and now it is quite tame, even humble. Clearly I have something it wants and thus far I have made no compromise. I do not fear it, but I hold it in healthy respect.

I have been pondering its origin but know nothing more. I do not pretend to understand where the creature came from, but creature it is. I am sure it is a natural part of the world. Elementals are evidently real, the source I expect of the myriad primitive myths and religions. I think it likely it was a djinn which tempted our Lord and supposed savior during *his* trials in the desert. Is it the fabled Shaytan? Meaning both adversary and evil spirit, or, in other words, djinn. Although my own djinn is not evil. Just damned persistent.

If indeed it was the Djinn that made ancient man believe in a higher power, or gods, then their influence has been staggering, infecting every society since the dawn of time with twisted perversions. Perhaps they are evil then, after all?

The djinn is back; the hair on my neck is prickling.

*No. It is not so. Not all of your peoples worshipped us. There was a time when Man and djinn lived as one. Long ago, but our kind still mourn the passing of the Atln.*

I am quite astonished. The djinn has spoken without demanding or offering something. I had not thought it capable of discussion.

"Tell me about that. How long ago was this?"

*For your kind, very long. For our kind, yesterday.*

I wait. Patience is required when talking with a djinn. Seeing that I will not ask more, it offers.

*More than twenty thousand cycles have passed since the schism.*

The schism. Some manner of split. Between mankind and the elementals? I assume a cycle refers to the time it takes the Earth to orbit the sun. Twenty thousand years ago. Before civilization. Back in the time of the caveman. It evidently knows my thoughts since I can feel its amusement.

*You know less of yourself than you do of me, Man. Your civilization is but a shadow of what it once was. The schism ended the peace between our peoples and your kind were destroyed. There are few of us now in this world.*

I don't know what to make of these revelations. After all, I am just a crazy man in the desert, hearing voices. Isn't that how religions start? I almost laugh at the absurdity and yet I am sure that there is more than a hint of truth in it. But my laugh becomes a cough and the djinn is quick to suggest that it could bring water, or wine. Its tone is more urgent, pleading, but I ignore the offer as always. I am still suspicious of its motives.

The air is so arid that if we sweat we do not know, as it is gone in an instant. The air sucks the moisture from our skin before it has a chance to dry. I look to Tajeddigt and my heart breaks. Her lips are cracked, and her eyes stare, unseeing. She will not survive much more of this.

It has not been a long day but already I need to rest and know Taj does also. I half expect the djinn to try to tempt me with a bevy of belly dancers and promises of peeled grapes, but it is silent, its curiously archaic speech absent. Perhaps it is learning that I cannot be persuaded with pleasures of the flesh anymore. As close to death as we are, I find myself tempted to push my limits just that little bit further.

And if I push too far, then at least Ibrahim need not bother himself. I am perfectly capable of ending my own life here in the desert without his involvement. I have no doubt he is somewhere behind us, searching out our trail in the shifting sands. He is smart, knows that I will avoid the main caravan routes. I am sure he too makes for the empty spaces.

Travelling due west we have already accomplished our day's goal. I see the top of date palms ahead, rising from the sand. As we approach the camels show their excitement as always in the near presence of water. I am excited too, I realize. The prospect of a drink has me sitting upright, straining to see ahead. Taj has not stirred. Even the promise of water no longer sparks her to life.

Those few palms aside, the oasis is a poor affair. As always we must push and bully the camels away from the pool to let us refill the water skins, dipping their hairy hides in the brackish water before letting the camels drink. They refill their own skins quickly enough and we hobble them loosely so they can wander a short distance as they forage about.

I had to help Taj from her camel. Now too weak to walk, she lies in the shade of a tree. I have bathed her face with cool water but she did not seem to notice.

Izem starts to make camp, his movements clumsy from exhaustion. I help. We prepare to settle in for the night. The camels are happy enough, with fresh water and the scant supply of grass and thorny bushes growing in the vicinity of the shallow pond. I am less pleased with our own victuals. We have only the little we bring unless we wish to try scorpion a la mode. Perhaps we should eat them. Avoiding them is such a tiresome task.

I make a noise, a strangled growl. Izem turns to look at me and I hook a finger and waggle it beside my nose. He laughs. He knows I am reminding him of the scorpion that I found basking on his face yesterday morning. They seek our warmth, which they are more than capable of ending with their sting. I had to snatch the armored arachnid by the tail just behind its needle, the only way to pick them up safely. Having grabbed it between finger and thumb, I pulled, and for a moment it hung eye to eye with Izem. One large pincer gripped his beard and it was a pretty little tug-of-war we had before I finally won. Not a nice way to wake up. Its sting is often fatal. A serious situation, much as we laughed about it later.

The oasis is small, but clearly well known to the Bedouin. How not? They know all the places where life may exist in the desert. I see spoor of both goats and camel as well as various signs of humanity. The dried droppings will come in useful though, and we make our supper in the same spot as the previous tenants, a ring of rough stone providing a perfect container for our campfire, which glows a deep red in the falling dusk. The smell triggers memories and I am taken back years, to a campfire in a field near Chiswick. I learned a song then. An old, old tune from a man who claimed to be part Apache. What was it he sang? A partial lyric is all that I remember but it is most apropos and I sing it to myself, albeit tunelessly.

> "And how we cook with buffalo chips,
> or mesquite, green as corn,
> if I'd once known what now I know,
> I'd have gone around Cape Horn."

It haled from the days of the prairie crossings in Oregon, when the Conestogas marched in endless convoys across the endless plain. I had never been in the prairies but was always fascinated by the American West, ever since I saw Buffalo Bill's Wild West Show. It must have been back in '04 or maybe '05. Aldershot. That was it. Visiting our cousins. It was their final tour of England, I am sure. Advertised as a congress of the rough riders of the world. I will never forget the amazing feats. The trick shooting from horseback. The trick riding. I was so taken that I went as far as to have an American-style saddle made, from which I fancied I could do everything a real cowboy could do. I doubt the claim now but as a young man I learned a few fancy tricks, including fast mounts and dismounts, turning in the saddle to ride backwards and even riding standing up.

The memories put me in a better frame of mind. By the fire we are relaxed and at ease. Even the djinn is away making mischief by itself in the sand, drawing odd shapes and symbols that appear as if by magic. I wonder what it is doing. It seems to be writing something. When it notices that I am looking, the marks vanish in a sudden a gust of wind.

Izem starts making rough dough from flour and water, while I put the kettle on a flat rock, placed over the glowing embers to make the most of the heat. This boils the water quickly. The heat is greater above the fire than in it. To save time, we put tea leaves in the kettle. Perfectly palatable but my dear mother, I feel sure, would consider this a vile practice. As the evening progresses we shall simply add more water to the pot, not minding the ever weaker flavor.

I have to help Tajeddigt to drink. She is as tiny and weak as a kitten, and I am ever surer that our enforced flight will kill her. Ibrahim will get his way after all.

Izem is restless. He keeps looking around, searching in the shadows. I see he still fears the djinn. The creature is far from harmless, I am sure, but it seems content to merely follow us and not interfere. I have learned to ignore its tiresome, predictable whispering. Although, if it were willing to discourse, it would make an interesting travelling companion.

I would very much like to talk more with it, about the claims it made. That man and djinn once lived as one. Before the schism, whatever that meant.

I twist a piece of dough in a spiral around a stick and hold it close to the heat. It browns quickly and I rotate the stick to save it from burning. Izem does the same.

The fire is burning low and Izem adds a few more pieces of dried dung. We collect the fuel at every opportunity since they provide the best chance of a comfortable night in the desert. My bread is ready and I pull it from the fire. It is delicious, made finer by the spice of hunger. I eat a piece, then break some off for Taj. She does not look at me but chews mechanically as I feed her.

The smoke of our small fire swirls and eddies in curious formations and I know it is the djinn, playing. It delights in such things. I stare at the rising gray pall and for a moment I see a face. A lean, bearded face, or perhaps it is a child's? Then it is gone.

I suspect that the djinn is indeed like a child. Capricious, wilful and very demanding. A child with a loaded revolver could not be more dangerous but when you have a tiger by the tail you do not let go. Now it has joined our little party we must get used to it, as perhaps it must get used to us.

Not for the first time, I marvel at my situation. So much in the world may be explained by the existence of djinn. I wonder how many of their pranks have been recorded as miracles?

The night grows dark and Izem and Taj sleep. Yet I cannot. I lie awake, staring at the myriad lights burning in the sky. There are often very many falling stars visible in the desert. But at that moment, one of particular brightness streaks across the sky. I wish the others could have seen it, to share in its luck.

In the early hours I have a premonition, a certainty something is wrong. I reach out and touch Taj on her cheek. She is cold.

Desperate, I sit up and feel for her heart, but there is no beat. No pulse of life. I felt her leaving me, I am sure. I knew her end was coming, but this was too soon. I was not ready.

I am too exhausted to cry. All I can do is moan my despair, as I lie back, supine, held down by the crushing weight of my grief.

*Hearken to me. It need not be like this.*

The whispering begins, as it always does. Offering me salvation. Offering me anything, so long as I agree and ask!

*I can take away your pain. Make you forget her.*

What use is this creature? To take away Tajeddigt would be to take the best part of myself. But an idea forms, and I wonder how powerful the elemental really is. It senses my intent immediately and becomes agitated, stirring up the dust in a frenzy of tiny whirlwinds.

"You have offered me your help, your strength. Come then, mighty djinn. You know what I need from you."

*It is forbidden.*

What care I for *forbidden*. The spark has fled my sweet Taj, and I will give my own life to restore her if needs must.

"If you want me," I whisper, "you know what I need. Bring her back."

I speak carefully, so as not to waken Izem. He slumbers on, oblivious to the pact that I am making with the djinn. With the Devil?

*I can make it so you forget. She will never exist in your mind. Better this way.*

My anger at this knows no bounds. I would kill myself before forgetting her. Suddenly, inspiration dawns. "If you do not do as I bid, then I have nothing to live for. I might as well die here too."

Am I mistaken? Was that a surge of panic from the creature?

*You want that I return to you the woman?*

"You know what I want. Give me back Tajeddigt and I will be yours. I will give myself to you."

I am willing to sign away my soul if it would give me back the only person in this world I care for. What manner of man would I be if I was not willing to give everything for her?

*Living energy is needed to restore her. A life, for her life. You agree?*

I glance at Izem. He appears to still be sleeping. A life for her life. God forgive me. I hiss my reply. "Yes!"

There is a sigh. The pact is made. A line has been crossed and now there is no going back.

*It shall be.*

A sudden chill caresses me, and for a moment I am suffused with a great energy. I feel as if I could fly should I just will it. But then, as quickly as it came, the feeling is gone. So too is the djinn. I feel that the creature is absent. Lately I have been able to sense its presence, but now there is nothing. The connection between us had grown stronger the more time passed, so much so that I had even began to sense its thoughts. And now that it is gone, perversely, I feel as if a part of me is missing.

Tajeddigt moves and I forget the djinn. She stretches languorously, as if having just woken from her night's rest. She is no longer sick, her skin is clear, her eyes shining. Her lips that were dry and cracked are now soft and smooth.

I laugh and weep and pull her to me.

"Jamez!"

I kiss her, my rough lips like splintered wood on her soft skin.

"Taj, my God!"

As I crush Taj in my arms, my tears wetting her face, I can feel the djinn's presence again, and for once I welcome it like an old friend. I feel an upwelling of gratitude beyond anything that I could have imagined. I will owe it forever. "Thank you," I say.

It knows the words are meant for it. It knows what she means to me.

The commotion has awoken Izem and he stands, trembling. He senses something has happened but he does not understand.

"Sayyd, what have you done?"

He falls to his knees, facing east in desperation, bowing low, praying. But I do not care. She has come back to me and that is all that matters.

I cannot stop touching her. Stroking her face, holding her hand. She is restored to her girlish self. Just as she was when we first met. We sit, side by side, and her head rests on my shoulder. I could stay like that forever.

Yet we must continue our journey. However, having succumbed to the temptation to use the djinn once, I find that I am less loathe to ask of it more. I know that when the time comes and we need food or water, I will ask it to provide them. Now that Taj is restored, I will not let her suffer. Never again.

She smiles and I laugh. Everything she does delights me. I give her my glass and she drinks the leftover tea from last night. I do not want to ask where she has been for those minutes she was dead, but in spite of myself I am fascinated.

"Taj. Taj, my dear. What was it like? Where you were?"

"What do you mean, Jamez? Where what was like?"

"You were gone Taj. For a little while. Don't you remember?"

She smiled the indulgent smile that you give to a child when he tries to tie his bootlaces for the first time. A mixture of patience and exasperation.

"Jamez, I have not been anywhere!"

The presence by my shoulder. The whisper in my ear.

*Hearken to me. She cannot remember now. It is better this way.*

I nod. Of course. How can one reconcile two different worlds like that? To be dead, then alive again? Resurrected in the flesh.

"Is this a dream, or is she real?" I address my words to the wind, and it answers me.

*She is real. As real as any of your kind.*

We break camp, and Taj rides with me. Sitting before me on the hard saddle. I try to defend her from the nips of the camel's teeth and she laughs. She is well used to the ways of camels. Izem will neither look at her nor speak to me. He is obviously wishing that I had left well enough alone. I do not think he knows of the bargain I was willing to strike. And while I have no doubt that Izem would die for me, I know that he would not choose to give up his life for one already dead.

But the words of the djinn are not easily forgotten. A life for a life. If not Izem, then who?

The house was old, red brick, the front covered almost entirely with a great swath of ivy, reaching as high as the slate roof. The gabled window in the attic was clear of the clinging vine, letting in a shaft of light from the late afternoon sun that ignored the faded, and ragged curtain that hung there. The light fell at an angle to the rough pine planking of the floor, piercing the gloom and illuminating the naked woman sitting, as if meditating, in the center of a large, geometric shape marked out in salt, meticulously aligned to the cardinal points. In each corner of the pentagram, a yellow tallow candle burned brightly. The five-sided star was encompassed by a large circle, around which dozens of symbols and ideograms followed its perfect curve. Ancient words in a nearly forgotten language, which Elizabeth Sandwell recited in an even voice. Her eyes were closed, her mind on the focal point. There, it was enough now.

Sandwell could feel power coursing through her, the lines and symbols of the circle amplifying the effect, focusing it. The energy pulsed in time with her heart, her life force attuned to the natural forces of the universe. Power unlimited, if she could only learn how to harness it. She would need the One's blessing for that.

Her Master would not come casually. The summoning took effort from her and there was considerable danger if it did appear. Sometimes she angered it, and it would hurt her. She could feel its pleasure then, while she writhed in torment, forced to watch her skin blacken and peel, as if horribly burned. Illusion, all illusion. But so real at the time that she would scream and scream until her Master was sated.

But not this time. This time she needed it to provide an answer. Elizabeth took the Athame, her sacred knife, and used it to cut thin lines on her forearm, criss-crossing until they formed a five-sided star. Evidence of other rituals marked her body. Small cuts and scars, showing faintly white against her pale skin.

Blood from the cuts flowed along her wrist, filling her palm, before dripping into a small bowl set before her. She focused her will and the blood thickened, clotting. Before long it was tacky, like putty. Elizabeth smiled in satisfaction and scooped it out, moulding it like dough. Pulling it into a rough shape with arms, head, torso and legs. She pulled and twisted at the homunculus until it was as perfect an imitation of man as she could make. Only a few inches tall, it rested in her palm. Raising her hand to her lips, she breathed into what would be its mouth. The tiny figure twitched. It quickened. A spasm went through it and it moved, arms and legs flexing, flailing, as if it wanted to run, to escape.

She held the tiny creature born of her blood and life essence enclosed within her hands, trapped like a firefly. Tiny shrieks could be dimly heard. Elizabeth closed her eyes and spoke. The ancient words were heavy in the air and they sucked the light out of the room, her voice taking on a deeper timbre as she recited the incantation of summoning.

As she finished the ritual, she forced her hands together, crushing the offering. A puddle of blood filled her palms and dripped down over her thighs. It was small as sacrifices go, but it had life, it would be sufficient. She opened her eyes. Inside the pentagram, in the only triangle of the star that was not aligned to a cardinal point, something formed. Nebulous at first, almost a shadow, it drew the dust in the room towards it and slowly began to coalesce. A thing of shadows, particles and darkness.

Sandwell observed this and a feeling of awe and terror struck through her. This was the most dangerous part. Her Master was unpredictable. She bowed her head in submission.

"My Lord," she said. "I have need of you."

When it came, the voice seemed to come from every direction, but thin, as if heard from a great distance.

"Speak."

"I need guidance, Lord. There are those that oppose me and I must have the strength to destroy them. I need to understand how the mortal, Entwhistle is a threat to me."

"We exist in time, as you. But we are not so blind. We see the threads, the probabilities. It is right to fear this lower creature, but how he opposes you is not clear."

"I need to defend myself against him. I did what I could to undermine him, but I need to be stronger."

"You would that I grant you power?"

"Yes, my Lord."

"Yet you know that no gift can be given. You must pay. What do you offer?"

For a moment she hesitated. There must be balance to the universe. In all things, there is give and take. If she wanted power, she would have to be willing to sacrifice something of equal value. But for her desires to be met, she could not give enough of her own blood to satisfy her Master's hunger; its need. She knew what must be done, and now that the time had come, she found that she was eager.

The darkness that was the voice pulsed. It seethed in formless agitation, growing impatient.

"Why summon me if you have nothing? Must I have my satisfaction from you?"

That meant torment, agony, possibly even death. Her breath shuddered. Sandwell placed her hands together in her lap, holding them firmly to stop them shaking.

"No, Lord. I will give you what you want." She shivered, not from fear now, but excitement. "I will give you a life of an innocent, if that is your will." One of her students: Cassy. She was obviously interested in her tutor. She could easily be persuaded to visit the house. Give just a hint that she desired the girl and the naive child would keep the rendezvous secret. Sandwell could persuade her to climb the steps to the attic and once here, she could do what had to be done.

"A child. I will give her to you, blood, body and soul. She will be yours for eternity. But I want to pierce the veil. Make me immortal, Lord."

"No. It is not enough. A human life is nothing. For what you ask, a creature of real power is required."

Sandwell was confused. A creature of power? Another daemon?

"I am sorry, Lord. I do not understand."

"Your kind are too weak. A higher order being is necessary. There are those among your kind that still bond with the baser elementals. Find one. They are closer than you know. Find an elemental and slay it according to my rite and I will grant you what you desire."

An elemental. A djinn? Where the hell would she find a djinn? But she could not back out. Her Master had told her there were those in the world who bonded with them. She knew this too, or at least had suspected it. But that was a far cry from having one in her power. It would not be wise to ask more from the One.

"Yes, Lord, I will do as you bid."

She spoke the words to end the summoning and the darkness dissipated, the room growing perceptibly lighter. She released a long whoosh of air as the tension left her. She had expected to be punished and was grateful that it had spared her. In times past it had been satisfied by her sacrifice, yet still tormented her body for its own amusement.

*They are closer than you know.* The djinn are dangerous. *Creatures of power.* This was no help. She already knew they sometimes bonded to humans. She had long suspected one had paired with that fool, the old man Francis. The eyes were the clue. The djinn, or their humans, cannot hide their nature. If there was just some way to winkle that fossil out of that fortress he lived in. But he had more magical defenses around him than she did. Which, now that she thought of it, was further evidence of his secret. She should have known. But so long as he remained in the cottage, he was quite safe from her. There had to be some way to get inside. Or find a way to draw him out?

She would need iron and salt to bind the djinn when the time came. That was certainly no problem. The challenge was to get the creature to manifest itself in her presence. She would need to find something, or someone it cared for. The old man, obviously. Or his protégé. Threaten the cub, and the mother comes running. Sandwell smiled, an idea forming in her mind.

Francis stepped forward quickly, taking Philip's arm as he staggered, the young man's face gray. The historian was clearly disoriented and dizzy, almost collapsing from the shock of the transition. Francis steadied him, his hand like an iron claw, gripping tight. Blinking rapidly, Philip took a deep, shuddering breath, then nodded once. He straightened up as if his strength was coming back, flowing into him.

"It's almost too much, Mr. Francis. I felt everything he felt. Everything!" He pulled away, overwhelmed by emotions, unable to keep still.

"I know, Mr. Entwhistle. I know. Perhaps it *was* too much too soon. It can take a while to get used to it."

"But how is this possible?" said Philip. He began to pace. "How can I see his thoughts? His memories?"

He stopped and faced the old man, his eyes searching. Francis looked away, then back again, the full force of his personality in his startling blue gaze. "Do you really have to ask that question? Don't you believe yet, Mr. Entwhistle?"

"I . . .Yes. I believe. The djinn was real. Is real. Is that how you are doing this?" His forehead creased, and with a slight shake of his head, his voice almost a whisper. "You are the djinn?"

Francis laughed. A short bark, not quite a guffaw. He exuded energy, even in his mirth. It was not the breathy laugh or the near cackle of an old man.

"No, my dear boy. I am not the djinn! What a foolish notion. I am just what I appear to be. A dying old man who needs a guardian for a certain inheritance. I had rather hoped you might be willing to take on the responsibility, so to speak."

"I think I need to sit down."

"Of course. Come into the library. There's a nice couch. You can have a little lie down and we can talk."

Francis patted Philip's hand as he led him from the portrait hall into a nearby room. A couple of comfortable chairs, a coffee table and a plush couch were centered around an old television set which, from the dust evident upon it, had not been used in a long time. On one wall was a floor-to-ceiling shelving, crammed to bursting with books. Philip caught a glimpse of some of the titles. They appeared to be related to particle physics, psychology and gardening. He sat on the couch at the old man's urging, while Francis put a cushion behind his back.

Jinny hopped up onto the historian's lap, and circled daintily before curling up into a vibrating ball of fur. Her purring calmed Philip's racing heart and he was grateful for the cat's attention. He stroked her luxurious, black-velvet body.

Francis sat in one of the easy chairs and regarded the younger man carefully. Gone was the mirth. There was no sign of merriment in his eyes, no hint of a smile. Without any preamble, he began. "Mr. Entwhistle, some gifts are so great, they cannot belong to any one person."

He was not expected to talk, but Philip nodded in acceptance of the statement. He hoped Francis would explain things more clearly. God knows he needed it.

"Many years ago a package came, by way of Tunisia. It was from my great-uncle, Sir James. He had sent some letters, some trinkets from the bazaar, the diary and a certain ceramic bowl that he was given by an old man in the desert."

Philip nodded, entranced, fingers itching for a pen and notepad. He considered again the twists of fate that had led him to this moment and how profoundly grateful he was to be in a position that no other historian would ever likely experience.

"The letters are a matter of historical record," said Francis. "The other items were quite ordinary. Or so we thought. A few pieces of silver," at this the old man fingered the pendant around his neck, "the diary and a dirty clay bowl. And the djinn."

Philip was feeling much better and desperately wanted to get his legal pad and pen so that he could make notes, but he dared not get up in case it disturbed the old man's train of thought. The last thing he wanted was to derail him right in the middle of a discourse on the djinn and the Francis family. However, he could not resist asking a question.

"So the fairytales are true? The genie is in the lamp? Or in this case, the bowl?"

Francis smiled wanly. "Not exactly. It is not so easy to explain. The bowl is nothing more than an anchor to our plane of existence. A focal point. If djinn wish to move within our world, they need to attach themselves in some fashion. This can be to a physical object, or even a person. Otherwise, it is a great strain for them to remain here and eventually they are forced out. There are natural laws that we do not conceive of yet and which I cannot explain."

He paused, as if collecting his thoughts. "The nearest I have ever come to understanding the phenomenon is this: imagine a rock climber. He is capable of climbing up a sheer rock face. But he cannot do it indefinitely. It takes a great effort to remain there. The climber needs help if he is to cling to the surface of the cliff, lest gravity makes its presence felt in a very unpleasant way." And with that Francis smacked his hands together. Philip did not need to imagine the effect of falling from a cliff. He was already afraid of heights. Francis continued.

"So the climber uses crampons and ropes and anchors himself firmly to the cliff. I think this is the same for djinn. Without an anchor, they risk falling. But the meta-anchor, the bowl in this case, is not the djinn. It does not contain its spirit. It is simply linked to it. When the old Bedouin gave Sir James the bowl, he did not really give him the djinn. That was a symbolic and necessary act. A pact between the giver and receiver. The bowl is a focus for the djinn to maintain its presence in our reality. But by accepting the gift, Sir James agreed to be linked to the djinn."

For Philip, this just brought to mind more questions, but he tried to quell his curiosity. He wanted Francis to continue with his tale. He glanced around the room, eyes resting on the wall of books. He was astonished to see one of his own titles there, next to a book on metaphysics. It was his biography of Zaghloul, which Francis had previously denied knowing about. Why would he lie? Did he already know who he was before he called? The old man saw the direction of his gaze and smiled, acknowledging the unspoken comment. He continued with his discourse.

"Now where was I? Oh, yes. My father did not tell me much. The location of the diary he took to his grave. At the time, I believed he had meant to tell me but it had just slipped his mind. Then he was gone and it was too late. I searched for it, of course. As you know, I never found it. But, thanks to the djinn, I have lived and traveled with Sir James many times over the years. Just as you are doing now."

He paused, his look inviting questions.

"Mr. Francis, as crazy and far-fetched as it all seems, I have to agree that there are things that can only be explained if one admits a supernatural aspect. So I accept that the djinn is real. My only question is, I suppose, where is it?"

The old man's smile was that of a mischievous schoolboy. He leaned forward and in a conspiratorial whisper said, "My dear Mr. Entwhistle, she is there, in your lap."

Philip froze, eyes wide. He could not have been more startled if a live cobra had been dumped on him.

"The djinn is a *cat*?" he exclaimed, leaning slowly away from the black feline that seemed perfectly content on his thighs.

Jinny. The cat. The djinn. He cursed himself for his slowness. Of course it was the cat. It drank from the old clay bowl, the same one he had seen in his first vision. The same one that Sir James sent back to his brother's family for safekeeping. It was able to assume any form it pleased. Why not a cat?

With a shake of his head, his world turned upside down, Philip Entwhistle idly stroked the djinn that was curled up in a purring ball on his lap. Part of him wondered how he was able to accept the situation. But after everything he had experienced, it did not seem crazy anymore. Unless, of course, it was *he* that was crazy?

One blue eye opened lazily and looked up at him, then closed. If he did not know better, he would swear that the cat had just winked at him.

"Now, Mr. Entwhistle, you know the truth. The djinn is real. It has been with my family for nearly a century and it enjoys the company of people. Some people at any rate. What I am proposing, is that you accept the djinn. Take responsibility for it. Be its guardian. I will not lie to you. It is not always a bed of roses. It can be capricious, jealous and often simply mischievous. But it can enrich your life in ways that you cannot imagine. I am old, Mr. Entwhistle, more than you may imagine and the time of my death is at hand. I do not have long and I want to ensure that Jinny will be cared for."

Philip was reeling from the revelation, but one thing the old man said caught his attention. "You really know when you will die?" He asked in a horrified whisper, as if it were a shameful secret.

"No need to be quite so shocked. I have known for over thirty years when it would be my time. It is terribly comforting you know. You don't need to go to bed wondering if you will wake up the next morning."

Incredibly, Philip found this funny and he smiled grimly. "I have rarely wondered, Mr. Francis, if I was going to wake up in the morning. Actually, I cannot say that I have ever given it any mind."

"Of course not. You're young. Only thirty, are you not? When you get a little closer to my age, you may start to wonder. Death is not something to be afraid of, since nothing ever really passes away. We simply change from one form to another. Death is transformation, not termination. However, it is nice to be able to make arrangements in time, so that one does not leave things in a mess."

A mess? Is that what this was? Francis was just trying to tie up loose ends. To find a new home for his companion. An otherworld entity with unknown powers. It seemed so absurd and yet everything he had experienced in the last days told him it was true. He was in the home of a man who had lived all his life in the company of a . . . what? An ultra-terrestrial? A genie?

But slowly, the preposterous nature of the situation dissipated and he started to imagine its advantages. Think of what he could learn! If the visions he had experienced could be replicated for any part of history, for any person of note, then nothing would be secret from him. He could discover the truth about any event. He could see Caesar and Cleopatra. He could BE Caesar! He would become the world's leading authority on any historic subject that interested him. He would be honored, lauded, respected. The University would be lucky to have him. He would get prestigious offers from other institutions. He could found his *own* institution!

And in the space of a few seconds he went through a gamut of emotions, desires and longing. All this would be possible, and more, if he just accepted the incredible and believed the impossible. His heart beat faster and faster and his head swam. He could hear the applause, see himself receiving prize after prize.

Francis was watching him closely, eyes narrowing. And with a sigh, he burst the younger man's bubble.

"Mr. Entwhistle, I am sure that you are thinking of what you could achieve with the power of a djinn at your side.

But, mighty as it is, the djinn is not all-powerful and omnipotent. It has limitations, which will curtail your, I suspect, wilder fantasies."

If Philip was disappointed, he did not show it. He was full of ideas of how he could make use of the creature. "Okay. I understand. It's not able to do everything I command."

"Actually, the first thing you will learn is that it does nothing at your command. It does what it wants, when it wants. It is entirely Ego, Mr. Entwhistle. If it does something that you want, that is simply because that too pleases it. It is not a complicated creature, but you need to know that you do not control it and never will. But you can live with it, you can learn through it and you can certainly benefit from the relationship in a myriad wonderful ways. But at no time will you be in charge. My great-uncle was quite strong and all he managed was a negotiated surrender."

Philip shook his head in wonder. Nothing was as it seemed. Western culture presented genies as amiable wish granters only desiring to serve their masters, and while that was obviously a naive representation, he thought there must be some truth to it. Apparently not. Clearly, everything he had ever heard about genies was wrong.

"What are they, Mr. Francis?"

"That is a question that took me many years to discover, and I do not believe I have all the answers, even now. Some things are just too secret. The djinn are not angels. They are not demons. They are not human."

"Are the djinn the source of the myth of angels?"

"Oh no. And those damned things are no myth, by the by. Djinn are not evil beings, forced to endure some kind of purgatory, nor are they spiritually enlightened. They exist in a multi-dimensional universe, as do we, but they are not so constrained by it. Meaning that they can interact in our world in ways that we cannot. They can manipulate energies and matter at a quantum level, which gives them the appearance of great power. According to Jinny, it is all a matter of perspective."

Francis stood and moved to the bookcase and started scanning the titles as he continued his discourse. "They can influence a man in his dreams, or they can choke him with a chicken bone. They have a degree of control over us, which they largely choose to ignore. And for those that abuse their abilities, the djinn themselves will usually stop them. Sometimes exorcisms work, and this will at least alert other djinn of trouble with one of their kind. Or with something else for that matter."

He found the book he was looking for. It was thick, heavy and bound in leather. He flipped through the stiff pages. "For the most part, they are not interested in us. They prefer their own company, rather than slumming around in our world. However, every now and then, one will crave the warmth of our emotions. I think they may want a family, contact with others. Some of them are not so different from us, in that respect."

At this, Francis found the page he was looking for. He held it out for Philip to see. It was covered in a dense handwriting that he could not understand, but there was a picture. A hand-drawn image that was instantly recognizable: The Vitruvian man. Or at least, some version of it. Details were wrong. In the center of the image was a circle, with the iconic figure of a man reaching to touch the edges. But it was not like the one Philip had seen in the Galleria dell'Accademia in Venice. The figure was not drawn with double limbs, as the original. It was just a man, reaching out, his hands seeming to grasp within two other circles that intersected with the center circle, slightly overlapping. On the left side there was a representation of what Philip could only imagine was meant to be an Angel, and on the right hand side, there was a series of esoteric symbols. The djinn, Philip supposed.

"What is this?"

"Da Vinci's understanding of the universe. The circles represent the realms, as he called them. Dimensions to you and me, I suppose."

"So he knew all about them?"

"Well, not all. Certainly more than most. It is quite interesting reading, once you figure out how to read backwards. And in reverse!" He laughed and closed the book.

"It's just so . . . staggering. I can hardly begin to fathom the implications."

The djinn were capable of doing amazing things. Sir James' elemental had performed miracles, restoring a dead woman to life.

Again, Francis seemed to be able to see his thoughts. He wagged a finger at him and tut-tutted. "Careful Mr. Entwhistle. Everything has a price. Everything. The bigger the 'miracle' the higher the payment that will be due. There are certain laws of the universe that cannot be broken, although for a time they may be bent. But there is always a price and one which you may find you cannot afford or do not wish to pay. And believe me, someone always pays."

He laid a wrinkled hand on the cat's back, and said, almost sadly. "Jinny, please show Mr. Entwhistle what happened to Sir James next."

Philip's vision blurred. He felt something twist in his mind and for a moment, he almost blacked out. Then he could see.


Fern looked around the University campus, taking in the hustle and bustle of the students as they flew from one class to another. As always, she was impressed. It was so much bigger than the schools back home. The clock tower rose majestically, the library looked properly scholarly and the red brick of the buildings gave it a certain air of gravitas. Not quite Cambridge, which she knew from a visit a few months previously, but still, it was solid and reassuring. The kind of place where you would get a proper education. But what *exactly* were they learning? Was someone teaching things they shouldn't? She would find out.

She walked slowly along the path, getting more than an occasional admiring glance from the many students, of both sexes. But Fern paid them no heed. Her focus was inward, creating a mental state that was close to a meditative trance. She needed to be receptive if she was going to feel any subtle changes in the energies here. Whoever it was she had felt previously, they had been quick and decisive, she could say that much. It was nothing like the fumbling of an amateur. The echoes from the release of energy had the feel of someone expert in the use of magic.

Like a spider at the center of its web, Fern reached out with her senses, trying to feel any subtle vibration that might lead to her quarry.

There was still a tension, but no overt sense of power, or confluence. At least, not close by. Fern was sure that she could sense something, but it was on the very edge of perception. She came out of her trance, shaking her head, her eyes regaining focus on the mundane world. It was no good. If that hint of energy was the meddler, then she was too far away for Fern to sense properly.

She took a deep breath and blinked rapidly. There was nothing here today. But one way or another, she was going to find the rogue. It was just a matter of time.

At the entrance to the Administration building, Fern could see Tessa. She was dressed far more primly than when she attended the circle.

Fern smiled. She would really have to get used to calling her friend and mentor, Mrs. Richards. It wouldn't do to be overheard calling the Head of Human Resources by her first name, not on campus.

"Mrs. Richards, Mrs. Richards, Mrs. Richards," she repeated to herself, with an amused smile, before heading over to report her thoughts on the hedge witch.

The camel jostles with its gentle rise and fall. Tajeddigt leans into me and it feels so natural and right, as if it has always been this way. I breathe in her scent, an almost nutty smell from the argan oil in her hair. My hand enfolds hers and she turns her head, smiling and I kiss her. I had never really believed that such love was possible. After all these years, and all the women I've known, who could have credited the possibility of such a thing as this? She is the true Eve, my very Eden. This is my home now, with her.

Even if she would agree to leave, I would not allow it. There are few of my friends that would accept her, and I will not make of her a prisoner. How can I sully something that transcended death itself? I will not take her to a place that would condemn us both simply because she is different.

*He has gone native,* they will say and sneer. And I have. Gladly and with all my heart. How could I do anything other? She accepted me into her world and her life, even though I was an outsider. She was betrothed, but she chose me. She risked her life to be with me. How can I turn my back on her?

My own people would shun us. We English, who think ourselves so civilized. What is to be preferred in the English and our vaunted manners? What need have I for a woman of class, of breeding? That woman would be dead inside a day, were she with me now.

I knew Taj would be my deliverance from the moment we met. When I think back, it seems like a dream. Before the nightmare set in.

The pendant is cool in my hand as I hold it. A silver chain from which hangs an Abalak cross. A talisman of great power, she said. I wear it now, as I always will. Seeing its familiar shape, silver glinting in the sun as I hold it up, I do feel protected. She turns her head and smiles, her teeth flashing white. Leaning further back, I hold the pendant to her lips and she blesses it with a kiss, then blesses me the same. When she gave it to me, I swore to never remove it.

I cannot stop smiling, even though my cracked lips hurt when I do. So many memories flood my mind, each of them bringing joy and therefore pain. They call getting married, *taking a tent*, as the tents were the property of the women. I was taking a tent and needed to conform to their rituals, which included being painted with henna. The women of the village paid me more attention than I had ever experienced before, painting intricate symbols and designs on my hands and feet. Both Taj and I had to undergo this and I found it quite enjoyable. The village women, giggling and laughing as they prepared me for the marriage, were a lot more fun than my brother's wedding in England. That was a stiff and formal affair, that I remember largely for its complete absence of laughter and giggling.

Our first nights and days were a languid time of love making and laughing. We were happy in a way that I never really imagined possible. There would be a price, of course. There is always a price.

Izem is doing his best to pretend that none of this has happened. I am quite sure he suspects the truth. He observes his daily prayers and I am sure says a few extra for my sake. But he will not look at Taj, nor me if he can help it. I am still more than a little ashamed of the deal I was willing to make, and in the cold light of day it seems incredible that I would betray my friend for my own selfish desires. But with Taj in my arms, I am not so blind to myself that I cannot admit that I would kill to keep her.

"Sayyd?"

I look up in surprise. Izem has broken his self-imposed vow of silence. I had not expected to hear him speak this day.

"There is a village ahead, Sayyd. Caution is required. It would be better if you both wait here, while I go alone."

I nod, appreciating that Izem still puts our safety ahead of his feelings towards me, or Taj. The ground hereabouts is stony, the sand giving way to rough grit and even the occasional fist-sized rocks. We are entering the foothills to a low range of mountains. It rears out of the desert for hundreds of miles. The highest point is probably not more than that of Snowdon, but to us, right now, it seems insurmountable.

I signal the camel to sit, tapping its neck with my riding stick and it folds itself in the incredibly ungainly manner of their kind. I jump down from its broad back and help Taj to the ground. She is like a feather. As I help her down she turns to look at me and her face registers surprise and puzzlement.

"Jamez, what has happened to your eyes?"

I blink them, rapidly, thinking that perhaps something must be in them. Some dust perhaps. God knows there is no shortage of that in the desert.

"They are blue, Jamez. Your eyes are blue, like the cheche of my father!"

I croak a laugh and shake my head. "You are mistaken, my little flower. I have brown eyes."

"No, Jamez, they are blue. Bright blue. What magic is this, dear heart?"

What magic indeed. I debate if I should tell her about the djinn. But her people are superstitious, and she would most likely be terrified. Of course, it is not really superstition if the belief is true, is it? They have a fearful respect for the elementals. But then, they have lived with them for a long time. Some of those fairytales I read as a child may even be true.

"Perhaps eyes can change color by themselves. When one loves another very much, it shows in the eyes, does it not?"

She laughs, knowing that I do not have a real explanation, but delighted by my answer anyway. We hug and kiss, and sit on the stony ground waiting for Izem to return. She lays her head on my shoulder and I wrap her in my arms. We cannot stop touching. In some cultures, this is a shameful display, if in public. Indeed here, it would not be possible were there others near. But I am not concerned. In the desert, there are few eyes to see and fewer still to judge.

Knowing that Izem will be gone for an hour or more, I get up and fetch a blanket. With a giggle, Taj joins me on it, and we lay together. Making love with Taj is beyond ecstasy. Perhaps for the first time in my life, those words have real meaning to me, as making love is more than physical. We connect on a level that is so powerful and holy, for a moment, just a moment, I think I might become a believer, as I see the face of God and she is smiling.

# We win much more than we lose

## 6

*Oh threats of Hell and Hopes of Paradise!*
*One thing at least is certain; this life Flies.*
*Yes, one thing is certain and the rest is Lies -*
*The Flower that has bloomed forever dies.*
                    *—The Rubaiyat of Omar Khayyam*

Professor Samuel Evans strode along the corridor, glancing at the doors to the auditorium as he passed. One of the students had taken a nasty tumble there, recently. Those stairs were a death trap. Too steep. One gets used to steps of a certain height and then they go and make them just a little bigger and some poor bugger trips over his own feet and breaks his leg. I suppose the students are used to them though. Not that the kid would admit it was his own fault.

Nope, it was no good blaming others for your own mistakes. Sam Evans had been brought up to believe that you had to take responsibility for yourself and your actions. There was just too much finger pointing in the world, for his taste. Shame about the kid's leg though. He wouldn't be playing football again this year. Perhaps ever.

But Evans had business and he pressed on. He wanted to talk to the candidates for the Professorship and get a feel for who they were. He preferred an informal chat, rather than an interview-style situation. Further along the corridor, Sam spotted his quarry. Several students were standing in a rough semi-circle around Dr. Sandwell. She was handing them flyers of some sort, pulling photocopies from her handbag.

"Just put them up on all the boards," she said. "Don't take other things down though. Squeeze them in where you can." The students took the flyers and hurried to their task, one of the girls smiling as she clutched the papers to her chest.

"Hello, Dr. Sandwell. How are you?"

Sandwell raised an eyebrow as she turned towards him. "Well, thank you. Dr. Evans, isn't it?"

"That's right." Sam ignored the questioning tone. She surely knew who he was. Was she trying to get one up on him? "I'd like to have a chat, if you have some time free. I am on the committee examining the applications for the associate professorship, and I wanted to get more of an idea about who you are, what you do, that sort of thing. Can you spare me five minutes?"

"Actually, I have a class starting soon, but if you want to walk with me, we can chat on the way."

"Thank you, yes. Let's do that."

They started to make their way through the myriad corridors. Her class was scheduled in a room located on the far side of the campus.

"You're history, aren't you?" she asked.

He chuckled. "Is that an observation on my interests, my age, or just a threat?"

She smiled too. "Your field of study, of course."

"Good. I would hate to think that I was past it. But, to answer your question, yes. You could say that. I run the History Department. Now, how are things on your end? You must be busy since Professor Jameson's accident."

The acting Department Head nodded, her face scrunching up in what Sam took to be regretful acceptance.

"Yes. I suppose so. Nothing I can't handle, but I can tell you that this was not how I wanted to get my own department. Not at all. I feel so sorry for his wife. She was devastated. They were married twenty-two years."

"Indeed. It was a tragedy. A most peculiar circumstance, I am led to believe. But you are doing well in the position, I hear. Very well indeed."

They walked slowly, students flowing around them as they rushed past on their way to lectures or to meet friends. The elegant, red-headed woman, with the designer clothes and handbag, and the stooped, portly man with thinning hair and glasses could not have been more different, but they both wore an air of authority that marked them as members of the same club.

"How many candidates are there for the position?" Sandwell asked.

"Only three actually. Yourself, one of mine, and one of the language fellows." Evans could not be sure, but at the mention of *one of his* he saw her eyes narrow and a look of anger flash across her face. It was gone in an instant. He continued, pretending not to have noticed.

"Naturally, I cannot say too much on the subject. But I will say you are highly thought of, Dr. Sandwell."

"Thank you, Sam," she said. "May I call you Sam? Sorry, I didn't mean to presume." She looked down, then her eyes flicked back to Sam's face.

"By all means, dear lady. By all means. Now, let's talk about your work. I think I have a basic idea, but why don't you tell me, what exactly *is* parapsychology?"

And as she started to explain what her field entailed, Sam watched her keenly. He watched her eyes, her mouth, her hands. He watched how she reacted to the students and how she carried herself. She was a fine figure of a woman. Very fine. What was it Philip didn't like about her? That mixup over his research notes hardly seemed worth making such a fuss over.

It was not long before they arrived at the room assigned for her next class. Sandwell stopped by the door, and fumbled in her bag. She produced a key, and Sam glanced down, not able to resist peeking into the private world of a woman's handbag. He frowned, confused by something he saw.

"Well, this is me. Thanks for stopping by to check up on me." She reached out and placed a hand on Sam's arm. "If you have any more questions, we can have lunch or something." She flashed him a brilliant smile as she pulled the door open.

"Yes, alright. Thank you, Dr. Sandwell." He spoke without conviction, then turned, and still frowning in puzzlement, strode off to his next meeting. There was a fountain pen in her bag. But it was exactly like the one he had given Philip for his birthday. A vintage Swan Safety pen. It was an antique, over a hundred years old. What were the odds of her having one too?

In the cottage, Philip Entwhistle lay on the couch, his mouth open. His eyes flickered wildly beneath closed lids. On his lap, the black cat lay curled, contentedly purring, while Francis sat in a nearby armchair, reading a book.

In Philip's mind, the world had changed. The sun was high in the sky and glowed with a malignant intensity that would quickly blind were you foolish enough to stare at it. He tied the bag on the camel's saddle, pulling tight the ropes that bound it.

"Make sure it is tight, Jamez."

"Yes, Taj, I will."

We have packed up the few items that we had been using for our comfort while Izem was away at the village. A rug, a pair of blankets, some glasses and a small bottle of grappa that we sipped and made ourselves tipsy. While we had the chance, we made good use of our time alone and enjoyed ourselves as every married man and woman should.

It was several hours before Izem returned and when he did, his expression was somber. We had prepared a little food for him, not knowing if he would be turned away or welcomed in the village. When he approached on the camel, we scampered about like children. Taj offered him bread, but he waved it away, still not looking directly at her. She is puzzled by his attitude, not understanding what has changed.

"Sayyd. There has been a death in the village. One of the old women, the wife of the headman's brother. They are having a funeral for her. It would be bad manners for us to seek hospitality now, as we are not of the tribe. I spoke with the headman though, and he told us to come at dusk. If we leave in another hour or so, it will be well."

"Thank you, Izem. I'm sorry to hear that. But there's a time and a place for all of us. Wa idha maridtu fahuwa yashfeeni." *And when I am ill, it is God who cures me.* "Did anyone else look sick?"

"No, Sayyd. There was no sign of sickness amongst those I saw. From what I could gather, it was a sudden and unexpected death."

"I see. Perhaps then she was just old and it was her time."

"Yes, Sayyd. Everyone shall taste death."

I recognized the verse. In my attempts to pass as a Pasha, I had studied the holy book, even if I did not believe in it. *Everyone shall taste death. And only on the Day of Resurrection shall you be paid your wages in full.* If he looked to Tajeddigt when he spoke, it did not seem to me an accusation. Indeed, Taj had tasted death, though she did not know it. If she was not a miracle of life everlasting, I cannot imagine what more Izem would wish to see. Perhaps the power of the djinn *was* divine? This was not a question I could answer, so I made an effort to focus on the more pragmatic concerns of our journey.

"Did you enquire about provisioning? We shall need more food."

Izem looked at his feet, then again directly at Taj. She did not flinch under his gaze but returned it steadily. There was no anger or fear in his look. Perhaps he has begun to accept the situation? I hope that this is the case as we need Izem.

"Yes, Sayyd. I asked. All will be well."

Out of respect for their rites, we waited until dusk before approaching the village and as Izem had said, the funeral had clearly only just concluded.

The wind started to pick up. The sand whispered and shifted quietly, an almost imperceptible rustling punctuated by the occasional bellow from the camels, or our own coughs. Izem cast a long look to the sky. "There is a storm coming, Sayyd. It will be bad."

Their headman was old, and he met us at the village boundary. The huts seemed incongruous after the unchanging face of the desert. It was the first sign of civilization for hundreds of miles, if you discount the goat dung at the last oasis. We dismounted, and I offered him my condolences, with hand on heart and head bowed.

"Father, we are sorry for the loss to your village. We are little more than poor travelers, but we wish to honor the one who passed."

"You are welcome, my son. All of you welcome," he said, hand on his own heart and head bowed, the scarf across his face held in place by his left hand.

"Please, lead your camels this way. I will show you to the water hole and you can care for your beasts. We have a hut that stands empty that you may use for yourselves. Some of our men have gone to fight the infidels in the west. We hope that they will return soon, Insha'Allah."

This is the first I have heard of revolution against colonial rule and I am surprised that it has reached as far as this tiny village. The French and Italians were quick to seize any opportunity they could to expand their empires, and the people they conquered were far from happy about it. This is no surprise. After all, did not the Britons fight the Romans? And yet, did not Britain in time become one of the most important parts of the Roman Empire? Even providing an Emperor or two? Somehow, I suspect that the Algerians and Tunisians and Libyans will not be quite so integrated into the empires of France or Italy or the Moroccans in Spain. The situation in India was just another example of colonial oppression but that was a sentiment that I tried to keep hidden, as it had become quite a bore defending my beliefs. To declare that a people be allowed to govern themselves was ridiculous. The prevailing wisdom was that colonial dependents were like children and could therefore not be trusted with anything as important as their own governing.

"I have heard of the fight against the infidel. It is like a jihad of old. What know you of this?"

The headman shook his head sadly. "Nothing good, my son. The glorious men of the tribes fight as best they can, but they lack a leader. They nip and bite at the heels of the great beasts of Europe, but cannot bring them down."

He seemed to be a gentle soul and I felt an immediate empathy with him. But the rising wind added a degree of urgency to our actions, so we hurried to see to our camels.

As we approached the well, Izem went to the bucket hanging over it and lowered it down into the cool darkness. The splash as it hit the bottom was easily heard in the silence of the night. Only the faintest noise from the villagers, wailing and singing, could be heard, drifting eerily in the twilight from the village proper, a half mile away. The voices of the mourners sometimes mixing with the howl of the rising wind.

Taj edged closer to me, her hand surreptitiously touching mine and signaling to the headman that she was my woman. His rheumy eyes did not miss this little interplay.

"It would be my great honor, if you would take my hut for the night." He motioned to Izem, who was now pulling up the bucket, hand over hand as he heaved on the rope. "Your companion may stay in the men's hut. He will be quite comfortable there, as I hope you will also be."

He does not mention Tajeddigt. He does not need to. It is a natural assumption that she must be married to me, otherwise how could she possibly be travelling with us? I do not like to be separated from Izzy, but it would not do to refuse what was generously offered and I placed hand on heart as I thanked him.

We penned the camels with the villager's livestock, including, I was surprised to see, a pair of Cuvier's gazelles amongst the expected goats. Once the animals were taken care of with a little fodder and fresh water, we slowly made our way to the village. The headman waved us into the crowd gathered around a raging bonfire.

"Please come, sit with us. Share our fire and food."

Being invited in that manner was diyafa, an obligation to hospitality taken very seriously and must be as seriously accepted. We sat on the ornamental rugs that were placed around the ring of fire and were handed small glasses of hot, mint tea.

The evening was full of songs and stories. People honor their dead in many ways in the world, and I have seen my share. But the desert nomads of the Sahara seem to me to have a goodly custom. They weep and wail, but in the end, they celebrate the life of the person and make small gifts, which I believed were intended for the deceased in the afterlife but Izem told me that these were gifts to the spirit to placate it so it would not return and do harm. They leave them by the grave to ensure the spirit's benign intent.

We had been sitting, drinking and eating and talking with our hosts for only a short time when I began to see something odd. Taj was with the other women, sitting separately, which is their custom, but I could observe them clearly from where I was positioned.

One of the villagers, an old woman, kept looking over at her. At first, I thought she suspected perhaps we were not married. A breach of custom, although not unheard of. She was whispering with some of the other old women and occasionally they would finger talismans around their necks or wrists. I had seen something like these before and I knew that they were to ward off the evil eye. It gave me an unsettled feeling.

After some time, they went back to ignoring her and I thought they had given up on their suspicions, but no. They were simply waiting. An ancient crone was led into the center of the group of women, several of whom jumped up to help her sit. As she settled down near the fire, the other women immediately formed a half circle around her and a conference began, with Tajeddigt clearly the topic.

There was much fingering of talismans and the old woman closed her eyes and seemed to fall asleep. The other women began to talk amongst themselves so I hoped that whatever concerns they had, were now forgotten.

Eventually, things began to quiet down, and we were taken to our borrowed home for the night. The headman showed us the way himself. The hut was small, but there were intricately woven rugs on the floor and plentiful soft cushions. I thanked the headman profusely, and we readied ourselves for the night. For us both, this was like a second honeymoon. A chance to know each other the way we had in her tent that first night.

Outside the wind had started to blow fiercely and the reed roof of the hut was buffeted in an alarming fashion, so we were doubly grateful for our refuge. Sand was flying and I knew that to be out in the desert tonight would be difficult. But inside the mud brick houses of the village we were safe, secure and comfortable. I felt a mounting excitement at the prospect of sleeping in comfort, of being warm and having my best girl by my side.

Taj and I took our rest, and took our fill of each other. We slept. I cannot remember ever sleeping so deeply, yet even so, at one point during the night, I was half awake and fancied that I could hear voices. But it was just the wind, blowing through the roof and any small holes it found into our warm nest. I rolled over and cupped Taj's breast in my hand, and fell asleep again like that. The morning came before I knew it.

Rough hands dragged me awake as they ripped the blankets from us, then yanked me from the hut. Tajeddigt screamed as two old men grabbed her arms, pulling her, still naked into the harsh light. An old woman, the one who arrived late the night before, stood at the front of a crowd of villagers. A bony finger pointed to Taj and she screeched a string of words I could not understand. Suddenly, something hit me from behind, causing white lights to explode across my vision. I fell to the ground, and as I lay in the dust and sand, too stunned to do more than moan, the old woman pulled a small knife from within her robes and while the two men held Taj, she swiftly cut her throat. Blood arced out in a scarlet fan as the men released her and Taj spun about, turning with outreached hands to me, falling to her knees, her eyes wide with shock.

I screamed and struggled to get to my feet, but a stone flew from the crowd of onlookers, and then another. The men behind me moved away and the people of the village grabbed up whatever rocks they could and threw them at me, their eyes filled with hate. I could feel the djinn near, but somehow I knew it was powerless to stop them. The stones struck me all about, opening gashes in my head, hands and face. I crawled to Tajeddigt and cradled her in my arms as her life's blood seeped away and her eyes closed. A rock took me in the head and mine closed too.

Philip cried out in anguish. His eyes opened wide, the pupils dilated with shock, his heart pounding almost audibly. Jinny leapt from his lap and took refuge near the old man. Philip's face was ashen as he sat up straight, rubbing the spot on his forehead where only moments before he had felt the skin torn away by sharp rocks.

"Oh my god. They killed her!"

He looked to Francis who regarded him with sympathy and compassion. Tears ran down his cragged face.

"I am sorry, Mr. Entwhistle. It is a hard thing to know the truth and the manner of it."

"I had no idea," said Philip, wringing his hands. "I have never felt such despair."

"Yes. Sir James twice lost the woman he loved. Loved more than life itself. It hardly need be said that it cost him greatly."

"How could he live after that. Didn't they kill him?"

"They tried. You can see for yourself, when you are stronger. It may not be too good for you to experience these emotions so soon after each other. Each of these *rememberings* costs you something too."

Philip breathed deeply, trying to calm the racing of his heart.

"It was just a dream, Mr. Entwhistle. These things happened a long time ago. That man died in the desert and all that is left are echoes. They are not real. It is true that these things happened, but not to you. You are just a guest who gets to glimpse another's life for a brief time."

"How does that matter?" Philip said, jumping to his feet. "She is real to me! I'm so angry. I want to smash things. I want to kill." He paced about the room like a caged tiger, looking for something to vent his wrath upon.

Francis nodded in understanding. "Yes, that was how I felt too. My father said that he never wanted me to experience these things and that is why the diary was hidden. But he did not know Jinny could remember just as well what had happened, and the journal was not required to spark the memories. Generally speaking, a catalyst is needed to perform a remembering. An object imbued with the spirit of the person whose eyes you wish to 'see' through. But Jinny was there when it happened. The djinn have long memories. You will feel better in the morning, I promise. Sir James, believe it or not, got over this. So you will too. Time is a great healer."

"And time can heal this wound? How will I ever forget that my wife was brutally murdered right in front of me?"

Francis grabbed Philip's shoulders and forced the younger man to look at him. "No, my dear boy. She was not your wife. You are too close right now. Go home, rest. Drink some wine. Read a book. Sleep as much as you can. Come back in a couple of days when your head is a bit more clear. You will see. This will fade and it will seem like a dream. When you have a little distance, you can pick up where you left off."

"I can't leave now. I have to know. What happened to him?"

"No. You've already been exposed to the past more than is good for you. You need a break. If you want to work a little, by all means, type up your notes, or write down your thoughts regarding the events."

Philip stood. He was angry with a white hot rage, but there was nothing he could do. The old man's words made sense, much as he wished to rail against them. Without another word he went back to the study. The diary was there, just as he had left it. He opened it and leafed through the pages until he found the entry that detailed the events of the vision that he just saw and felt. Tears filled his eyes as he read the few words that failed to convey any semblance of the reality.

*July ___ I know not what day it is. They have taken Taj from me a second time. I cannot cry, I have no tears left. No water to spare on mere misery. I will find a high place and throw myself down. This journal will be all that is left of me soon.*

Philip shook his head in dismay. He read the words again and again. *They have taken Taj from me a second time.* It was the merest shadow reflecting the horror of the past and it wrenched at his heart. He typed up what he had learned. Making notes on his notepad for things to check up on, or review. Soon he was finished, and without the strength to read more, he put his things away.

Entwhistle was exhausted beyond anything he had previously experienced. It was not so much a physical strain, but the emotional toll that got to him. The trauma of re-living another man's emotions was excruciating. He drove home in a daze, knowing he had not lost her, that Tajeddigt was not his wife, but feeling the pain regardless. It was all so real. Frankly, it was inconceivable that a man could take that much and survive. How could Sir James live with himself after that? But he did live, at least for a while.

Somehow Philip managed to get back to the city, and now he found himself in his busy street. He drove slowly, looking for a gap big enough to park in. As he approached his own building, he saw one. An ample space out front, but someone had tried to block it off using a pair of cheap kitchen chairs. Stretched between them was brown tape, the kind used to seal moving boxes. Was the lout on the first floor finally leaving?

There was nowhere else to park, unless he wanted to try some of the other streets in the neighborhood. Philip was about to drive on, but something inside of him said no. That was not going to happen. He got out of his car and picked up one chair, then the other, and placed them on the side of the road. In plain view of all the windows in the house, including Paul Sumpter's. He stood there, defiantly, for a moment, then got back into his car.

Philip then reversed into the very generous space. He smiled thinly, wondering what the consequences would be for his provocative action, but not really caring. The way he was feeling now, he would welcome a beating. It might distract him from his emotions.

As he climbed out of the car and locked it, Paul Sumpter, head gleaming from being freshly shaved, came barreling out of the building, his face a mask of fury.

"You've got to be fucking kidding me!" he screamed, spittle flying from his lips. He snarled his rage, drew back his right fist and let fly with a wild haymaker. Philip observed all of this from a detached, almost uncaring perspective. Through his mind thoughts meandered. He noted the stain of spilt ketchup on the other man's T-shirt, the pervasive body odor that spoke volumes of his hygiene and the hairy knuckles belonging to the fist that was making its way towards his face. As it approached, he wondered if it were best to just let it connect, or simply move his head out of the way. After another moment's consideration, he opted for the latter.

The fist missed him by scant millimeters, and the snarl of rage from his opponent slowly turned to an expression of rank surprise, before transitioning into a look of concentrated malevolence. He stalked closer to Philip and reached out his hands to grab the much smaller man by his jacket lapels. Philip observed this new tactic and deduced that Paul intended to butt him in the nose with his prodigious forehead. He had never been assaulted in such a manner before and he wondered how it might feel. But a part of him declared that this was not a time for experimentation. He had to defend himself. It was time to stop allowing the bully to intimidate him and strike back.

And as the bigger, heavier built man moved his head back in preparation for the strike, Philip lunged his own head forward, crashing his brow into the skinhead's nose. He felt the other man's cartilage crumble and he could hear the sound of the flesh being brutalized as the nose was all but crushed by the impact. It was not a pleasant sensation, but nonetheless, it gave him a warm feeling of satisfaction.

The skinhead staggered back, howling as he reached for his nose. He tripped over his own feet and fell heavily onto the pavement, eyes wide with shock and dismay. He looked up at Entwhistle, impotent in the face of fearless opposition and Philip could see the man's cowardice clearly in his face.

"You fucking bastard," croaked Sumpter, as blood started flowing freely. "You broke my nose."

The words came out muffled, spoken through his hands as they attempted to staunch the bleeding. Philip noticed, in a detached way, that the blood blended quite well with the ketchup so that he could no longer tell where one stain began and the other ended.

"I'm terribly sorry," Philip said. "I really don't know what came over me. I think I may have had as much of you as I can stand." He stepped over the prone man and entered the building. Mrs. Hardy poked her head out of her first-floor apartment and gave him a big smile and a sharp nod.

"Good for you, Mr. Entwhistle. I told you the only way to get through to his sort was with a boot up his ass." She gave him a glance that held more than a hint of admiration. "There's more to you than I thought." And with that she closed her door.

As Entwhistle ascended the stairs to the third floor, he could not help but wonder how he had come out of it unscathed. He felt . . . different. Not that he could explain how exactly, but he could feel a change in himself, as if there was nothing left for him to lose. He felt stronger, more dangerous. He smiled.

Philip entered his apartment and placed his satchel on the table in the hallway. Then he regarded himself in the mirror that hung above the table. He didn't look different. He had the same blondish brown hair. The same green eyes with the purple bruises below, and now a slightly crooked nose, thanks to Sumpter. With a shrug, he looked away. Now that the moment of excitement with the thug from downstairs had passed, he was awash with adrenaline, so much so that his hands trembled. Clenching and unclenching his fists to ease the shaking, he walked into the kitchen and took a beer from the fridge. He twisted the cap from the bottle and took a long, hard pull, luxuriating in the liquid coolness as it slid down his throat, suffusing him with a deep sense of satisfaction.

Now that it was all over, he was suddenly, ravenously hungry. Opening the fridge again, he peered at the mixed contents, looking for something that could plausibly constitute a meal. The events of the day had been a roller coaster of emotional and psychological horror, yet his stomach was threatening revolt. Digging out a block of cheese, he cut himself a thick slice, and munching on the yellow cheddar he went into the living room. He pulled his laptop and his notepads from his satchel.

Sitting down at his table, he read the notes that he had written during the day. Then he read them again, adding some additional thoughts to the pages from time to time, tapping his pen against his teeth as he contemplated what he had learned. He fired up the laptop and opened the file that was the genesis of his new book. He started transcribing his notes, fleshing them out with additional information.

He had been working for only a short while, when there was a soft knocking at his door. He was tempted to not answer it, thinking it could only be his pugilistic neighbor, Paul, come back for round two. Still, his curiosity got the better of him and he got up. He tensed slightly as he opened the door.

"Well, are you going to invite me in?" said Dr. Sandwell.

Philip was astonished and made no effort to hide it. "What are you doing here?"

She pushed past him, her plastic smile firmly attached as she looked about his rooms. "I heard a rumor that you were on a sudden sabbatical. I thought I'd stop by to see how you're doing."

She raised a bottle of white wine and brandished it, as if it were a talisman that would counter his protestations at her almost forced entry.

"I want to put the past behind us, Philip. Start again. You know that I've always liked you. It's a shame things are so strained between us."

Without waiting for a reply, she marched into the kitchen. The sound of drawers being yanked open told him she was looking for a corkscrew. Philip hurried to his laptop and slammed shut the lid, putting his notepads into the satchel. The last thing he wanted was her poking her nose into his affairs.

"Dr. Sandw . . . Liz. I'm a bit busy right now. I have some work to do. Perhaps we can do this another time?" He started walking towards the door but she was not going to be so easily thwarted.

"Nonsense. Let bygones be bygones, I say. Come on, have a drink with me."

She had found the bottle opener in one of the drawers and was busily removing the cork. He sighed, accepting the inevitable, and took a pair of glasses from a cupboard. Perhaps if he just played along for a while, she would say what she wanted and then leave? She poured for them both, then put the bottle on the counter. Raising her glass to her lips, she sipped, all the while her eyes roved about, taking in the shabby furniture, the unmade bed visible through the open door to his bedroom and the laptop on the table in the living room.

"What are you doing here really, Liz?"

"Drink your wine, Philip. We need to talk."

Her tone of voice left no doubt that she was all business. He picked up his glass and took a sip. It wasn't bad. He moved into the living room and sat in his chair, facing the heater that stood duty as a fireplace. He did not own a television, so the typical arrangement of furniture found in most houses did not work for him. He had one chair facing the large windows, overlooking the front street, and the other facing the wall with the electric bar heater. Sandwell turned the other chair to face him and sat down, crossing her slim legs and leaning back. She looked at him steadily, eyes searching his out. He was not at all sure what it was she expected to see but she seemed satisfied and looked away, taking her glass and sipping.

"So? What do we need to talk about," he said.

"I'll make this easy. I want to know what you found in the stacks."

"And what makes you think I found anything?"

"Don't be coy with me, Philip. You don't email your department head informing him that you're not going to be able to come to work for at least a month unless you found something. Then you run off home and the next day you visit the only surviving descendant of James Francis. I want to know why."

Philip kept his face neutral. He would not give anything away to her. And frankly, he was tired of tip-toeing around.

"Dr. Sandwell, whatever I am doing is of no concern to you. I am following a lead on a subject that I have been working on for a while and I interviewed Mr. Francis as part of that. And how the hell do you know who I've been talking to? How this possibly pertains to your work in parapsychology, I cannot imagine."

She leaned forward, her violet eyes burning. Was it his imagination, or were they brighter than usual?

"No, I do not think you can imagine how it pertains to my field. You are not able to make that distinction. Only I can do that. Tell me what you found in the stacks and what you got from the old man."

And with that it was as if a switch was thrown. Usually he was able to contain his anger and he rarely let it out, keeping his emotions close. But he was done now. If it was not the bully downstairs, it was the bully in his apartment. Well, she could intimidate others, but not him. Her ability to hold a grudge was part of campus lore. But whether it was his success with Paul Sumpter or something else entirely, he did not care. He put down his glass with a bang on the table by his chair and stood up. Crossing to the door he flung it open and stood silently, his anger palpable. She smiled and this time it looked genuine.

"Oh, so the little puppy has teeth, does he? Well, so do I."

She put down her own glass and walked over to him, hips swaying. Pressing her face close to his, so close they could have kissed, she hissed a last warning. "Be careful, Philip. I don't like to be disappointed."

She walked through the doorway, and he watched her back as she disappeared down the stairs. With a feeling of foreboding, Philip slowly closed the door. He was quite certain that he had not seen the last of her. He went back to his chair and picked up his glass of wine, carrying it out to the kitchen where he poured it down the sink. Suddenly, it tasted like ashes in his mouth.

# And survive the trials and the tests

# 7

Nearly all men can stand adversity, but if you want to test a
man's character, give him power.

*—Robert G. Ingersoll*

The conference room was small, but there were only three
people seated at the oblong table. Sam Evans, Entwhistle's
mentor and nominal boss, the dour-faced Tessa Richards
from Administration, and John Gillings, head of the
Physics Department. Each of them had a short stack of
three files, bearing the names of the three applicants;
Sandwell, Entwhistle and Congreve-Symmonds. The clock
on the wall showed a quarter after nine.

Mrs. Richards cleared her throat and shuffled her files.
She looked at the two men. "The three candidates all have
various merits to consider, however, two are clearly more
senior and have more potential. If you do not disagree,
gentlemen, I propose that we dispense with Congreve-
Symmonds. He's still a bit on the young side, so it will
come as no surprise to him that he did not get it."

Both men nodded at the suggestion. It made sense. Why
spend an hour talking about him, when the fact was he had
no real chance. It was either Sandwell or Entwhistle.

"Fair enough," said Evans. "Let's start with Sandwell
then. Dr. Gillings, you are the most familiar with her work,
yes?"

The balding, myopic physicist shrugged. "I know what
she does. If that means I'm familiar with her work, then
yes."

Mrs. Richards interceded. "John, we know all too well
your feelings on the subject of parapsychology. The
question is not what you think of the subject, but what you
think of the researcher. Hmm?"

"Alright. Sandwell is a dedicated teacher. She has a good track record of publications in" —he paused as if searching for an acceptable adjective— "popular journals. She teaches post-graduate and undergrads and has helped develop a number of projects that received funding. All in all, she is pretty solid from a track record point of view. As for her, personally, well, she and I get on well enough, when we are not discussing physics." He started to rap on the table with the tip of his index finger, as if hammering home a point. "Why she insists that I only have a partial understanding of my own subject will never cease to astound me. I mean, she takes her work seriously, but it's parapsychology for God's sake. It's not science." He ended with a frown, then sat back and folded his arms his eyes daring the others to disagree with him.

"Well, science is not the be all and end all, is it?" replied Evans.

"Thank you, John," said Mrs. Richards. She turned to look at Sam. "Dr. Evans, you have been Dr. Entwhistle's direct supervisor now for two years. You recommended him for Associate Professor. Would you care to explain why?"

"Certainly, Mrs. Richards. Philip is a fine historian. He is popular with the undergrads, a good teacher, and has published a number of scholarly articles. In addition, he has written two books and is currently working on a third. And I am informed that this latest will be something of a humdinger. He specialises in nineteenth- and twentieth-century historical figures, and is best known for his work on Saad Zaghloul, the Egyptian statesman. He is a sound researcher. Very methodical. Leaves no stone unturned."

Mrs. Richards was scanning her file as Evans spoke. She looked up as he finished. "Well, that all sounds good," she said. "Now, we have to consider various aspects when choosing the most suitable person. If I might sum up, in brief?"

Both men nodded, the physicist looking particularly pleased that things might move quickly.

"Both the applicants under consideration can perform with excellence and independence. Both are highly motivated and well-published. Both can teach at undergrad and postgrad levels, although there, I perceive that Sandwell has a slight edge."

Evans reluctantly nodded his agreement.

"You say that Dr. Entwhistle is currently writing another book," she said. "What is the topic?"

"Actually, I am not entirely sure. It's all a bit hush hush."

"Hush hush? Isn't that a bit unusual Dr. Evans?"

"Yes, I should say so. It's most intriguing!"

"And when can we expect this *humdinger*, as you call it, to be completed?"

"Well, Dr. Entwhistle assures me that it will be done inside a month. So, I have made arrangements for his T.A. to take over his classes, while he focuses on the writing."

"I see. If there are no other extenuating circumstances, then let's put it to the vote."

Before anyone could speak further, the telephone rang. Mrs. Richards picked up and listened, her face becoming grave. She did not speak, except for a final word of thanks. After a moment she placed the receiver back on the table. She looked to the two men and sighed.

"There has been a complication. Sandwell has made some serious allegations. About Entwhistle."


Philip sighed in exasperation. He looked up at the ceiling, wondering for the umpteenth time when they would let him go. It was one thing to help police with their enquiries, but quite another to be interrogated.

"Listen, I told you three times already. Nothing happened. She came to my apartment. She asked – no, demanded – access to my research. I refused. She threatened to make me sorry. And she has! Did it not occur to your keen inquisitorial intellects that the fact we are competing for the same promotion might suggest a tiny hint of a motive? Indeed her timing was perfect – the day before the selection committee meets, she makes an outrageous allegation and lo and behold, here I am."

Philip gestured around the grubby interview room. Stained walls, coffee or blood? Who could tell? Fluorescent lighting that was oppressive as it was bright.

Detective Hanlon leaned across the table, her eyes searching. Her expression was one of bored professionalism, as if she had heard every excuse under the sun and this was nothing new, but her eyes were intelligent and sharp. She made a tone of exasperation, shaking her head with short, savage jerks, as if denying his every word.

"As I see it your motive story cuts both ways."

"How so?"

"Precisely because there is so much motive, as you are quite capable of working out. It could be a reverse smear campaign. You figured that you could do practically anything you wanted to her, and get away with it. And if she did complain, well, out comes your ace in the hole, *it's a smear campaign. She's out to get me.*"

The last words made in a whining voice, like a petulant child's. Her partner, Topley laughed. The overweight officer clearly thought it a good imitation of Philip. Hanlon continued.

"Now, do you take *my* point?"

Philip tried to keep the anger from his voice but they kept asking the same questions and it was wearing him down. He began to understand how some people would admit to crimes they had not committed, just to stop the badgering. The interview room was getting smaller, the walls looming. Was he ever going to get out of this grimy, claustrophobic hellhole? The two detectives looked quite at home. Topley wore an expression of smug self satisfaction, as he towered over Philip with his hands crossed over his prodigious stomach and Hanlon's eyes glinted in a feral manner.

"You know what I think? said Hanlon. "I think you made a pass and she turned you down and you didn't like it. You got rough. You thought you could get what you wanted and she couldn't stop you. You tried to force yourself on her, and when she resisted, things got out of hand."

"Is that what she says? Because that's not how I remember it. Look, I know you have a job to do and you need to investigate her story. But that's the point. It's just a story. Her word against mine."

Detective Hanlon leaned back, the look she gave her partner evidently conveying something as he snorted derisively in response to the unspoken comment.

"Okay, Mr. Entwhistle," Detective Topley said, waving one hand magnanimously. "Let's just say you're right. That you did nothing. Why do you think that *impugning* your honor would get her that promotion you mentioned?" The smirk on his face left little doubt in Philip's mind that whatever answer he gave was unlikely to convince the fat detective, or his partner. The two plain clothes officers were diametric opposites. He was older and obese, she was young and petite. Philip knew in his gut that it was Detective Hanlon who would need to be convinced. But what else was there, if honesty was not enough?

"She's trying to eliminate the competition. We're both in line for associate professor, but only one of us can get it. And if I'm under a cloud of suspicion, then the University isn't going to give it to me. Seems to me like a perfectly good motive, don't you think? Maybe you should bring her in and ask her yourself?"

Again the two detectives made it clear that they did not consider his argument reasonable. Topley snorted again while Hanlon shook her head in obvious dismay at his pathetic attempts to wriggle out of the mess he was in. Philip felt his temper rising. He leaned forward, and with an effort of will, controlled his voice.

"All I know is that she came to my apartment and made demands. I refused. The next day, here I am getting questioned. You still haven't told me what she claimed happened. And more to the point, whatever she claims, it's just her word against mine. It may not mean much to you, but my word means a lot to me. If there was some way to prove what happened right here, right now, I would do it. You want to hook me up to a polygraph, then fine. Wheel it in. I'm game."

Philip leaned back in his chair, arms crossed. The posture was defensive, but he couldn't help it. He felt attacked, exposed, vulnerable and more than a little sorry for himself.

"OK, Mr. Entwhistle," said the obese Topley. "You're right that it's just her word against yours, but we have to cover our bases. We checked you out. You have no record. There are no warrants outstanding. You've never even gotten a parking ticket. So, for now, you're free to go. But I would advise you to keep your distance from Elizabeth Sandwell."

"Hah! You don't need to tell me twice."

Philip stood and straightened his rumpled shirt as best he could. It was the same he had worn the day before, not having had time to find anything else. He had not expected to be roused from sleep that morning by a pair of plain clothes officers, and he would never have dreamed that they would drag him down to the station in order to sweat him for an hour in an interview room. It was Kafkaesque. But at least they had allowed him time to dress.

Being detained by the police, was bad enough. It had left him shaken. But to be displayed in front of his neighbors as a criminal was worse. He just hoped that no one had seen him being led away.

He had clearly underestimated just how far Sandwell was willing to go. It was one thing to be ambitious, but quite another to wreck someone's career.

He was not being melodramatic. It was as difficult for him to prove his innocence as it was for them to prove his guilt. The only problem was, Sandwell did not need him to be found guilty of anything. He just had to look like he *might* be guilty. The mere fact that he had been picked up and taken to the station for questioning was enough. Now, as far as the review committee was concerned, he was probably out of the running. After all, there's no smoke without fire.

And clearly, Detective Hanlon did not believe anything he had said. She gave him a look that conveyed a desire to continue the interview, possibly with a length of rubber hose. But she opened the door for him anyway, and he stepped through, surprised at just how much sweeter the air was outside the little room.

"Follow me, sir," she said through gritted teeth. She looked like she had just eaten a lemon. "I'll find someone to drive you home."

"Hi, Fern. This is Steve. He's got the van I told you about." John motioned to his taller, and somewhat younger friend, who was standing outside the door to her apartment.

"Hello, Steve." She shook his hand then motioned for them to enter. "Thanks for the help."

Steve's eyes roved about, taking in the various boxes and bags. "Yeah, no worries. Doesn't look like it'll be a problem. We can squeeze this lot in the truck. She's a beaut. Merc Sprinter. Should be big enough."

The accent was as Australian as his tanned and grinning face.

"You sure you're fine?" John asked. "Everything's in order with the new place?"

"Oh, yes. Absolutely," she replied. "It's quite close to the University, bigger than here. Perfect really."

John waved his hands around the apartment in vague gestures. "Is there anything about the place that I should know about? You know, dodgy plumbing, that sort of thing?"

"No, no. It's just the same as in your bachelor days," Fern said. Well, not everything. She had placed some charms in the small apartment. Little sprigs of juniper that would help attract a positive energy, and she had performed a spiritual cleanse, to help give him a new start.

Just her way of paying him back for his kindness in allowing her to stay there, when things had been difficult for her.

"How about we make a start with the boxes now? Get them loaded up, then come back early tomorrow and pack the rest," Steve said, jiggling his keys. He was never still, like a little boy in a man's body.

"Sure" said Fern. "That's fine. I'll make us some tea."


Finally arriving back at his place after the grueling fiasco with the police, Philip had no wish to go anywhere. He stayed home typing up his notes and proofing the completed chapters. The day passed quickly enough and as the evening came, cooler than expected. Philip got to thinking that he should inform Sam about the recent events with Sandwell. He took his phone and settled into his armchair before the electric fire, beer in hand.

With the phone cradled against his ear, held there by hoisting one shoulder as high as he could, he pecked at the laptop balanced on his knees, as he listened for the ringing tone. As the call connected, he took the handset and straightened slightly in the chair.

"Yes?" Sam's voice, annoyed.

"Hello, Sam. It's Philip. Sorry to call you at home."

"Philip! Uh . . . how are you doing? I was just talking about you."

"Nothing bad I hope."

There was a pause. "Actually, this morning Professor Sandwell made some allegations."

So. Not just the police. The University too. It was to be expected. "I see. Attacking on all fronts, then. I was just calling you to tell you the same thing. Actually, I spent a couple of hours with the police this morning."

"My God! Really? She claims you invited her to your apartment yesterday evening, tried to get her drunk and sexually assaulted her."

"Sam, you can rest assured it's nonsense. She's playing the system. Trying to get me off the committee's radar and onto HR's."

"Well, that's what I thought. Or at least, hoped. But it's a sticky situation. You know how it is these days. Thank God your sabbatical means the question of temporary suspension hasn't even come up. How's the big secret, anyway?"

What? How could Sam know about the djinn? Then he relaxed. The 'secret' was the Fortescue book. He had almost forgotten it.

"That's why I'm calling. I'm onto something here. Something, well, almost incredible. I can't talk about it, yet. But trust me – this is big."

"How intriguing. Not even a hint?"

"I really can't say, Sam. But it's a primary source. You have to give me a little more time. Just another couple of weeks."

"What do you mean, you can't say? What's going on, Philip?"

Philip, desperate to tell him and keep his hopes alive, was opening his mouth when Mr. Francis' words rang in his ears. *"You will tell no one what you are working on. You will most especially not mention the diary."*

He sighed. "I made a deal. Sorry."

"Come now, Philip! The committee will meet again soon. It might help your cause tremendously if we knew what you're working on."

Philip was torn. If Mr. Francis was right about when he would die, then permission to reveal his work would come a week too late. The committee was going to make a decision before he could even show the members that his research was not only important, but potentially historic.

Sam pressed his advantage. "You're in a tight spot. Something really special could make a big difference."

But, he *could* show some of the stuff predating the diary. Years of work, mostly covering Sir James' life before Africa.

"How about I show you the first couple of chapters. You can let me know what you think so far. Perhaps a rough outline of the next couple of chapters as well, but the period of his later life will have to wait. I'm still studying the, uh . . . source."

In spite of his resolution, he had almost blurted out the word diary. He would have to really watch himself.

"Oh, come now, Philip. At least tell me what it is. Do you want the promotion or not?"

"Sorry, Sam. No go. I made a promise, which I intend to keep."

He slammed shut the laptop lid in frustration. But a deal was a deal and he would honor it. Philip was a little surprised that he actually meant what he said. Not just about the diary, but the whole thing, including protecting the djinn and preserving its secret. If it meant losing the promotion, well, so be it.

"Alright," Sam replied reluctantly. "Send me what you have so far. I look forward to reading it."

"I'll send the file now. Check your private email account."

"I'm logged into the office account, just use that one."

"No, I don't think so. I don't quite trust that our work systems are secure."

"Come now, Philip. I thought that I was the one into all the cloak-and-dagger stuff."

"I just have a feeling, that's all. There are just a few too many coincidences that are neatly explained if you assume that some of our communication channels are, well, bugged."

"Remember Occam's razor, old boy. The simplest explanation, what?"

"Sure, Sam, I get it. I'm crazy. Just humor me, would you?"

Philip hung up. His method was to create a file for each chapter and a partner file for notes. He emailed Sam the first two pairs. For himself he had no doubt this work would make him the pre-eminent authority on Sir James

Francis, but Sam had to see it too. He was nervous, but eager to hear Sam's response.

At that moment, he heard a commotion in the street. A man shouting, the string of expletives he used making it all the way to Philip's third-floor apartment. He crossed to the window, beer in hand, and looked down on the shaved head of Paul Sumpter trying to load a couch into the back of a moving van with the aid of his long suffering girlfriend, Traci. She was struggling, and as Philip watched, dropped her end of the couch into the dirt of the gutter, prompting a new outburst of abuse.

He was still holding his end of the heavy furniture, so all he could do was color the air. Then he looked up. When he saw Philip, his face twisted in rage. Philip was tempted to step back from the window, but he held his ground, staring down at the ugly man.

If it had been anyone else, Philip would have gone to help. But not for Sumpter. Not now. By the look of hatred Sumpter shot at him, the skinhead harbored more than a simple grudge.

Once he would have retreated in fear from the thought. Paul had terrorized the house for years, but his reign was over. Philip hoped the new neighbor would be friendlier. He raised his bottle in salute to the gods of good fortune. The action was not missed by Sumpter, who dropped the couch, and raised a finger in response. Philip smiled.

The next morning Philip headed for the cottage, eager to resume his work. He was disappointed that he had not dreamed, but suspected he was being given a little time to get past the emotional events that had transpired. Seeing Taj so cruelly . . . he could not even think of it. But he would have to. He would have to deal with it, just as Sir James had.

The sight of the now-familiar red barn and horses restored him. The ordinary things. Life goes on. He needed that. Francis met him at the door with a gentle smile.

Neither spoke. Philip made straight for the study and pulled the laptop from his bag. Within moments he was deeply immersed in the diary, his mouth set in a line of grim determination.

Taj has been taken from me a second time.

It hurt to read it, but Francis was right. The beginnings of disconnection, as if it *were* just a dream. Surely now he had pushed through the worst Sir James could throw at him and the end was in sight. Perversely, he felt bad that he did not feel worse. Jinny entered briefly, seemed satisfied, and stalked out again. Philip got to work.

*July 5. The djinn returned Taj to me. Just as she was when we were first together. I am grateful to it, more than I can say and in my heart I have pledged myself to the elemental. I sense it knows this and is pleased. This is what it has wanted all along. The price of my obligation was hard and I can feel its weakness now. Nonetheless, I suspect it needs this bond. Perhaps without a human connection it would just float away? But my shame over the bargain I was willing to make does not leave me. I will make it up to Izem somehow. He gives no hint that he knows what I would have been willing to give for my Taj. We ride. The heat is oppressive, our thirst is great, but I relish every second of it. Taj and I smile and laugh and sneak kisses when Izem is not looking. We are like youngsters knowing the first bloom of love. We are making good progress; I calculate that we are two weeks due east of Marrakech.*

*July 6. We have seen a village. I sent Izem to talk. They were in the middle of a funeral for an old woman, holding the rites and mourning her with great pomp. It may last a week. We are allowed to stay the night and receive every honor they can bestow. Taj and I have been offered the headman's hut and we are as happy as ever.*

*July — I know not what day it is. They have taken Taj from me a second time. I cannot cry, I have no tears left. No water to spare on misery. I will find a high place and throw myself down. This journal will be all that is left of me soon. I cannot live without her. I know not what fate befell Izem, but I fear the worst.*

*July –– The wounds have closed. The stones bit deep but somehow I heal. Stoning and beating was not enough, and they dragged me behind their horses into the desert and left me to die. How many days since, I do not know. I would not disappoint them but the djinn forbids it. If I die, so will it. This is unexpected but changes nothing. I would walk into the desert like the old man. The djinn tells me that it is not my time. Will it or not, my fate hangs over me. It finds water and brings it. It tells me I will live. That there is value in life. I do not see it.*

*July –– I have faced my trials. I am through them but not unscathed. Losing one's great love twice, in so short a time, no man should have to experience. But a grim humor has taken me. I let the djinn mother me now. It is determined to keep me alive and I allow it. No longer seeking death for its own sake I have become reckless beyond measure. Taunting scorpions and sand vipers is just sport to me now. I pity Ibrahim if ever he catches up with me.*

Philip looked up as Francis entered with a tea tray bearing two cups and set it on the desk. Philip smiled ruefully. He was being mothered too. Of course, Francis had no one else, the last of his family. The last keeper of his great-uncle's secret, the final guardian. It came to him, the understanding of what that meant, the burden. A lifetime of secrecy and no one to share it with. Then Philip had knocked on his door, just in time.

The old man, it seemed, was now openly reading Philip's mind. His mouth crinkled up into a smile and he said, "There have been others before you. I have tried to find a new guardian for Jinny a couple of times in the past. But not everything works out. Most people are just wrong. A very few, just right. You, sir, are of the latter party."

Philip smiled. "Who have you tried to tell about the djinn? Anyone I know?"

"I do not think so. The others were interested for the wrong reasons, I think. There are ways one can detect an elemental. Some people are drawn to them as the higher creatures are drawn to us. This house was once a bit busier than it is now, but those days are gone. All things must pass, eh Mr. Entwhistle? One day you will be just a memory too."

Philip looked at him sharply, but the old man's eyes were kind and his smile warm. He nodded reluctantly. Francis continued.

"That is why Jinny reminds me to tell you to find a wife. You will need progeny if you are to be its protector."

"Protector? I was under the impression that the djinn were powerful."

"Oh, they are. But not invulnerable. And Jinny is a gentle creature at heart and wishes only to live in peace. However she will do anything to protect me and I would die for her. And there, as they say, is the rub. If I die, so will she. We are conjoined now, completely dependent upon each other. There must be a ceremony. A transfer of title, if you like, though Jinny is not a thing to be possessed or owned. More like a wedding ceremony, perhaps. You must dedicate yourself to the djinn and she will dedicate herself to you. I am guessing, hoping, that you are willing."

Francis regarded him with a steady gaze. Philip nodded slowly. From what he had understood from the diary, this made sense. The relationship between human and djinn was almost symbiotic. At least, the elemental seemed to need the human to survive, if not the other way around.

"I understand. But what would happen to me if Jinny died?"

"Why, Mr. Entwhistle. It would break your heart, I think," he said with a smile. Then, his voice lower, somehow darker, he continued. "And then your mind."

Break his mind. What did that mean? He decided to change the subject to something a little less worrying. Though he would come back to it. "Why do you refer to it as a she? Do they have gender?"

"No. They don't. It is just the affectation of an old man. She has been my only real company for a very long time. It would be rude to think of her as an 'it', don't you think?" Philip reciprocated his smile.

"So how does this ceremony work?"

"Oh, it is no great thing. I will simply ask you, when the time is right, if you wish it. If you are willing, then you receive a gift from me. A small thing, of no value. You take the gift, which symbolizes your acceptance of the djinn, and it is done. Easy."

"And when will this happen? I guess what I am saying is, when is it your time to walk into the desert?"

"Mr. Entwhistle, so poetic you are. In a little over three weeks. I shall be quite prepared, you will see."

"Mr. Francis, I have to know. Why me?"

The old man sighed and looked to the cat. "You were not my first choice Mr. Entwhistle. But you passed all Jinny's tests. And Jinny assures me that there is iron in your heart. By which, I understand that you have some gumption."

"Appearances notwithstanding?" They both smiled. "But what tests? I don't recall having to jump through any hoops."

"No, you did not. But the first day you were here Jinny planted in you a strong desire to possess the diary. You were tempted, were you not."

Philip glanced away. "Yes. I was, I am ashamed to say."

"Had you succumbed you would have, shall we say, disqualified yourself."

"And that was a test? I passed, I take it."

"With flying colors! That was a big test, and to fail that would have seen you . . . inconvenienced in the extreme."

"Why do I get the impression that is a euphemism."

"Because it is, Mr. Entwhistle. Had you tried to steal the diary, Jinny would have put you someplace out of harm's way."

Comprehension dawned. The masterfully forged face of the door-knocker. The suggestion of a rotund face, mouth agape, trapped in the iron of the garden trellis. Previous candidates, the ones who had tried to steal the diary, were now dead. Or worse. He shuddered.

Francis nodded, his eyes never leaving Philip's. He was coming to terms with the realization that his thoughts were transparent to the old man and strangely, he did not mind. And while this wonder seemed miraculous, he had overdosed on miracles lately and was in no way surprised or shocked. Nor at the fact that there were souls locked *out of harm's way* in the house.

"I see," said Philip. "You've killed to protect the secret. How many times?" But he shook his head violently. "No, don't answer that. I don't need to know. But was it necessary? Did you have to do it?"

"Mr. Entwhistle, it is not in us to see the future. Well, not all things, anyway. But certain events can be predicted with a measure of certainty. One such, is that a man with a bad heart will easily find justification for using the djinn to further his ambitions. Usually at the cost of others. By which I do not mean that he will magically know the next winning lotto number. No, he will begin to harm others. Starting with his enemies, but invariably adding to that list his friends and even family." He paused to sip his tea, then sighed in satisfaction. "You have heard, I am sure, that absolute power corrupts absolutely. This is not exactly a truism, since some people appear to have a latent goodness that tempers the corruption. But when that is missing, or, as in Sir James' case, confused by grief, the consequences are invariably dire. Sir James accepted, eventually, that he was the cause of the horror in that village. And repented it, deeply."

"And you think that I have a good heart?"

"I do. We both do. But just to clarify. Those that failed Jinny's test are not, in the strictest sense, dead. They are simply inconvenienced . . . more or less permanently."

Francis picked up the cat and caressed it with long strokes on its rich black fur. It regarded the historian with an affectionate gaze and for the first time Philip began to believe he was meant to be there. Part of a world that held elemental creatures, beings that needed a man with a good heart to help protect them. And, like the Francis family for a century, keep a secret that they had, for all practical purposes, killed to protect. Soon to be his responsibility. He wondered if he would be willing to do whatever it took in order to preserve the secret of the djinn.

It was a difficult question. But he knew in his heart that if it came to it he too would be willing to go to extreme measures to protect it. How not, when the alternative might be to allow it, *her*, to be exploited by someone unscrupulous? There was more than enough evil in the world already. And the consequences of the wrong person possessing the djinn were unthinkable. He would do what was necessary. Then he remembered what Francis had said about ways to detect an elemental. This was not just a possibility. Sooner or later someone would try to exploit him. Or worse. Well, so be it.

*Thank you, little man.*

Philip sensed rather than heard the voice. He gave a start, eyes wide with wonder.

"I heard her, Mr. Francis! In my mind. I heard the djinn."

"Oh yes, she will talk to you now. Jinny was never a chatterbox, but in time she will likely bend your metaphoric ear."

He could talk to the creature! He could not even begin to guess what might be possible to learn from it. Again, Francis sensed his thoughts.

"If you want to know more, Mr. Entwhistle, why not simply ask to be shown?"

Philip swallowed hard, chewing his bottom lip. He was afraid. The reality of living another man's life, of feeling his emotions, the entirety of his being. Yes, there was indeed a price. But he would pay it. At least, one more time. With a deep breath, he said, "I'm ready."

This time there was no sense of dislocation. The vision came quickly and he was simply . . . there.

I stagger onwards, not looking where I put my feet. Not caring. For days I have walked or crawled. I would rather simply lie down and die, get it over with. But then it whispers, encouraging me. Always there.

*Hearken little man. You must rise. You must live.*

"Live for what? What have I to live for, now that she's gone?"

My voice is hoarse, my throat dry as the sand under my feet. I sound like death. Not that I mind. But I struggle to rise and carry on, putting one foot in front of the other. Taking a breath, keeping my heart beating. The djinn has become closer to me in these last days. Somehow more intimate. I sense it, vividly. I wonder if it is my proximity to death? Am I more real to it the closer I get to the other side? It is not quite inside my head but I know it is always near. I sense its feelings and I catch glimpses of its memories. They confuse me sometimes with their strangeness. Other places, other times. Many faces, each of which belonged to one like me. Men, women, children. The djinn has known many of our kind, over thousands of years. It is like a lost soul, forever condemned to an eternity of wandering. But it needs us. A terrestrial conduit or spiritual channel to link to it. To anchor it.

Sometimes the thoughts or memories are those of my predecessors. At first this was peculiar, but not as much as one might expect. Even the djinn dreams. True, it is a creature of another plane but not entirely different from us poor earthbound mortals. It has hopes and desires. And, to my sorrow, it shares with me the guilt of what I forced it into. But in one respect the djinn differs greatly from me. It fears death, which it believes to be near at hand, whereas I long for its release.

But still I struggle on. The sun is merciless. It scours me, illuminating the blot on my soul. Should I find a cave I would crawl inside it and let Mother Earth consume me forever. But there is no cave. The sun will not let me go so easily. If I am to find relief from its searing gaze I must carry on.

Near the top of a low rise I see the surrounding desert for miles in every direction. No longer great dunes rising like elegant waves of sand but a plain of rocks. Little scraggly bushes as well, nibbled to nothing by goats and camels.

I cannot blame the creature for the events of the past days. It is my fault, my doing. I know it and I accept my punishment. It did not want to restore Taj to life. It objected, it argued: I forced it to obey. I named the price of the pact without which it would be lost on the winds; I wanted nothing in this world other than her. And now she is gone and I am left to die. Or live. Is there a difference?

The djinn forces me to drink. My own hand does not obey me. We made a bargain and my life is not my own to take. I don't know why I rail so. My arguments with it do not end well. It always has an answer.

*Would you rather have not had her at all? Would it have been better to put her in her grave?*

"Better that you put me in there with her!"

*No. You are mistaken. It is not better. You are needed.*

"What do I care for your needs now?"

*It was not I who killed her. And if I could, I would have saved her and your man too. My strength is gone. It will be many moons before I am as strong again.*

My strength is gone too. We are a sorry pair. A voice on the wind and a man as close to death as possible, yet still living. The villagers took almost everything from me and expected the desert to do the rest. They betrayed their honor to exact revenge. And had I known that the life taken for Taj was that of the headman's family . . . what? Would I have chosen differently?

The villagers took their revenge. Blood for blood. As is their right, by their customs. But still, they risked much to take us while still under the protection of their hospitality. They have a shame now almost as deep as the one I carry.

I wonder again if Izem knew what was coming. Did he suspect? The old woman died suddenly. Of course they would suspect sorcery or dark forces at work. It is in their blood, part of their nature to believe in spirits and magic. The djinn have made their home in many parts of the world, no doubt, but there is something about the great desert that gives them more focus. More power. Something here that allows them to exist in greater numbers. If the old tales are true then man and djinn have had dealings from the dawn of time.

Believers in magic and the hidden spirits of the desert are ten a penny here. I am one of them now; a true believer at last. The djinn has brought me some of the things that the villagers took. I wake up and there they are beside me. My notebook, the clay bowl, my kettle and the bottle of grappa. Most of the other items in our luggage have been destroyed by the people of the village, to remove any temptation for our souls to return as evil spirits.

I still have Taj's talisman; her gift. It hangs around my neck and I will not part from it, even in death. I will pay the ferryman with a twist of its links before I let it go. The djinn whispers and whispers. It cajoles and threatens when it must. It brings forth water from the stones, needing no staff to strike the rock. I drink, and in spite of myself, I find that I am not ready to die. Not quite yet. Something inside demands that I take my fill and restore my body. And I replenish the husk that was once a too-proud Englishman.

Day after day I am forced to live on. Forced to walk alone in the desert. Am I become Sisyphus, that my torment never ends?

*Hearken. There is another village, not far.*

I care not, truthfully. Another chance to be stoned to death and I am more afraid than I would like to admit. But I stand and follow its voice. It takes the whole day before I stumble into the collection of huts whose desolation mirrors my own. The few people I see stare at me, eyes blank and wide with fear. They make signs with their fingers to ward off evil. They think me a creature of the desert too. Perhaps one possessed. They are not wrong. No one approaches. No one talks. But no one stones me either and for that I am grateful.

There is a small basket, lying at the edge of the village. A gift to appease the bad spirits. To make me leave. I seize a small flatbread and a handful of dates and carry my prize away. I respect their desire to not have me amongst them. I am not fit company for any society, no matter how rough or mean.

I have poured what remained of the grappa away. I do not need its taste again when the memory of how Taj and I drank on our last night together is still so fresh. Instead, I fill the bottle at the spring that the djinn called forth. Its taste is peculiar, but it is water. The bottle is small, holding only enough of the precious fluid to keep me alive for a few hours.

*There is more, soon. You must keep west. You will find sanctuary.*

I eat the dates and the bread as I walk, growing stronger in spite of my best intentions. The djinn has its way and I live. It suffuses me with whatever energy it can spare. We are partners now and it needs me to stay alive as much, I regret to say, as I need it. But I accept, willingly now. I would not have its death, too, on my hands.

When night falls, it warms me. It brings forth fire and the rocks glow amber. I know not how it can do such things. Magic has always been the stuff of fools and charlatans but I find I am now quite a believer in the impossible. The djinn can sense my thoughts.

*The man is ignorant. It knows nothing of energy. Of binding forces.*

It is right. I do not. Nor do I care. It lives in a universe vastly different from ours, I think. But it looks to our world with desire. As the days and nights pass, we learn more of each other. Or at least, I learn more of it.

"What are you, djinn?"

*We are like Man. But not like Man.*

"Are you one of God's creations? Like it says in the Recitation? The Qur'an? Or did your kind evolve, as many believe that we did?"

*I cannot say. We are. We have always been.*

"But why are you here?"

*The lower mortals are many. They glow brightly. They burn. We see them, burning in our minds. Your kind are like the sticks of fire that you strike. They flare, then gutter and are gone. The realm of Djinn is vast and cold, but we are few. For some it is enough. For others, we need more. We need the flame. The realms above are colder still, and we care not for them, or for those you call the Seraphim.*

I had read the sura for the djinn. I know it well. I know the holy book of Islam as well as I know the King James. A necessity, to pass for a Pasha, often under close scrutiny. The sura says the djinn are made from smokeless fire. I do not put much stock in this for all it is the holy word of a great people. But the djinn are real as we are real. To hear that the seraphim are real too is unsettling. But I am not going to believe in an omnipotent deity just because angels exist, if indeed, that is what seraphim really are. If the djinn are a natural part of creation, a result of Darwin's evolution as I am sure mankind is, then the seraphim too must be a natural part of evolution. Natural selection by adaptation. What characteristics, I wonder, can have been of advantage or disadvantage in such unimaginable spheres? I doubt the djinn knows. It is an unsettling thought to imagine that there are beings of supernatural power in the universe, and yet that is what so many millions believe. I was at ease with the view of angels as manifestations of mankind's need to believe in something greater than itself. To discover that they exist, living lives beyond our understanding, is almost worrying. In terms of their powers are they to us as we are to ants?

"Did men worship your kind?"

*Some have worshipped us. Thought us gods. Many of my kind think it is our right. But we have our own gods too.*

"Do you worship the ones above? The angels?"

*Not the seraphim. They are like us. The higher orders are different.*

Higher orders? And it used the plural. Gods, not God. Are there really many gods? Is there a pantheon, like the Norse once believed? Or the Romans and Greeks? Monotheism is a relatively recent idea, I suppose. Going back to Yahweh and the Jews in the post Babylonian period. But even that God once had a female consort, long forgotten now. Asherah, the mother Goddess. Also known as 'She who walks on water.' There are several mentions of her in the Old Testament. Josiah ripping her statues from the temples of Yahweh and defiling the altars with burnt bones.

Whatever the origin of the djinn and regardless of what they believe, they are creatures that exist in a world separate from ours and may enter only by anchoring themselves to one of us; a flame. Without me, the djinn would be forced to return to its own realm. But it fears death. Perhaps, once here, a djinn may not return? I wonder if that is the purpose of the old bowl. Does it somehow provide an anchor for the djinn? Why else is it needed? The djinn does not reside in it. There is no rubbing of the magic lantern to call it forth. And yet, I sense it is important. As if it is a necessary part of its being. That it *needs* a physical aspect, as well as a spiritual one. It seems to me that the djinn, having a taste for the material, would happily eschew the spiritual. Or is it the ephemeral? I wonder, have our holy men all got it backwards? We are not drawn to the divine, the divine is drawn to us.

Days pass, and I am keeping the diary again. At first words are hard to come by. If there will be a time when I will read these pages I hope they will only be echoes of the feelings that encompass me now. And while I no longer wish to kill myself, I can imagine a dozen ways that I would court death and be indifferent to the outcome. Russian roulette seems entirely too childish. I would prefer a game with higher stakes. I find that I am growing eager to meet Ibrahim again.

# Then fall to a dark witch's hex

# 8

How sad is a heart that
does not know how to love,
    —*Rubaiyat of Omar Khayyam*

The days passed quickly in a cycle of work, sleep, dream, rise and start again. But this day was different. It started badly, with a summons for Philip to give his side of the Sandwell sexual harassment story. Philip knew full well he was facing the loss of his job, his reputation in tatters. He might never teach again.

His knuckles showed white on the steering wheel. The whole thing was getting to him. No doubt that was what she wanted. He needed to calm down, think of something else. He took a deep breath and forced his hands to relax, his mind going to the previous day's vision. All the visions were extraordinary but this one laid out Sir James' understanding of the higher orders of life and that was a revelation. Then, another episode sleeping at his computer and waking to find thousands of words, his own planned chapters all written. Neat and concise, as if he had typed every word himself. Perhaps he had? The words were his own, of that he was sure. The phrasing, the sentence construction, all uniquely his.

But the things he was being forced to believe were perplexing. Philip kept trying, and failing, to reconcile them with his own beliefs, or rather lack of them. He took the view that life evolved to fill all available habitats and become singularly suited to them. Perhaps, since the universe was comprised of elements, held together by some kind of energy field, life could evolve from energy fields alone, without matter of any kind? He sighed. It was quite beyond him. Even assuming that was what the djinn were. And the others too, of course: the seraphim.

154

Philip's knowledge of physics was superficial, to put it mildly. There was that Professor Derringer, the theoretical physicist. He could track him down and offer to buy him lunch, although what he would ask escaped him for the moment. Imagine how that conversation would go. "Professor, a being that can transcend space and matter, but not time, what would it be made of, do you think?" He smiled wryly. At least it was taking his mind off Sandwell.

Traffic was light and twenty minutes later he was walking the corridors in the Administration wing, approaching the Human Resources department. Passing the stern, forbidding portraits of the college's former presidents gave him a feeling that he had not felt since he was a schoolboy, sent to the headmaster's office for playing truant.

At the end of the corridor he found Sam Evans waiting, his foot tapping in time as he hummed a nameless tune.

"Hello, Philip. I thought I'd stop by. You never know, you might want a character witness." He smiled as if it was a joke but it was not a bad idea. It was Philip's word against Sandwell's, and Sam Evans was influential in the small world of the university. Philip was touched and grateful.

"Thank you, Sam, I appreciate it."

"Well, I want to support you, Philip. I know this must all be some sort of misunderstanding."

"It's no misunderstanding," Philip declared, shaking his head. "This is a smear campaign, plain and simple. She warned me, now here it comes. I promise you, there is no truth to this. Quite the opposite, in fact."

They stood outside a door marked with gilt lettering. Tessa Richards. Director, Human Resources. Sam nodded towards it. At Philip's shrug, he knocked and opened the door. Inside, they were met by Tessa Richards, dour and prim, and a man wearing glasses with 'lawyer' written all over him. Inevitable, Philip supposed.

He had only ever met the head of HR once before, when he first took the job and his first impression had not been favorable. Now, even less so. She was very blue stocking.

She stood and indicated the two chairs arranged before her desk.

"Sam, good to see you. Dr. Entwhistle. Please sit down. This is William Turney. He is a lawyer. You should be aware, Dr. Entwhistle, that he is the University's lawyer, not yours. I apologize. I should have advised you of your right to have your lawyer present. My oversight. I will be quite happy to give you the time to arrange one. The union will help you with that, I'm sure."

"Thank you, Mrs. Richards, but that will most certainly not be required. I am quite sure your office will get to the bottom of this. I look forward to it."

"Yes, Dr. Entwhistle. It will. Of that, have no doubt. You are quite sure? I don't want you to feel pressured."

"Quite sure. Thank you."

"Very well." She looked around the table. "Shall we proceed?"

She exuded confidence and a no-nonsense manner. Philip found that, in spite of the circumstances, he was impressed. She pulled four sheets of paper from a slim folder and distributed them.

"Dr. Entwhistle, this is the statement made by Dr. Sandwell. With your permission, I'll summarize. She alleges that you invited her to your apartment, where you plied her with drink and then attempted to force yourself on her. Now, can you please tell us, in your own words, what you believe happened?"

Philip ignored her use of the word *believe*, but he feared his initial assessment of her may have been all too accurate. He spoke quietly, but with conviction. Nobody interrupted. "Of course. Dr. Sandwell did come to my apartment, but not by invitation. She came in an attempt to discover my current research topic. This is of great interest to her. For some reason, which she did not disclose, she thinks the subject has relevance to her own field. She brought a bottle of wine, walked into my kitchen, opened it and insisted that I share it with her. I could hardly refuse. She asked for, no, demanded that I not only tell her what I was researching but share the entirety of my research with her. Naturally, I refused. She then tried intimidation, making scarcely veiled threats. I stood my ground. After a few more words back and forth, she left. No one touched anyone. No one made any kind of offer or demand of a sexual nature. Our entire discussion consisted of her demanding my research and my refusal. However, her final words to me were, and I quote: *Be careful, Philip. I don't like to be disappointed.* I took this to be a threat of some kind. Obviously, I was right. I am quite prepared to take a polygraph to verify this statement and I would be very interested to know if Dr. Sandwell would agree to the same."

Mrs. Richards made some notes. Her face and manner gave nothing away. Although he realized the danger of protesting too much he felt it necessary to add an additional point.

"There is one more thing. I know that this is going to sound . . ." he paused briefly and cleared his throat, "more than a trifle paranoid. But Sam, did you forward any of my emails to Sandwell?"

"No, certainly not," he replied, his forehead creasing. "Why on earth do you ask?"

Philip pressed on. "Or anyone else? Concerning my sabbatical?"

Again, the older man shook his head. Philip smiled thinly. "And did you discuss my sabbatical with her?"

"No. Philip, what are you getting at?" Sam cast a look at Mrs. Richards and the lawyer. Both wore puzzled, slightly impatient expressions. He took a deep breath and raised a finger.

"Sorry. One last question. Did you tell Sanjay how long I would be away, and why?"

"No. I just told him you needed him to step in for a while. He didn't ask any questions, I assure you. Just grinned and shook my hand, pleased as punch, and raced off, probably to phone his girlfriend."

Philip exhaled slowly, overcome with relief.

"When Dr. Sandwell came to my apartment, she knew I had requested, specifically, a month off to pursue a vital research topic. Only you were aware of this, Sam. Now, I can understand that she might have got wind of the fact that I was on sabbatical, but first," – he started to count the points on his fingers – "how did she know I would be gone a month, second, how did she know it was for research and third" – he turned to face his friend – "how on earth did she know I had emailed you? Emailed, not phoned? Or discussed it in the corridor, face to face? How could she possibly know about the email, Sam?"

Sam Evans shook his head slowly. "I didn't tell anyone that you'd emailed me. And I certainly didn't tell anyone how much time you had requested. Nobody asked."

Philip nodded, his mouth set in a thin line. "That's exactly what I thought. It is my firm belief that Dr. Sandwell has hacked either your, or my university email accounts. Perhaps both."

Mrs. Richards and the lawyer exchanged glances. The man had said nothing so far but now leaned forward, slowly. And with very conscious, deliberative movements, he took off his glasses and polished the lenses on a handkerchief.

"That," he said, "would be a very serious matter indeed, if true. Not the sort of thing that you should idly put out there. If you are thinking throwing a bit of mud back might be to your benefit, Mr. Entwhistle, you should seriously reconsider. Right now."

Philip knew he was on thin ice. But he had a hunch. He had suspected Sandwell since the Disraeli affair. As far as he was concerned, this confirmed it. He nodded, never once taking his eyes off the lawyer.

"I stand by my statement. If I am wrong, then I will take whatever sanctions you feel appropriate, without complaint. By all means, fire me if you must. However I believe that Sandwell has provided the answer herself. You tell me, how else could she have known the details of my private correspondence with Dr. Evans, unless she had seen it? If you accept that she knew facts specified only in a private email what other explanation is there?"

Mrs. Richards looked at him and nodded. Whether because she agreed with him, or simply because she was acknowledging him damning himself by his own testimony, he didn't know.

"How indeed. Well, Dr. Entwhistle, I think we have enough for now. Thank you for coming in. We appreciate your time."

Philip and Sam both stood. Mrs. Richards reached across her desk to shake hands with Dr. Evans. "Sam, it was nice to see you again."

Sam gave her an affable smile and without another word they turned and left the office. Just as Philip was pulling the door closed he heard Mrs. Richards pick up the phone. "Phyllis, please ask the head of I.T. to join us."

Sam Evans gave his younger friend a wry smile. "Okay, Philip. Now it's in the record. I just hope you're right about that email business."

Philip buried his face in his hands, then steepled them in from of his mouth, as if in prayer. He sighed. "So do I, Sam."

They walked back to the campus gardens and Sam gave him a pat on the back. "By the way," he said. "The chapters were good. Now why don't you tell me about this mysterious discovery of yours?"

Philip shook his head. "It won't be long, Sam. Until a certain event transpires I am not at liberty to reveal anything more than I already have."

"Ahh, shame," Sam replied. "I'll play for time but there's only so much I can do. I just think it would be a pity if you missed the boat, so to speak."

"Yeah," said Philip. "Me too."


Elizabeth Sandwell knelt on the rough pine of the attic floor, the air dense with smoke from tallow candles, incense and dust. With the light from the candles and the little that filtered through the grimy window it was not quite dark. She poured salt, a fine line of white crystal, in a broad, precise circle enclosing a cluster of shapes and symbols. Each of the four cardinal points was marked with a smaller circle, in each of which stood a candle. It was a tricky rite, one that would have been easier with others to handle some of the energy, to help with focus. Her solitary nature came at a price and she took extreme care over the placement of the ritual objects. Any mistake could be disastrous, even fatal. But then, that was the nature of the science.

Sandwell, probably correctly, believed her method to be unique to herself. Unlike other practitioners of witchcraft, she used a rigorous scientific approach to test and validate every aspect. She kept detailed records, repeated experiments, used statistical methods to filter out the superficial and ineffective. It was her strong belief that the occult mysteries were in fact an extension of physics. The hidden mysteries were only mysterious until they were understood. After that it was science, plain and simple. After years of diligent research she had developed a system of magic which she called Metaphysical Geometry, a term borrowed from a heroine in a fantasy book that she had loved as a precocious young reader.

Sandwell considered herself, with some justification, light years ahead of current thinking in physics. Early pagans had intuited the principles she now used, but had confused them with all sorts of hocus-pocus. But if you stripped away the nonsense what was left was . . . powerful.

Over time she had created a synthesis of traditional methods and her own deductions, proven by experiment, to produce a hybrid science that demonstrably worked. She could have written a book on the subject and provided the first robust evidence that magic *was* science but her ambitions were far higher than mere fame. She had no intention of sharing her discovery. To be first of many had its attractions but to be unique was sweeter still.

The salt circle on the floor was almost finished. She poured it carefully in a clockwise direction, making sure to leave no gaps. It must be a perfect circle, an unblemished ring, and in the heart must be an object of power. In this case, it was Entwhistle's personal notebook, filled with his handwritten notes on Disraeli and the remarkable meeting between the nineteenth-century British Prime Minister and a Sufi mystic. The same notebook she had removed from his office, leaving behind a virulent virus on his laptop which wiped his hard drive within seconds of his turning it on the following morning. She smiled.

He was so indignant when he accused her of taking his work; he was almost comical, carrying on as if that had been the most dreadful thing that one person could do to another. If her current strategy failed, he may yet have to be taught that stealing his work was far from the worst she could do.

With the foundation elements in place, Sandwell was ready. All she needed now was the cover of night, for him to sleep and to be physically close to Entwhistle when she recited the incantation. This was crucial and Sandwell frowned in irritation. To be so limited when she knew what the potential was. What *her* potential was! But that would change. One day the rituals of metaphysical geometry would no longer be needed. One day she would transcend the physical. Then she would know true power.

The meeting with Administration had gone well enough but the loss of valuable research time was frustrating. The manuscript was proceeding in leaps and bounds and his close analysis was proving the diary a mine of information. Any time not spent working on it was wasted as far as he was concerned. Sam had even given his manuscript the nod. Now he needed to get it finished.

It was already past twelve when he reached the cottage. He would not get much done now, starting so late in the day, but he would throw himself into it as always. Francis was trimming the lawn edge with a pair of long handled edging shears. Something like a pair of giant scissors set at right angles to its long handles. Nifty, thought Philip. Just the thing for an old man. Francis shuffled along snipping at stray blades of grass, maintaining the knife-sharp borders Philip had admired on his first visit. Could it really have only been two weeks ago?

Francis waved. "Hello, Philip. Bit of a late start today. Nothing wrong I hope?"

Philip crossed the lane and entered the garden. He shook the old man's hand in greeting. "I had a bit of trouble at the University," he said. "Not a big deal, but it cost me the morning."

Francis swapped his shears for a sharp-tined garden fork. He sank to his knees at a flower bed with an ease belying his age.

"How unfortunate. Why don't you go in and get started? I made you a sandwich. I didn't know if you would be coming so I wrapped it in plastic. It's in the fridge."

Francis started to dig vigorously, pulling weeds and turning the soil with almost youthful vigor. Was his frailty an act?

With a mental shrug, Philip went inside. The mention of the sandwich reminded him he was starving. He found the sandwich in the fridge and took it through to the study. The diary was in its usual place next to the old phone. On impulse, he went back to the garden. Francis was still on his knees but not working. He was nursing a hand which dripped blood at an alarming rate. The fork had evidently turned on its master. Philip rushed to his side.

"Are you okay?"

"It's fine. Just a scratch."

Philip helped the old man to his feet and pried his hand away. There was a deep cut, running across the palm. Philip was not faint hearted, but the ragged gash left him feeling queasy.

"That's going to need stitches. I'll drive you to the Emergency Room."

"Oh, don't fuss. It's nothing. Jinny?"

The cat was there by his feet. And then it wasn't.

Philip was suddenly aware that the djinn was hovering close. Moving like a soft breeze between them, flowing over the old man's hand. He saw a faint shimmer, like hot tarmac in a heat wave and he could detect an unusual smell, like a summer evening after a lightning storm. The bleeding slowed, then stopped, and the wound closed, leaving a smudge of drying blood on an otherwise perfect palm.

"That's . . . I don't believe it. It's not possible." Mouth agape, he leaned forward to examine the now perfectly healed hand.

"Oh, it's something alright. I have become quite blasé about Jinny's abilities over the years. A miracle is still a miracle, but if you see it every day, you stop being awed by it."

Philip laughed nervously. The cat was back, winding itself around his legs. It looked up, its blue eyes incomprehensibly deep.

"It still hardly seems real to me. Everything is normal then, pow!"

"Perhaps that is for the best, eh? I wouldn't want you taking Jinny for granted."

"No. Nor would I." Philip regarded Francis speculatively. "How does she do it? Heal your hand, I mean."

The old man looked at him for a moment, his eyes thoughtful. "Are you familiar with quantum mechanics? Particle theory? String theory?"

Philip frowned and shook his head. "No, Mr. Francis. Not even slightly."

"Come now, Philip. We are on first name terms by now, surely?"

"Thank you. But I don't even know your first name."

"Indeed not. I have never told you!" Francis seemed particularly delighted with this point, as if it were a tremendous witticism. He smiled. "It is James. All the male descendants in my family have been called James. It is something of a tradition."

"I see," said Philip, one hand going to his chin, his finger tapping his bottom lip. "That's quite a tradition." The finger now pointed to the older man. "So you are James Francis, too." Philip laughed, lightly. "My father was called Herbert. I'm happy to have been spared."

They both smiled, then James Francis settled onto the nearby bench absently rubbing his palm. Jinny settled at his feet, stretching herself out in the sun while the old man talked. Philip sat beside him.

"So back to my point," said Francis. "Without advanced physics you won't even have the language to grasp the principles. At least, as I understand it. Keep it simple. Miracles."

Philip recalled the books he had seen in the cottage's library. He made a decision to start studying at the earliest opportunity. It irked him to be so ignorant that he could not even understand an explanation if one was made. As if he were a child and too young. His mood was not lost on the old man, who patted his companion's hand.

"Never mind, old boy. You will have plenty of time to figure things out. I did. I have had a good life, Philip. Better than most. And a long one. I have seen everything I ever wanted to see and done pretty much everything I ever wanted to do. I have very few regrets, but I do wish I had had children. I lost my wife a long time ago and I would not, could not remarry. And with me passing, there are no more of the Francis clan to carry on the traditions. No more guardians. You are a very necessary surrogate, Philip."

The old man leaned forward and stroked Jinny's rich, dark fur, his eyes fiercely blue. Like Jinny's, thought Philip. He felt he should say something, but nothing seemed adequate. Not for the first time he felt humbled in the old man's presence. Francis had lived. He had tasted life. Philip felt more than ever the narrow constraints of his daily routines.

"Philip, I have spoken to my lawyer. Everything will go to you. The only condition is that you should live here. Jinny is at home here and I think in time so will you be."

He waved his hand vaguely around. "There is the cottage, some land and a few bits and pieces. You will not have to work again, if that is what you wish."

"What? Are you sure, James?" he asked, hesitantly. "I don't want to take advantage. It wouldn't be right. I will be the next guardian if that's what you call it but I don't need to be bought."

Francis frowned and snapped, "I have no intention of buying you, boy." Then his shoulders slumped, and he looked at Philip, eyes glistening, a single tear running down his cragged face.

"For her. For Jinny. Please, Philip?"

Philip, wretched, wished he could take his words back. "Of course, James. You know that I'm grateful. It's all just a bit, well, overwhelming."

"I should hope so. It's not every day someone gives you a house, is it?"

They both laughed and any tensions between them were dispelled. James wiped away the tear from his face. Philip leaned over to stroke the cat. Jinny purred loud enough to be heard above the droning of the insects in the flower beds. Again, the almost voice.

*Thank you, little man.*

"You will get on fine, together here. You'll see. And don't worry about death duties. I have taken care of that too."

"It is lovely here. I grew up in a small town bordered by countryside, you know. I will be honored to look after the place. But I doubt I'll do such a good job with the garden."

"Oh, you'll pick it up, don't you worry. You can continue to work from here, of course, follow whatever line of research interests you. And I meant what I said about you settling down. Find yourself a young filly and raise a family. It would make me happy to know that you will continue where I left off."

Philip nodded, smiling. He had not been in a serious relationship for some years. There were just too few opportunities to meet anyone he clicked with, except for the occasional student, a fruit forbidden by ethics and custom and for good reason. Philip stood. "Alright, I'll keep my eyes open. And James? Thank you."

Francis waved away his thanks and leaned back on the bench, closing his eyes, face to the sun. Philip went inside and settled into the chair behind the desk but struggled to engage. He could hardly believe what had just happened. To be the next guardian of the djinn was exciting, wonderful, but came at a fearful cost. His mind flew again to the door-knocker and the trellis. But this, a lifetime of independence, was being handed to him on a plate. His head was spinning. Turning away from the desk he surrendered to his thoughts. Never work again. No. That, he now saw, was not something he wanted. To never again stand before a class and meet the freshness of young minds. To have no place in the world. And he would miss Sam and some of his other colleagues. Whatever the future held, he would continue to work. Decision made, he picked up the diary and continued reading.

*I have lost track of the date. The days all run into each other. One is the same as any other. When I waken, the djinn gives me water and I eat whatever food there is. A few withered dates for this morning's repast. When I am ready to walk, the djinn spirits away my few paltry possessions. No need to be encumbered when I have the very latest in travel accessories. A djinn porter to carry my luggage, such as it is. I wonder why I need walk at all. There are very few limits to what the djinn can do, at least according to the legends. But then, she is weak. She has extended herself beyond the limits of her strength in order to bind me to her. And it worked. I can no more part from her, than her from me.*

*August 1 The djinn informs me that this is the start of the new cycle, by man's reckoning. I take this to mean it is the first day of the new month. There is no way to know for sure, but I prefer to put a date to my musings. My strength has returned, and to a degree, so has the djinn's. I wonder if our fortunes are so closely linked that what affects me, affects her. I am tempted to test the theory, even were it to put my life in peril.*

Jinny padded silently into the office, stretched extravagantly then sat, curled her tail neatly around her feet and began to purr. Philip continued reading, making notes and occasionally typing on the laptop but he could feel her watching him. Eventually he gave up and turned to meet her gaze. And froze. In his mind the world began to tumble, merging one over the other, then coalescing with all his senses tuned to Sir James Francis. The waking vision held him, his eyes still glassy, but in his mind another world and time unfolded.

The sound of a rider approaching disturbs the still air. The stony ground carries the sound further than I would have imagined, but eventually he comes into view. I am not worried for myself. I would care little enough were he to offer me harm. But the chances of that are slim unless it is Ibrahim, or his agent. I am now just what I appear to be. A poor wretch, deserving of pity, not a rich man to be robbed.

The rider slows as he nears. Clearly Tuareg, with the blue cheche across his face and around his head leaving only the eyes visible, his clothes stained with travel and countless days exposed to hard sunlight. He salaams and dismounts, leading his horse by the reins.

"Who are you?"

This is no courtesy. He demands an answer. I am on the land of his people and he has a right to my name.

"Salaam aleykum, brother. I am Ibn Musaafir, from Damascus." Son of a traveller it means, a not common name, but most apt for my pretense.

"Wa alaykumu s-salam. How are you here? Where is your horse? Your camel?"

"They are lost. Raiders took everything. I barely escaped with my life."

He pulled aside his scarf, and spits on the ground. An act of contempt for me and my story or for the men who robbed me?

"My sympathies for your loss. There is a village near. You can be assured of hospitality there."

His eyes scoured the surrounding countryside as if he expected my retinue to suddenly catch up. "You are Arab?"

"Yes, from Damascus. I have been making a Haj. I travel to the mountains." I point in the general direction where I believed my destination lay. The other man nodded, accepting my story.

"I am Amnay. I have a little food, if you would like to sit with me," he said.

"My thanks. That would be most welcome."

"Then come, let us find some shade and you will tell me your story. It is not every day that I meet a lone wanderer in the desert. I am amazed that you have survived. But it is the will of Allah, is it not?"

"We live the days we are allotted. No more, no less," I agreed.

We walked and talked until we came upon a wadi where an ancient stream had carved itself into the living rock, cutting a narrow passage like a corridor. It was cooler in its shaded depths and we took our ease under an overhang of rock. The rider passed me his water skin and I drank deeply. He broke in half a loaf of dark bread. We ate in companionable silence. From time to time he would ask a question, probing my story. I felt a sense of dissatisfaction. He did not entirely believe me.

"You do not look Arab," he said.

"You mean my eyes?"

"Blue is not a color we see very often. At least, not unless you are French."

"I am a Pasha. I serve. My people are Albanian originally but we are brought up in the traditions of the Empire, of Istanbul. There are many like me in service." I cannot tell him the real truth of this matter, of course. Why my eyes are blue when once they were brown. He would believe me, were I to do so, but it would invite entirely too much interest and possibly worse.

"You mean you were taken as a child from the infidels? You are blessed indeed." He looked at me and a pained expression crossed his face. "Unless you were . . ." He left the question hanging.

Unless I was gelded. A eunuch. There were many in the Empire, even in this day and age. I smiled, shook my head.

"No. Praise be to Allah the All-merciful, I am a man as any other."

He seemed relieved. He laughed and chewed the rough bread. He sounded like Izem when he laughed. The pain from the sudden reminder that I would not see Izem again does not surprise me. But for it to come from hearing another man laugh is a low blow. How can mirth cause this pain? I try to think of Izem and his smiling face. His feeble jokes which he was always so certain I did not understand, else why did I not laugh too?

My notebook is tucked into my belt sash and the horseman notices it. With a nod to it he asks to see it. I could hardly hide it now, nor refuse to give it to him so I pass it to him. He opens it but is clearly puzzled by its contents.

"What is this? This is not Arabic. Not anything I know."

"It is the language of my first people," I lied easily. "I first learned this as a child. Now, a simple device to confound prying eyes."

"It is strange. Like the marks a bird makes in sand."

"Indeed. A most primitive script in comparison to our own."

To demonstrate, I traced a few letters in the sand, the smooth swing of their lines beautiful in comparison to the Latin alphabet that owes some of its origin to the need to carve in wood and stone. The Arabic script is a wonder of elegance in comparison.

Amnay did not seem particularly impressed or indeed convinced. So I took the notebook from him and produced the pen from the pocket of my trousers. With care, I slowly drew a complex pattern of intersecting Arabic letters on a clean page. Arabic calligraphy is more beautiful than any other script and can be formed into calligrams. Shapes, made from the weaving of words into and around each other to form patterns. I had once practiced this art most diligently, partly as a necessary attribute of an educated man from the courts of Damascus, but also because I found it most relaxing.

I soon reproduced a well-known calligram I had first seen in Istanbul. In the name of God, Most Merciful, Most Gracious. The words entwined around each other in a pattern reminiscent of an arrow head, pointed at the top, over a broad base.

Amnay nodded and sighed in appreciation of the skill. He spoke in a dialect different again from the one I had been learning but I understood it well enough. "By Allah, that is amazing."

I replied in his own language, shaping the vowels somewhat to match what I heard him use. "My thanks. It is a gift."

He looked at me with wonder when I spoke his tongue. "You are a man of rare talent, Ibn Musaafir."

"Thank you, Amnay."

"How long have you been learning my language?"

"Since I came West. Perhaps a month or two." I replied in the same tongue.

He nodded, impressed. "I am sorry, but I must return. But follow the wadi and you will reach the village. You will be welcome. I will leave word. It is perhaps two hours' walk. I leave you with regret but we fight the infidel and I have duties."

He left as quickly as he came. Probably to report my presence to his superiors. I had no doubt that he was a scout. The gun holstered on his horse was a modern carbine, a military weapon, not the traditional long rifle of the desert dwellers.

Then the djinn was with me, its voice echoing softly, like a fading whisper.

*You must not go to the village. There is one there that would seek to harm you. You must go around and not be seen.*

The yellow glow of the street lamps only partially pierced the dark; small islands of gloom in the night. But an observer would still have seen the tall, red-haired figure striding purposefully towards the three-story Victorian building. She ignored the admiring or envious glances of passers-by. She was a beautiful woman, knew it and thought nothing of it.

It was nearly time, the moment when her power would reach its peak, although still barely enough for the task. She must be as close as possible. She stopped, hugging the shadows opposite Entwhistle's house, and looked up. Her eyes glowed with a pale violet light as she fixed her gaze on the third-floor window. Her enemy dreamed. She could feel his mind, and though she could not see his dream, she got a sense of it.

Smiling, she subtly steered his thoughts towards a woman; towards urgent desire. She did not have to conjure a specific fantasy, he would do that himself. Desire was all that was required.

In the dark room Philip lay tangled in blankets and sheets. He smiled, rolling over onto his back. The dream vision this time was sweet and he felt a sense of peace. But it was different. In every previous dream Philip had been subsumed into Sir James, his own identity lost, a silent observer of the actions of another, seeing through his host's eyes, experiencing his emotions. But this time it was he, Philip, who felt the dry heat of the desert and the loose flow of robes about his body.

The sun was setting and Philip stood, admiring the serene beauty of the great globe of burning orange as it hung on the edge of the world before slipping below the horizon. This was the best time of day, an interlude of perfect temperature. Twilight, an exquisite balance between day and night. He watched the sun disappear, its last light lingering.

He heard Tajeddigt calling and turned to see his beautiful young wife step from her tent. She called to him in her language and for a moment Philip did not understand. She spoke again and this time the words were clear.

"Come, my husband. It is time to eat."

She disappeared into the shaded confines of the large tent and he followed. It felt normal, his daily life. He knew he was not Sir James. He was Philip Entwhistle, historian and teacher. As his eyes adjusted he could make out the slight form of Tajeddigt setting out dishes on the rug-covered floor. She smiled, her brown eyes, dark with kohl, looking up at him with adoration. "Sit, husband. You must eat well, for you shall need your strength."

Her mischievous smile made her meaning clear. Philip, suddenly, hungered not for food but for her, but sat and accepted the rough bread and seksu – what Philip knew as couscous – with the stewed lamb.

He ate with his fingers as she served him, offering him wine and then more bread. His hunger for her grew as he took her in – the high cheekbones, the luminescent skin, the fine blue line of her siyala, tattooed from her lower lip to the tip of her chin to foster fertility and be a talisman against evil. What would it be like to kiss those lips?

Tajeddigt stood and shrugged off her robe. She pulled the scarf from her head, freeing a lustrous black river of hair flowing down her back. With every garment she removed, Philip's enchantment grew until he thought her the most beautiful creature he had ever seen.

She wore only a loose fitting cotton shift now and Philip held his breath, imagining the magical designs tattooed between her breasts and the arcane symbols on her belly. He ached for her. He put down his cup, wiped his fingers carefully on a cloth.

"Thank you, my sweet. It was delicious."

She nodded, smiled and giggled. She had not eaten. She would serve his needs first, satisfying his hunger before she dealt with her own. That was her way. He stood, eyes never leaving hers, and shrugged off his own robe. But before he could release the crimson sash around his waist, she was there tugging at the material, unwinding it, helping him out of his loose trousers. She looked up at him, smiling. Seeing, and feeling, his urgent desire.

She caressed him gently and pulled him down to the soft rugs on the sand. She ran her hands over his chest and kissed him, her tongue probing for his. He matched her passion with his own, rolling on top of her, thrusting, almost mad with desire. She laughed and pushed hard, rolling him onto his back.

"Hemmleɣk," she said. *I love you.*

"Hemmleɣkem," he replied, caressing her small breasts as she leaned over him.

She straddled him, leaning forward to kiss him, her young body, supple and lithe. She wriggled out of her shift, and freed her body to his touch and gaze. Grasping her shoulders, he pulled her down onto him. Smiling, she arched her back as he thrust deeply. She gripped the skin of his chest, nails digging. Philip reached up and grasped her breasts in his hands, squeezing the tender flesh, causing Tajeddigt to exclaim in pain and pleasure. The delicate patterns of the tattoos between her breasts swirled, rising up to her throat, promising eternal joy and great love making.

He had never been harder, never more passionate, never more in love than now. He was a stallion, but it was she that had mounted him, riding him to her pleasure, her hips thrusting. Her nails continued to dig into him as she moaned, her lips open, eyes closed. It was the most intense pleasure he had ever known. Grasping the fullness of her breasts, he too closed his eyes. Her fingernails dug deep and he arched his back in pain or ecstasy, he did not know which. He was reaching his climax. Getting closer. Tajeddigt's hair, deep red, falling into his face. She moved his hands away, then leaned forward, pushing a nipple into his mouth. He sucked, feeling it stiffening, drawing forth fluid, filling his mouth with her milk.

No. Something was wrong. Red hair? It was like trying to grasp fog but try as he might it eluded him. His eyes opened. But was he actually awake? The days of visions and dreams had taken their toll. He could not tell. He saw the slim, red-haired woman crouching above him, pushing him down, filling his mouth with her breast, her milk. But not milk. His chest was slick with blood, deeply gouged. Her mouth was twisted in a cruel smile, violet eyes glittering with delight at his pain.

Twisting beneath, he arched his back, trying to dislodge her but he was too weak, his efforts ineffectual. She pinned him down easily, smothering him, her breast choking him, and held herself there as she rode him. Bitter, hot fluid filled his mouth, sliding down his throat. She cradled his head gently as he continued to suckle, thick black ichor dribbling from the corner of his mouth. His eyes were wide open now and staring, the pupils small. She pulled her breast free, one hand across his mouth, forcing him to swallow. Her smile was wide, genuine in pleasure. She had him now. He was hers. The knowledge sent her over the edge and she arched her back, riding him harder until her orgasm overtook her, his seed filling her belly at the same time.

Elizabeth Sandwell climbed off the supine man and looked down on him with a sneer. He stared sightlessly at the window. Something dripped. Her hands were wet, and she smeared her breasts and belly with the blood from the deep scratches on his chest. Entwhistle lay, dazed, his eyes open but registering nothing. His strength of will was surprisingly strong, but for now, he was hers. With a word, she closed down his mind.

"Sleep," she said.

It would not keep him under for long, she knew, but the command was accepted without a fight. He closed his eyes, instantly asleep. Sandwell walked into the other room, her eyes darting, seeking. Her lips curled in a smile at the sight of his notebooks and laptop on the table. Everything he had unearthed, would now be hers.

She sat and opened the computer but as she reached to switch it on she heard a knock at the door. A voice came through the thin wood, muffled, clearly belonging to a young man.

"Mr. Entwhistle? Mum told me I should come up. She said you needed my help with something." When there was no answer he spoke again. "And maybe we can look at my revision notes, Mr. Entwhistle?"

The knocking continued. Sandwell's face twisted in rage and frustration. She had taken too long. She should not have used the man like that. He was not the priority. In the bedroom, Philip was stirring, the banging on the door waking him. She heard the creak of the bed. She whispered the command for him to sleep but the noises from the bedroom continued. With a hiss she closed her eyes and spoke three words. She began to fade, quickly becoming unsubstantial, like a shadow. In a moment, she was gone. Only a sense of something unpleasant remained; a lingering smell of chamomile, caraway and something rotten, both sweet and putrid at the same time.

The voice beyond the door muttered something muted and incomprehensible then the sound of footsteps could be faintly heard, walking away.

# Our open minds may not agree
## 9

He was oppressed, and afflicted,
yet openeth not his mouth: he is
brought as a lamb to the slaughter,
and as a sheep before shearers is dumb,
so he openeth not his mouth.

*—Isaiah, 53:7*

"What do you mean, it's no longer available? I'm moving in!"

Fern was standing on the pavement outside the building of her new apartment, phone in hand. John, her erstwhile landlord, and Steve were already unloading boxes from the back of the van, stacking them at the side of the road.

"Yes, I'm sure you are. But what exactly am I supposed to do now?" She sighed and looked heavenward. This was not exactly what she had expected when she asked the universe for support.

"Alright. Well thank you for that, at least. Please call me as soon as you know something." She put her phone away. "Guys, hold it. We have to put it all back on the van."

"What?"

"That was the estate agent. There's been some confusion. She says this place isn't supposed to be available for another two weeks. They have some workmen coming in tomorrow, to rip the floors out."

"Jesus fucking Christ on a crutch!" said Steve. "That's bloody bad timing, that is."

"Well what're we gonna do now?" asked John, concern clearly written on his face. There was no way they both could live in that tiny studio apartment. It was barely big enough for one.

"I don't know," said Fern. "She said they had others on the books and would ring me back. Wait, I suppose." And say a prayer to the Goddess for good measure.

"You got any friends who can put you up, Fern?" asked Steve. "We could put the boxes and whatnot into storage. Just grab what you need for now."

"I could ask one of my . . . colleagues." She had nearly said coven.

"Alright," said John. "Let's load it back up again."

"Can you guys take care of this? I'm really sorry but I'm needed at work."


Philip stared at the horses in the field opposite the cottage. How did he get here? He had driven, evidently. His car was parked in the usual place. He walked slowly up the stone path to the red door with its morose knocker and shiny brass numbers. The door opened with a suddenness and ferocity that would have alarmed him if he was not so utterly drained. Its massive weight swung wide, slamming into the inside wall. Francis stood there, shaking, his rage palpable, one claw-like hand pointing in accusation.

"You have some explaining to do, young man," he said, as Philip entered. Francis faced him, blocking his entry. "Before you take another step, tell me how long this has been going on."

Philip stared at the old man, puzzled. He was tired, in a daze. His mind was unable to focus as it should. Everything was hazy. Even the old man's voice sounded distant.

"What? What has been going on? I don't know what you mean." Philip stepped around him and made his way into the study. He put his satchel on the floor. The desk was as he had seen it on the first day. Just the telephone, isolated and alone on its expanse. The diary was not visible.

Francis followed him in. Jinny was suddenly there too, her back arched, a ridge of fur standing up.

"You," said Francis, his finger stabbing pointedly into the historian's chest, "have been keeping something from us. Tell me. Exactly what arrangements have you made with *her*." He spat the last word out as if it was poison. Philip frowned, lost in a fog of confusion.

"Mr. Francis, what are you talking about?" He looked blankly at the smaller man.

"You know what I am talking about. You have a relationship with that woman, Mr. Entwhistle. That harridan. Why don't you tell us about it?"

"Woman? What woman?"

"With Elizabeth Sandwell. A colleague of yours, I believe?"

"Well, yes, I know her. Dr. Sandwell works at the University. But I don't have a relationship with her. I mean, apart from the fact we both work at the same place."

Francis' eyes blazed, fiercely blue. "That is a lie, boy. You were with the harpy last night, and worse, you brought her sin into my home."

Philip Entwhistle shook his head in surprise and denial. He had not been with anyone last night. That was ridiculous. He was at home, alone. He didn't have any visitors. What sin? What was Francis talking about? He had spent the night working as he had since he first came to the cottage.

"No, there's been some kind of mistake. I wasn't with anyone. I don't know what you're talking about, James. I was alone the whole night."

The old man did not reply. He held Philip in his gaze, as if gauging the truth of his reply. Then, with a speed that would have shocked Philip if he could think clearly, his hands lashed out and gripped the historian's shirt. With a quick jerk, he ripped it open. A button tore off, clattering to the wooden floor as the young man's chest was exposed, revealing deep, ugly scratches. Francis' mouth curled in disgust as he pointed again. There, clear as day, were the livid scars of a pentagram, carved into his chest.

"That," he said, his mouth turning into a thin, hard line.

Philip looked down at his exposed skin. What? He saw nothing. That was his favorite shirt!

"Mr. Francis," he said, exasperation evident in his voice. "Would you please be good enough to tell me, just what in the hell you are doing?"

At this the old man looked thoughtful. He turned to regard the cat, which had jumped onto the window ledge, assuming a regal pose. Then in an almost human gesture, she cocked her head to one side, as if listening to something only she could hear. The air around her seemed to shimmer. Philip felt a sudden savage pain in his chest. He burned. Looking down he gasped in horror at the raw flesh, crusted over with blood.

"What in hell? How did that . . . " He could not finish the words. His voice left him at the same moment his legs buckled and he fell heavily against the old man, like a marionette whose strings had been cut. Francis grabbed the bigger, heavier man and held him easily, lowering him gently to the study floor.

Tessa Richards held the transcript of computer terminal logins, showing date stamps, IP addresses and user IDs. It meant nothing to her.

"What am I looking at?" She asked, in a voice just short of annoyed. She dropped the printout on her desk and speared Kevin Fisher, the hapless head of I.T. with a fierce gaze. Thin, with wire-rimmed glasses and a nervous disposition, he was more comfortable around computers than people, especially powerful women, but Tessa was in no mood to mollycoddle.

Cautiously, Fisher pointed to the user ID, and the time. "There," he said, finger tapping the printout.

"Very well. There. What is there?"

"That is Entwhistle's IP address. We use fixed IP addresses for all the staff, so we know exactly who posts what, or who sent what. No question, that is Entwhistle's terminal. That shows that someone logged into the network from his office. And they did it," – the finger moved across to the next column – "at exactly that time."

"Someone? You mean Dr. Entwhistle. He must do that every day, at least."

"Not with the System Administrator login and password, he doesn't."

Mrs. Richards sighed. So Entwhistle was right. Someone did indeed appear to have been hacking his account. He had named a name, one she was inclined to dismiss, but then Sam Evans had come to her with a story about a pen. Was it possible? His tip gave her something to work on though, and it did support Entwhistle's theory. Albeit barely.

"Also," Fisher continued, "I checked the CCTV over both entrances to the building for two hours either side. Lots of people came and went, but not Dr. Entwhistle. I also checked gate security. He didn't use the car park at all that day."

"So, you are saying that at exactly two twenty-three, on that day, someone broke into his office, logged into his computer using an ID and password they should not have had. And then read his emails."

"Well, I'm not saying anything as to why they did it, but I can tell you that somebody did. And yes, the application logs showed the email account being accessed." He took a step back from the desk, wiping a hand on his brow. "And it was not me, or any of my team. This leaves the very serious possibility that our systems have been compromised. When I saw this, the first thing I did was change all the Admin passwords."

Tessa smiled. "Thank you Kevin. You have been extremely thorough. Now, who did it? Any clues?"

"Well, that's just it. It could be anybody," he said with a shrug. "There are CCTVs inside the building too. Even one on his floor, but nothing covering the part of the corridor where his office is. But I can tell you this: it's somebody who can pick a lock."

"I beg your pardon?"

"Whoever did it either had a key or picked the lock. There was no evidence of a break in. I asked security to take a look," he said, looking pleased with himself. "They examined the lock and the door frame. All fine. The lock is a pin-and-tumbler type so the hacker must be quite skilled."

At Mrs. Richards' blank look, he elaborated quickly. "Apparently this is a difficult lock to pick, and all the offices use this type. More likely though, I think, is that it's someone with a master key. Apparently, the maintenance and security guys have a special key that will unlock every office door. That's most of the doors in the university it seems. If the hacker has one, he can literally go anywhere."

"I see. That is interesting. So what we know is that someone may have the capability to gain entry into any locked room and certainly can hack anyone's computer. And they may have been doing this for a while."

Fisher exhaled with a wheeze, nodding. "The way I see it they could have been doing this for the best part of a year. But they won't be doing it anymore, I can tell you. We've reset all the admin passwords. Not unless" —he took out an inhaler, put it to his mouth and took a dose, then tapped one finger on the side of his head— "they can read minds."

"Yes. Well, that aside, I need to see a list of people with access to the master keys. They never give them out to anyone, do they?"

"I don't know. You'll have to check with Maintenance."

"Very well. Thank you, Kevin. You've been very thorough. As a last favor, could you have security send me the afternoon's CCTV footage from Entwhistle's floor?"

The system engineer nodded, visibly glowing. He turned to go but Mrs. Richards raised her hand.

"Kevin, come and see me later. I think I have something that will do wonders with your asthma."


Philip's eyes opened tentatively. He was lying on the study floor, with a pillow under his head. He stared at the ceiling, noting the cobwebs in the corner and the small crack in the plaster. He breathed deeply and slowly sat up. Francis' silver necklace hung about his own neck, the amulet lying cold against his bare skin. Chillingly cold. He looked at it with a puzzled frown, then gasped as his memory came rushing back. He opened his shirt. The hideous marks were gone, the skin unblemished. He wondered if it had been a dream.

You did not imagine it. It was real. So too was she.

The voice in his head was strange, odd. Almost metallic. But he had heard it before. The djinn.

Then, in a dizzying flood, more memories poured through his mind. The dream where he was both Sir James and himself. The meal in the tent, making love with Tajeddigt and then finally, *her*. Sandwell. He started to dry retch. She had put her breast in his mouth and made him drink . . . something.

At the sound of the younger man gagging, Francis entered with Jinny. With a few slow, shaky breaths, Philip managed to suppress the nausea. He looked up at the older man, gasping, and spoke.

"What happened to me?"

"It seems that your colleague, Sandwell, paid you a visit last night. She put a geas on you, Mr. Entwhistle."

The historian climbed unsteadily to his feet. Almost immediately he wobbled, his head spinning. He slumped into the chair. Absently, he started to do up the buttons on his shirt.

"A geas? You mean, like a hex? Witchcraft?"

"Indeed, Mr. Entwhistle. Very much like a hex. In fact, you could say that you were under her spell."

"But that's impossible. I don't believe in any of that . . ." He stopped, realizing how foolish he sounded. In the last days Philip had been made to understand that the world was not the black and white, relatively simple place he had taken it for. The line from Hamlet came to him. There are more things in heaven and earth, Horatio, than are dreamt of in your philosophy.

He sensed amusement from the djinn. *You have no idea, little man.*

Francis seemed to know his mind as easily as the djinn but at least he was not laughing.

"Yes. It is so. Most people see the world as they would like it to be. Others perceive it as they fear it to be. Few see it as it truly is. And the truth is far, far different from anything dreamt by your philosophy, or indeed mine. Witchcraft is real, rest assured of that. But it is not quite so prevalent as it once was. There are few in the world today who could do to you what she did."

"What *did* she do to me? What was this?" he gestured to his chest. "There was a star there. What happened to it?"

*It offended me. I removed it.*

Again the voice in his head, the sense of something not human, yet oddly, not entirely alien either. Francis nodded, as if in agreement with the unspoken words.

"That was her mark, Mr. Entwhistle. A pentagram. Jinny took care of it while you were . . . indisposed."

Philip nodded. He remembered the incident with the fork in the garden. In spite of the situation he was a little sorry he had not observed the djinn healing him.

"But why would she do that? What on earth did she want?"

"Why? So she could own you, Mr. Entwhistle. Nothing less. While you were under the geas she could see through your eyes, hear what you hear, feel what you feel. As for what she wanted, well, that was not the first time she has tried to gain entry into this house, but this was the furthest she has ever been. She is probably very pleased with herself. But she will also know that she has lost you, too, so perhaps not. She neither saw nor heard anything of importance."

Philip looked at the amulet that lay against his skin. It was very cold, as if it had just come from the freezer.

"Why did you give me this?" he asked, holding up the silver necklace.

"You are young. Her control over you will diminish in time. Eventually your spirit will fight it off. But right now the hex is very strong. The talisman is protecting you, blocking her, so to speak. So long as you wear it, she has no influence over you. At least, not more than you allow."

Philip nodded. He did feel different. Less fuzzy. Memories were sharp again. Some he would rather not have. He felt the bile start to rise in his throat again.

"I think she was in my head. I dreamed of her last night."

"No, Philip. Not exactly. It was not a dream, as such. Not a vision either. She was there last night. Or at least, a part of her was."

Philip shuddered at the memory of what had occurred. His stomach continuing to rebel and resume its attempt to vomit. He shook his head in horrified wonder.

"And you say she wants to control me. Why?"

"For what she has always wanted of course. Power. You are a threat to her, Philip, even more than you know. You oppose her. That makes you her enemy and she is perverse and cruel. She will delight in ruining your life. You need to take care. If Sandwell cannot control you, she may well try to destroy you."

The old man smiled and a prankish look came over him. "But she might find that hard to do. You have a great power now. Or at least, you will very soon. You will have no trouble resisting her when you are Jinny's guardian. In fact, she would be well advised to leave you alone."

Philip could not help but think of the unfortunate Professor Buckley, the previous head of Sandwell's department. He had swerved into oncoming traffic and collided with a truck. At the time it was thought he must have fallen asleep at the wheel. Now Philip was not so sure. Just how far was Sandwell willing to go, in order to get what she wanted?

He looked down at the cat and the cat stared back. Suddenly he began to understand what was really happening. What he was really doing there. Why Francis had allowed him to study the diary and more importantly, why he had asked the djinn to show him the past, the visions. There would soon come a time when the djinn would be his, or vice versa. The prospect was dizzying and terrifying. Did Sandwell suspect something? She could not know anything of the djinn as he had not written a single word about it. If she had somehow gone through his papers or what was on his laptop then all she would know is the facts, without any hint of a supernatural agency. As far as she knew, he was researching Sir James Francis and had been welcomed in the ancestral home. Anything else would be conjecture on her part. Of course, that was the reason she had . . . assaulted him. Because she wanted to find out not just what he knew, but also what he didn't.

*It is so. She suspects you are chosen, even if she is not sure if you are aware of it yourself. You have much to learn and very little time. I feel it has been hard for you, little man. I am sorry for that.*

Philip was not perturbed to hear the djinn in his mind. There was a sense of comfort in knowing that something was watching over him now.

"If I keep this," he said touching the amulet, "am I safe from her, even face to face?"

Francis nodded, but his eyes narrowed slightly, as if suspecting what was on Philip's mind.

"Then I think that it is high time that I paid Lizzy a visit. Let her know she can't intimidate me. And that I'm not going to hide from her. If she wants to come at me, bring it on."

"Well said, Mr. Entwhistle, well said. But if I may offer you some small advice? Inject a little sanity, perhaps? Do not, for one moment, think that the only danger from that woman is mystical or supernatural. It is not. She is perfectly capable of running you over with her car. Just remember that."

Entwhistle drove straight to the campus, teeth gritted all the way. Once there he strode through the campus like a man possessed. He ignored the affable greetings of fellow academics, and the shy hellos from the undergrads. None registered. He marched with a singularity of purpose, cutting across the lawns, where normally he would follow the winding paths.

He passed a slim, dark-haired woman with a slight scar on her upper lip, as she stood in the middle of the lawn with her hands held out slightly. She cast a sharp glance in his direction, but he paid her no heed, skirting around her, then entering the red brick building belonging to the Humanities, and the Psychology Department. He took the steps two and three at a time and strode down corridors until he was outside Sandwell's rooms, the poster advertising a conference on the paranormal telling him he was in the right place.

He flung the door wide and strode in. Sandwell looked up from her desk, surprised. She lowered the paper in her hand.

"You went too far last night, Sandwell," Philip said forcefully.

She smiled up at him, showing even, white teeth. "Well, well. What a pleasant surprise. And so soon. What, no flowers?"

Her smile changed to a sneer, and he found that he preferred it. He closed the door behind him so firmly that it rattled the glass.

"It's one thing to steal my research, but what you did last night . . . that was beyond the pale. You disgust me. Leave me alone or you will regret it."

She laughed, her smile one of pure delight in the face of his moral outrage.

"Oh, get over yourself, Philip. You haven't come to any harm. And you seemed to be having a pretty good time last night. You should be grateful. When was the last time a woman even looked at you?"

Philip was not blind. Sandwell was beautiful, but looking at her made him feel slightly ill. The biblical phrase 'whited sepulcher' came to mind. Yes, that was it. A beautiful container of every kind of rottenness and corruption. He loathed her, felt sick to have been with her.

He longed to wipe the sneer from her face. Unconsciously his hands clenched and unclenched, aching to take retribution. Sandwell arched an eyebrow and one hand made a gesture, her fingers tracing an intricate pattern in the air.

Philip's retort froze in his mouth. His tongue became wooden and his head felt like it was being squeezed in a vice. An overwhelming desire to please her washed over him. To give himself to her, totally and completely. Yes. She was a goddess! Philip started falling to his knees and her sneer became a smile, lascivious in its triumph.

It seemed the old man's protection was not enough. A distant part of his mind understood but he was powerless to stop it. Then the amulet around his neck grew cold, so cold it burned, and the feeling passed. The smile faded from Sandwell's face. Philip straightened; chin jutting in defiance and provocation.

More gestures, frantic now, her eyebrows furrowed, her violet eyes burning into his. He met her gaze with a grim smile.

"Well? Is that it?" he challenged, satisfied to see unprecedented confusion on Sandwell's face. For the first time since he had met her, Sandwell was thrown, unsure of what was happening. Her gaze fell upon the amulet, seeing it for the first time, her eyes widened with—yes, Entwhistle was sure—fear. She obviously knew what it was. Protection against the evil eye. A shield against dark forces. Against her. Her features relaxed.

"So, you have a benefactor. An initiate. I would like to meet your friend. The old Mr. Francis, if I am not mistaken."

"I don't think he would want to see you. In fact, I will make myself clear. I do not want to see you again either. I do not want you to contact me, and I certainly do not want you paying any more visits. Rest assured, I will take very good precautions in case you decide you want to drop by in the future."

Sandwell stood and walked around her desk until she was standing before him. She was tall and slender, but there was strength in her, more than in most. She smiled again. Then her hand flashed out, her fingers four claws aimed for his eyes. She was fast. Entwhistle was faster. He caught her wrist and held it locked in his hand. She struggled, trying to pull free but his grip was iron. He felt power coursing through his veins, strength of purpose and the will to achieve anything. She hissed her frustration and made to strike with her other hand but then looked into his eyes. Her own widened in response and the fight suddenly went out of her.

Her face changed, becoming a mask that revealed nothing. She tried to pull away. Entwhistle felt a pang of regret. He had exposed his power, given away something important. But what alternative did he have? Now wary, she backed off, her look more thoughtful, calculating as she regarded him.

"I'm sorry, Philip. You are right. It was wrong of me, I can see that now." She moved behind her desk, placing it between them. "I am just used to getting my way," she said, "and when I don't, well . . . perhaps I over-reacted."

There was a gentle knock on the door and it opened a crack. Philip turned to see a young student, glasses and dirty hair peeping into the room.

"Oh, sorry. I didn't mean to interrupt. I just wanted to ask you something," said the young woman, looking at her tutor.

"Why don't you come back later, Cassy?" Dr. Sandwell said. The student withdrew and she sighed. The interruption seemed to come at a perfect moment. Philip was ready for a fight but her surrender had taken the wind out of his sails.

"You just forget you ever heard my name and we'll be fine," he said.

"Don't worry. I won't bother you anymore. And I'll withdraw the accusation. You can forget about that."

"Good. See that you do."

He turned to leave, then stopped and looked over his shoulder, one hand on the doorknob.

"And stop hacking my email."

She smiled ruefully, the expression of a child caught trying to steal candy.

"Fine. Level playing field, fair enough?"

He nodded, satisfied, and left as abruptly as he had entered.


Sandwell sat slowly in her chair, her carefully composed expression dissolving into shocked disbelief at the brief blue flash she had witnessed in his eyes. But it couldn't be! That milquetoast had been granted what she had always desired? Disbelief turned to a jealousy so intense that it hurt. She knew exactly what the momentary change in his eyes meant. The mark of the djinn. That old man, of course. So he *did* have a djinn after all.

Sandwell had tried for years to cultivate him, but to no end. Then Entwhistle just turns up at his door and suddenly it's all fatted calves and prodigal sons. That spineless old fool!

Yet, perhaps this might work for her in the end? An avaricious smile spread across her lips as the pieces came together in her mind. The time was nearly at hand and the tools of her ascension had quite literally just walked into her office. All she had to do was reach out and take them. Take what she needed. And deserved!

She must take care. Entwhistle was made of firmer stuff than she had anticipated. But no matter. It would be all the sweeter when she destroyed him. And she knew exactly how to do it. After her little visit the night before, she had no doubt that Entwhistle was not exaggerating when he said that he would take precautions. No doubt Francis or the djinn would help secure Entwhistle from any further magical intervention. But there were other, simpler means.

Most people, when dealing with the occult, started to see it as the ultimate tool to achieve their purpose. They were fools. There were other methods that would work just as well.

Elizabeth took up her mobile, which lay on the desk. She searched her contacts and selected one. The call connected.

"I have a job for you. And this time you had better not let me down."


Entwhistle's hands were shaking. He doubted he would ever be comfortable with confrontations, and he was definitely not comfortable with dealing with what he had learned about Sandwell in the last twenty-four hours. The woman was capable of things that once he would have scoffed at. Now he was acutely aware that he was completely out of his depth and it scared him. He had extracted a promise of a truce from the parapsychologist, but that was probably worthless. He would have to keep his guard up, now more than ever.

He walked back through the campus grounds, stopping to hide the talisman under his shirt. He took in the kids walking, laughing and just starting to learn about life as they flowed around him, like water around a rock. How recently there had been so little difference between him and them. He almost wished that he could go back to how it was before. Ignorance, evidently was bliss. What he had seen recently amazed him and filled him with wonder. But it was also terrifying. A barely concealed world had been revealed to him and it changed everything.

He drove back to his apartment, stopping to buy groceries at a nearby store. His cupboards were almost comically bare –he was down to things in tins he did not even know he had. A good dinner and a quiet evening, that's what he needed. Tonic for the soul and a chance to get back on an even keel.

An hour later, as he was pulling into his street he spotted a large, white truck double-parked outside his building. Two men were wrestling a heavy couch through the door. He drove past wondering about the new tenant, hoping it would be someone a little friendlier than Sumpter. For a moment he was almost curious about what had happened to the skinhead and the downtrodden Traci. Wherever he was, he was probably causing trouble.

He parked in an adjoining road. The plastic shopping bags were too heavy for their handles and were stretching alarmingly. He picked up the pace, hoping to get home before one of them broke. He had almost made it when he narrowly avoided running into a woman exiting the building.

"Oh, sorry. My fault," he said, deftly dodging, feeling a handle stretch even further. She was slim, with a scarf on her head covering long, dark hair. He noticed a small scar on her upper lip that pulled her mouth up on one side. The woman from the campus.

"Hey, don't you work in the library? At the University? Your name is Fern, right?"

"Hi," she said with a smile. "Yes, I do and it is! Do you live here?"

"Yes. I'm on the top floor. So you're just moving in?" He could have kicked himself. How banal. He put down the shopping bags before they gave way.

"Uhm . . . yes?" she replied, nodding towards the open door of what had been Sumpter's apartment, and they both laughed. Now they were both doing it. Two men worked their way past and clambered into the back of the truck. Entwhistle indicated his shopping.

"I need to get this upstairs. Perhaps I'll see you later?"

"Sure. I'd like that," she said with a quick smile. She turned back to the van.

He gathered up his shopping and went inside, stopping at the bottom of the stairs and turning for another look. Fern was outside staring back, openly watching him. He smiled tentatively and proceeded up the stairs.


James Francis stood in his garden, head tilted back, watching the clouds gently scudding across the sky. It was bright, with late afternoon summer sun. Not quite the

Sahara but it satisfied a need. He wondered why he was not scared or sad. That would have been . . . *traditional.*

In fact he felt the anticipation of one about to embark on a journey. And wasn't he just! The undiscovered country awaited and who knew what lay beyond? He watched the sky a little longer before going inside.

A tall man in a gray suit stood as he entered and Francis waved him back to his seat, the same one Entwhistle now habitually used. Francis sat opposite and Jinny stalked to his feet and sat looking up at him. The man in the suit put on his glasses and picked up a stack of papers.

"I had to pull in extra resources to get everything done by today," he began, "But you insisted, and I am happy to say it is complete. Everything."

"Very good. Thank you, Benjamin. I have so appreciated your assistance over the years. And your father's. I will suggest to my successor that he retain your services, but of course you understand it will be his choice."

"Yes, sir. Naturally. And thank you. It has been our pleasure. Now, are you ready to review everything?"

James nodded and Benjamin Rappaport walked around the table and presented him with the first of the papers. The rest he carefully fanned out in front of his client. Nodding to the paper in the old man's hand he said, "This gives me Enduring Power of Attorney, passing to the beneficiary upon probate. Basically, I will control all your assets in the interim. But with everything so neatly in order, probate should be a formality."

The old man nodded and the attorney presented Francis with a pen. He signed the document carefully. They worked through the forms in sequence, sometimes Francis asking questions, querying this or that, while the attorney presented various contracts, agreements. Finally, only the last will and testament remained.

"You made the changes I asked for?"

"Yes, sir. All done, but check, please."

A few minutes silence followed while James Francis read, nodding and grunting approval.

"Good. Deliver the item tomorrow morning along with the will and whatever papers you need him to sign."

"Yes, sir. I understand. If you would just sign one more time . . . here."

And that was that.

"Thank you sir," said the attorney. He swept up the papers and put them in his briefcase, closing the lock with a snap.

"A pleasure to see you as always, Mr. Francis. And so nice to get out of the city now and again. Until next time."

Francis shook his attorney's hand as Rappaport picked up his briefcase.

"I believe that this is the last time we will meet, Mr. Rappaport."

"I am sorry to hear that." The attorney looked down at the table, unable to meet the old man's eye. There was fondness under the professional front. "I feared that might be the case. You know I am not one to pry, but if there is anything I can do?"

"Actually there is." Francis said. He pulled open a drawer and removed a polished wooden box, and a tiny but elaborate silver key.

"This is the item that you must give Philip, tomorrow. Directly into his hand and no other's, under any circumstance. It has enormous sentimental value. Mention it to no one and make sure nothing happens to it."

Rappaport nodded. "I will. This is the unnamed item specified in the will?"

"It is."

"I will take great care of it."

He placed it inside his briefcase. "Is there anything else, Mr. Francis?"

Francis sat down, ran a hand down his face and muttered to himself for a few seconds.

"Yes. Yes, I suppose there is." He spoke up, looked at the lawyer. "If anything should happen to Dr. Entwhistle in the interim, should he become unable to take up his inheritance . . ."

The lawyer leaned forward, concern for his ageing client revealing itself.

"Yes?"

"The item must be cremated. With me. In my coffin. You promise?"

Rappaport failed to notice the cat stalking out of the room, tail in the air.

"Really? Are you sure?"

"Promise. Please."

"Very well. You may count on it."

"Thank you, my friend. You have done well, very well. I thank you."

Francis stood, patted Rappaport's arm and with the gentlest of pressures propelled the attorney towards the door. He watched him go, then turned his gaze to Jinny, an anguished expression on his face. The cat had returned, agitated, its tail whipping back and forth.

"It will be alright, you'll see. What else could I do? Without Philip it's all for nothing, anyway."

Jinny did not seem to take much comfort in his words. She stalked between the table legs, emitting a mournful cry.

Philip had unpacked his shopping and put everything except a packet of spaghetti and a jar of sauce away. He took a beer from the fridge, flipped the cap and took a long pull as he contemplated the day.

His thoughts turned to Fern. That was a funny name. It was very . . . earthy. But there was something about her. The moment when he had met her in the library, he had felt an instant attraction to her. Not that it made any difference. When it came to women, he was not exactly Don Juan. Philip accepted that the attraction was probably not mutual. Still, he could ask her for dinner. She was probably too busy with unpacking, and might not have time to deal with food.

Decision made, Philip went downstairs and found her in the hallway thanking her helpers. She embraced them both, a quick, cursory hug for the younger, and a longer hug for the older, balding man.

"You just call if you need anything, Fern," he said.

"I will, John, thanks."

The two men left, the younger twirling the keys to the truck in his hand, whistling tunelessly.

"Hello again," she said, turning to Philip, a slight smile on her lips.

"Hi. I was, uh, just about to make some dinner. Nothing fancy, but I wondered if you would like to join me?"

She seemed undecided. Philip pressed on. "I mean, since you're probably under the gun a bit, you won't have time to cook." He nodded towards the open door to her apartment and the stacked boxes and bags. She nodded.

"Yes, thank you. That would be nice. I've not even started unpacking or organizing things though. How long do I have?"

"How long do you need?" Philip said, with more confidence. "Just come up whenever you're ready and I'll start cooking. I'm on the third floor."

"Alright. I'll see you in a little while. Just want to make a dent in the unpacking first."

Philip nodded. He stood awkwardly for a moment, trying to think of something to say. Then with a last glance at the slender woman, he turned and trotted up the stairs, taking them two at a time.

So nice that someone normal was moving in, he thought. Not that the rest of the tenants weren't normal. Philip hardly knew anyone except Mrs. Hardy and her son, but Fern seemed nice. An ordinary young woman, and that was perfectly fine by him.

Fern watched him climb the stairs. The smile now gone, her face serious. There was something very odd about him, she thought. He was clearly not the one responsible for the emanations perceived by the covens. Yet there was an aura of energy that followed him. He was involved somehow, that was clear.

Fern had already planned to investigate Entwhistle, after having seen him earlier that day. When he had stormed past her on the University green, Fern had felt his power like a thunderstorm coming. It was not at all the same feeling as the other magic she had perceived within the University, so clearly someone else on campus was practicing the arts. And if he was not involved, maybe he could shed some light on just who was. Asking her to dinner was a golden opportunity. She would be able to see who and what he was far more clearly within his own home.

She returned to her apartment, surveyed the chaos, picking up a box marked Kjøkken. She carried it into the kitchen and began sorting it out.

Fern pondered again the remarkable coincidence of ending up downstairs from Entwhistle. It had to mean something. Immediately after he almost ran into her on the campus green, the estate agent had called, offering another apartment in exchange for the one that had become so mysteriously unavailable. Fern had jumped at it, sight unseen, trusting it was the universe looking out for her. And hadn't her faith been rewarded!

But what a shock to see Philip Entwhistle here. Luck, or the universe pulling strings. Or could it be . . . something else? The thought stopped her in her tracks. What if someone else wanted her here? Could that be?

She must at least try to find out. Fern went into the living room and pulled a suitcase out from under several boxes and carried it into the bedroom. She unzipped the suitcase and rummaged inside, removing a floral patterned dress. She slipped out of her habitual baggy sweater and jeans into the figure-hugging dress. Then she brushed her long, dark hair, tying it back with a thin strip of leather.

Wherever possible she used natural materials and absolutely no metal.

Grabbing a bottle of wine from one of the boxes, she made her way upstairs to the third floor. He had not told her which apartment but the child's stroller outside one of the doors gave a clue. She knocked at the other. When it opened she smiled and raised the bottle.

"You like red?"

"Sure," Philip said, with a smile. "That will do nicely."

She passed him the bottle and entered, looking about with interest. No television. She approved.

"Nice place," Fern said, and headed straight to the bookshelves, always a treasure trove of information about a person's character. She perused the titles while Philip went into the kitchen.

"So, what do you teach?" she asked, her gaze skimming over the books.

His voice came back, slightly muffled. "History."

Fern nodded, taking in the notebooks and the open laptop. "And you write, I take it?"

"Yes. History, again, I'm afraid. I'll get that wine open, shall I?"

She walked into the kitchen and found him inserting a bottle opener. With a little fumbling, he managed to extract the cork without breaking it. He poured the wine into two glasses, filling them halfway.

"Thank you," she said, taking a glass. She raised it up. "To . . . new beginnings."

She watched him as she sipped her wine and winced at the expression on his face. Not a great vintage, positively acerbic in fact. Slightly embarrassed, she grimaced.

"It was cheap, but I had hopes for it," she said, with a wry smile. "Never mind."

"It'll be better with the food," he said. "Though perhaps we should add a little extra garlic? Perhaps a lot?"

197

MJ Kobernus

She laughed. He was funny in his way. Not quite what she had expected. Philip busied himself with opening a packet of spaghetti.

"Why don't you sit down," he said. "I'm sure you've had a hectic day."

Fern nodded. It had been a lot to deal with. She smiled ruefully.

"It's been crazy. I was supposed to be moving into another building, but something went wrong and the rental company said I couldn't have the apartment for another two weeks."

She sat down on a chair by the small kitchen table as Entwhistle stirred pasta into a pan of boiling water.

"So I was literally homeless. Well, for a couple of hours, anyway. Then they called back and said I could have this place. Same rent, which was lucky, but it's a bit further from the campus. By the time they called, I was thinking I would have to use one of the cardboard boxes and sleep under a bridge somewhere."

"Like a troll?" said Philip. He had an impish smile on his face. She chuckled. Had he figured out she was Norwegian?

"No, not a troll." She stuck her tongue out at him. They both burst out laughing, suddenly eight years old again. He began chopping mushrooms. Fern cocked her head to one side, watching him, her thoughts turning to the Tarot. Their meaning was clear and the cards never lied. The Lovers. Relationships, choices, union and passion. Very well then. A little frisson of excitement blossomed in her chest.

"Anyway, this place has a much better view," she replied with a look that left no doubt what she meant. Fern watched, fascinated, as a blush ascended Philip's neck.

"Sorry. I didn't mean to embarrass you."

"No, it's fine," he said, looking at the floor. "I'm just not very good at this sort of thing."

"What sort of thing?"

He shrugged, his eyes avoiding hers. "Flirting."

Fern stood up, smiling and took two small steps to be by his side.

"That's okay. I am."

She put her hand over his, gently laying down the knife, then pulled him around to face her. Fern looked with fascination into his eyes. They were hazel and green and beautiful. She leaned in and kissed him, first on the cheek, then lightly on the lips. Philip responded, putting his arms about her pulling her in close. She could feel his desire growing, and she chuckled again, then pulled away.

Philip was breathing heavily. "I'm really glad you did that," he said. He leaned in again and kissed her hungrily. She responded. After a minute Fern pulled away again, this time breathless.

"Phew. You may not be much for the flirting, but you know how to kiss," she said.

Philip grinned. "Thank you. I could say the same for you."

He took the bottle, poured more wine into her glass, then his own. They both drank silently, reappraising each other in light of their first kiss. This time, neither seemed to mind the bitter taste of the wine.

The pasta was soon ready. Philip strained it, then served them both, spooning a generous helping of sauce onto them. He put the plates on the kitchen table, and they sat down to eat. Fern was hungry and tucked in with pleasure.

"So how do you like working in the library?" Philip asked.

"It's okay," Fern replied between mouthfuls. "But it's just part-time. I also teach, and help run a holistic spa when I am not on campus."

"Holistic? Is that a new age kind of thing?"

"New age, old age. It's all the same. I believe that much of what we know today is ancient wisdom. We just like to dress it up with a fancy title and pretend it's modern. As if labelling a thing helps us understand it. I don't mean technology, so much. But some aspects of science certainly."

"So what do you teach?" he asked.

"Philosophy, sort of."

Philip's eyes widened with surprise and he looked at her with what she though was respect. "That's interesting. And unusual. What sort of philosophy?"

He sounded eager to hear about her work, and she liked that. A man that took a real interest in what she did was not common, in her experience.

"Well, it's more a question of teaching a certain lifestyle, although there are philosophical elements. I am part of a small circle that teaches what you might call the old religion. I'm a Wiccan. A witch, if you prefer."

Philip jerked back, as if electrified. He slapped his fork down on the table, his mouth turning into a grimace. "I see," he said, his voice strained. "I'm sorry, Fern, but I think you had better leave."

Now it was her eyes that widened in surprise. "What?"

"You need to go. I'm sorry, but I have no interest in having one of your kind in my home."

"One of my . . . Philip, are you religious?"

He regarded her coldly, his mouth a thin, hard line. She did not flinch, but held his gaze steadily. Suddenly all the warmth that had existed between them was gone. The flirting, the kiss, it was as if they had not happened. Fern could sense anger, confusion, *fear*.

"No. I am not religious. I don't believe in an all-seeing, benevolent God, if that is what you are asking."

"Good," she replied. "The parts of the King James Bible that refer to Witches are translation errors, you know."

"Yes, I know. But that is not it."

"Did something happen to you, Philip? Please, tell me. I want to understand."

"I don't know you, Fern. How do I know what your motives are?"

"Philip, I don't have any motives," she hesitated a moment, "other than simply liking you." She felt guilty; it was not entirely true.

Philip picked up his wine, stood and walked away from her, distancing himself. Fern could see him looking down at the liquid as he swirled it around in his glass. He breathed deeply, his chest heaving as if he were having a panic attack. Then he drank the wine, draining the nearly full glass before putting it on the kitchen counter. He stared at her, his eyes unreadable.

"Please, Philip. You have nothing to be afraid of. Not from me. I just want to understand. Maybe I can help?"

She did not try to charm him. That would be a mistake. But she spoke from the heart, her eyes beseeching him to listen. He took a deep breath, then nodded, slowly, a decision made. His voice was hesitant, almost shy.

"I recently had an . . . experience. With a woman. I believe she can only be described as a witch. She did things to me. She hurt me. More than that really, and she would hurt me further if it were not for this." He pulled the silver chain and the talisman from under his shirt.

Fern stared at the pendant, leaning forward to get a better look.

"Excuse me." She stepped back, eyes closed, and extended her left hand, palm out, towards it. She shuddered and her eyes snapped open.

"My goodness," she said. "It has enormous power. Arabic?"

"Tuareg."

"I don't know much about them. I must learn more. And you needed this to protect yourself?"

"Yes. Well, after the fact. Someone gave me this when they found out that I had been," he struggled to find a word that could encompass the horror of that night and failed. "Compromised."

She shook her head in wonder. So, he *was* involved. But a victim. She felt oddly relieved.

"Who are you, Philip? Why would anyone try to hurt you?" Her eyes closed for a moment as she studied him closely, getting a feel for his character, his energy. There was something strange about him. He exuded power, but it was not his. The talisman, of course.

"Who tried to hurt you, Philip?"

Philip looked down at the floor. "You'll think me crazy."

"No, I'm probably one of the few people who will not."

His voice a little shaky, Philip started to relay the key details of his relationship with Sandwell. He spoke about their conflict, emphasizing that it was simply an attempt to intimidate him because he was competing for something she wanted. He explained how she had appeared in his dream, and then how she was there, in his bed. How she had carved a pentagram into his chest and how she had laughed in his face when he confronted her.

By the Goddess! The woman was more powerful than anyone Fern had ever heard of. If she could really translate in multiple locations . . . Fern could feel the blood drain from her face. She drank her wine in one long swallow, putting the almost empty glass down on the table.

"I'm sorry, Philip. That was awful. Let me ask you a question. If a man owns a knife, is he a bad man?"

"No, of course not."

"What if he used that knife to hurt another? Is he bad then?"

"Yes, I would say so."

"Is it the knife that is evil, or the will of the one who wields it?"

"The one who uses it, of course."

"Okay, please understand. Witchcraft is like that. It is a tool, as much as it is a way of life. I do not call it a religion. We do not worship a God. In fact, we do not even call it witchcraft. We are Wiccans. Our ways are quite different from most modern religions, but we have certain beliefs that are common to most, that are echoed in many of the mainstream religions. Where do you think they got them from? Like in the Bible, Galatians, verse six. You may know this one. *You reap what you sow.* It is part of our philosophy, our way of life and it is much more ancient than the Christian or even the Jewish faiths. We believe that what you put into the world, comes back to you. It is as fundamental a part of our nature as breathing."

She tried to appear calm, but she was flustered. That someone would use what they knew of her beloved Wicca and then pervert it!

"So if a person uses a tool to cause harm to another," she said "they are ultimately hurting themselves. But are all those that possess a similar tool equally responsible?"

Philip shook his head. "No."

"We would condemn that woman, utterly. And if we can, we'll do something about her. We do not believe in standing by and watching as evil enters the world."

She stood and paced about the small kitchen. "It was a great wrong she did and I am grateful there was someone that could help you." She snatched up her glass, drinking the dregs before setting it on the table.

"Since you told me your story, I will tell you a little of mine. I have been looking for this person. I did not know who she was, but many covens have been feeling her influence, and they are worried. I was given the job of finding her, so she could be . . . curbed."

Entwhistle nodded. He let out a deep breath, but he seemed to be calmer, more at ease.

"She is dangerous, Philip. More than you can know."

"You're not wrong," he said. "But my friend believes that this will stop her from being able to do anything else." He fingered the talisman. "No more magical interventions."

Fern stopped pacing. Relationships, choices, union and passion. Well, it certainly seemed that Philip fit the bill on all of these options. She made her decision and spoke earnestly. "You have another friend who will protect you now, Philip. I will ensure that Sandwell cannot reach you here. I will place wards about the house that will prevent her from seeing you, or worse." She looked at the half empty bottle on the kitchen counter.

"Why don't you pour the wine," she said. "I need to make a phone call."

# On becoming what we want to be

## 10

And we have sought heaven but found it filled
with powerful guards and burning flames.

*—sūrat l-jin, Qur'an*

"Dr. Sandwell, do come in. Can I get you anything?"

Elizabeth Sandwell sat gracefully. Behind the simple desk the neat and orderly Mrs. Richards observed her with keen interest. Given recent events it was not surprising to be summoned in this way, she thought. But still, she had to keep her guard up. Elizabeth had a feeling that the head of Human Resources was more than she seemed, and that made her wary.

"No, I am fine thank you. What can I do for you?"

The older woman smiled thinly and gazed at her without reply. Sandwell was not intimidated. Since her teens, she had been using her looks to her advantage. Manipulating people was second nature to her now. She was so used to doing the intimidating she barely recognized it when someone else tried.

"I have some questions regarding the allegations against your colleague, Dr. Entwhistle. Also some questions of a more . . . general nature. I would like to record this discussion. You don't mind, do you?"

So there *was* an agenda. Sandwell masked the sudden rage that flared. The other woman's eyes narrowed slightly; she had not missed the momentary lapse in composure. Elizabeth cursed herself for the slip. She had to be more careful.

"By all means, Mrs. Richards. Go ahead. I have nothing to hide."

"I am not suggesting you do. We just need to keep careful records when things get to this level. Now then, Dr.

Sandwell, you have made allegations of a serious nature against a colleague. Naturally we began an investigation. However, earlier today I received an email from you withdrawing the allegations. Were you pressured into doing this?"

Sandwell was relieved. She considered using this as an opportunity to smear Entwhistle further. To claim he had threatened her if she did not recant. Not that it would be a lie, at least not entirely. He really had given her something to think about in her office and there had been more than a hint that he would retaliate. Push it a little further then? No, not this time. She had promised him a truce and she would stick to it. Let him think she was playing by the rules. Until the time came to break them.

"No, there was no pressure. I think I just over-reacted. I'd had some wine and we were talking. I guess I'm so used to people hitting on me that I see it everywhere. On reflection, I believe that Dr. Entwhistle did nothing wrong. It was simply a misunderstanding. I have already apologized to him and I hope that the whole affair can be put behind us."

"Well, that's very good, Dr. Sandwell. I'm pleased to hear it. So you will sign a statement to that effect?"

"Yes, of course."

"And you have withdrawn the report you made to the police?"

"Well, it's my understanding that they can't proceed with it anyway, as there's no material evidence. But for what it's worth, yes. I did withdraw it."

"Oh, it is worth something, I'm quite sure. So, just to be clear, let me recap. Dr. Entwhistle, at no time, sexually assaulted you?"

"Correct. It was all a misunderstanding."

"I see. Very well. Now, perhaps you can help me with my other question. Dr. Sandwell, how long have you been breaking into offices and hacking University computers?"

Sandwell was unprepared for this. Her calm mask of composure began to crumble. "What . . . I . . . what?"

"Dr. Sandwell, we have video surveillance footage which shows you entering Dr. Entwhistle's office. We have computer logs showing you used an administrator login and password on his computer. We have eyewitness testimony that you were privy to information that could only be obtained by reading Dr. Entwhistle's emails. What can you tell me about that?"

While Mrs. Richards was speaking, Sandwell used the time to think. They could not have video footage of her entering Entwhistle's office. The cameras did not cover that section of the corridor. She had checked this most carefully. But saying that would reveal that she knew about the cameras and the areas they monitored. Why would anyone know that if they did not need to know? The best course of action was to bluff.

"I'm sorry. But I have literally no idea what you are talking about."

"Dr. Sandwell, I have asked members of campus security to attend this meeting. They are waiting outside. I am quite willing to call them in at which point this becomes official. But for now I will refrain. I assume that you have either learned to pick locks, for which I commend your initiative, or you have managed to obtain a master key from our maintenance staff. I am reliably informed that one day last year, you had such a key in your possession. So I rather think it must be the latter. You either made a copy of the key or you have somehow obtained one. Either way, you will no doubt have either lock picking tools or the master key on your person or in your bag. Either turn them over to me right now and we will deal with it off the record, or I will ask the security chaps to come in at which point you will be given no further options. The choice is yours."

Sandwell sat in stunned silence. It was not possible that she had been seen in Entwhistle's office, and yet this old hag seemed to know everything. Well, almost everything. Mrs. Richards had clearly figured out that she had been in the office, she knew about the admin login, and she knew she had a master key. There was no real choice left. She would have to *charm* the bitch.

Her fingers automatically started to trace the arcane symbols to create the power needed for the simple spell. The older woman was not going to be easily persuaded to forget anything. The best course of action would be to implant a sense of completed achievement in Mrs. Richards' mind. If she could do that, then she could possibly just smile and thank the old biddy for her time and walk out She completed the spell. Nothing happened. No surge of power, however small. How could that be?

Her eyes darted about the room. There, on the shelf, just visible behind a photograph of a group of six kids, was a small bottle holding a sprig of Hazel. There was something in the bottle. A coin. A silver coin? Sandwell's eyes widened in surprise. That was a defensive ward. Was Tessa Richards a witch?

Before she could try the spell again, the door opened and two burly men entered, accompanied by an equally burly woman, all dressed in the blue uniform of campus security. Mrs. Richards sighed.

"Well, we have no choice but to proceed," she said. "Dr. Sandwell, I am officially required to search your handbag under the terms of Section 17, clause 2 of your employment agreement, authorizing personal search on suspicion of theft. Miss Jenkins, would you please?" She indicated the bag on Sandwell's lap.

For a second Sandwell considered making a run for it. Mrs. Richards seemed to know everything already and denial was pointless. But she did not have to give them the satisfaction of seeing her squirm. Sandwell raised her head and slowly, deliberately, reached into her bag and took out the key from the zippered pocket within. She laid it on the table with a metallic click.

"I believe this is what you are looking for," she said with as much dignity as she could muster.

Philip had already been working for several hours, having arrived at the cottage before nine. The weather reports all said the same thing; the hottest day of the year. And it was stultifying. Even the birds, normally voracious with their songs and calls were struck dumb by the sudden heatwave, the study eerily quiet, even with the window open. Only the drone of a single bumblebee could be faintly heard as it went about its business.

Philip thought back to the previous night. He had not flirted with a woman for . . . who knew how long. But Fern interested him, in spite of the fact that she was a witch. And to find that she seemed to reciprocate his interest caused him to smile involuntarily.

She was very straightforward and Philip liked that. No games at all. As she was leaving, she had given him a kiss on the cheek and a lingering look that left him in no doubt about her own interests.

Entwhistle curled and uncurled his fingers, clenching his fists in an effort to relieve the cramps that had begun to plague him. He had been writing every day for a month, often for ten hours or more, and he was exhausted. He was pushing the limits of his endurance. He wanted to get the first draft of biography of Sir James completed today. Sure, he'd had a good start, with plenty of stuff already developed. But with his new insight into the man, Philip found that much of what he had previously written was wrong. He had started again, and this time he was getting it right.

Had it really been almost five weeks since he began? Five weeks since he turned up at the front door and believed the old man senile? When Mr. Francis had claimed to know the hour of his death, Philip was quite certain he was a little unhinged, to say the least. He smiled ruefully at that. Mr. Francis was as sharp now as he ever had been. He just liked to mess around with his protégé.

The book was almost finished. There were just a couple of unanswered questions. Sir James was notorious for openly supporting Egyptian self-rule and had gotten himself into hot water with Lord Milner, the British colonial secretary, over some statements he had made to the effect that Africa was for Africans, and Egypt was for Egyptians. Obviously, he was sympathetic to the nationalists' desire to end British occupation in the country. When a warrant was issued for his arrest for agitating unrest, he was forced to flee. It would have seen him deported, certainly. But then he left Cairo for Khartoum and that was the last anyone knew of him. There were simply no other records. Until the diary, that is.

And after only five weeks of work, talking with Mr. Francis and the combination of the diary and the djinn-induced visions, he had reached the end of the known story. But there was still a key component missing. The diary ended abruptly and gave no hint as to Sir James' fate in the desert.

Knowing now what he did about the djinn, how it affected a mortal's eyes, he knew that the portrait of Sir James hanging just outside the study must have been painted at a later time than the events portrayed in the diary. There was no doubt of that. Clearly, Sir James had lived, at least long enough to send various items home. But where he went and what he did when he left the desert was not yet clear. Philip resolved to ask the old man. There was still something not quite adding up.

If Sir James did not die in the desert, then where? Did he make it to Algiers, as Mr. Francis claimed? Only to send letters, the bowl and a few trinkets? Where did he go after that?

Philip typed some more, the words flying from his fingers in a way that still seemed magical. But if the djinn was giving him help, then why did his fingers and wrists ache so much? He began to worry that he might be developing carpal tunnel syndrome. He smiled when he realized that Jinny could probably fix that anyway.

Philip finished the sentence he was working on, typing the final period with a flourish. He got up from the desk and stretched, before making his way to the kitchen where he found Francis, staring out at the garden. But he turned when he heard Philip enter, eyes bright.

"Ahh, Philip. It's good that you came now. I was about to call. It's almost time, I am sorry to say. I had better tell you everything while I still can. There is no need now for any more secrets."

Philip was alarmed at the thought that the appointed hour was at hand but he took his chair at the table. More secrets. What could Mr. Francis still be hiding? Even after everything that had happened, he still marveled that the old man had yet another trick up his sleeve.

"Do you feel something happening? How do you know?"

"Never mind about that for now. We have more important things to discuss."

More important than his imminent death? This will be interesting.

"Okay," Philip said, waiting expectantly. He knew better than to try to hurry the old man. After weeks of visiting Francis nearly every day, they had both fallen into certain habits and patterns. Like a very odd, old couple.

"I told you that Sir James died. But first he sent some items home."

Entwhistle nodded. This was what he had been waiting for.

"Well, that is not entirely correct. He did not send the items home, he brought them."

"What? He came back to England?" Philip almost leapt from his chair in excitement. Francis waved him back impatiently.

"Sir James Francis returned to England on October ninth, 1922. Three years after he had set off for Egypt. Most of that time was spent in Africa, in one part or another. But when he came back to England after that trip, he never left again."

Philip shook his head in amazement. If this was true, it was a revelation. Sir James was buried somewhere in England. That was the last place he would have imagined.

"I have not been entirely honest with you, my boy. I have kept some things from you for your protection, as well as my own. What I tell you now, might seem incredible, but there are those that would kill for this information. "

Philip stared at him in rapt fascination, his heart beating faster. When Mr. Francis took it upon himself to reveal something, it was invariably shocking. He waited, every sense alert.

"You see, Sir James did not just return to England. He created a new life for himself. In time, he grew to love that life, if not quite as much as he would have loved sharing it with his wife. But you play the hand you are dealt. I have told you a couple of things that are . . . well, lies or half-truths. The first was that Sir James sent certain items home from Algiers. That was not true. He brought them home, as I said. The other thing was that there is no family tradition to name all the first male heirs James."

At that Entwhistle risked an interruption. "But if your name is not actually James, then what is it?"

"I said that there was no tradition, and I meant it. But my name is indeed James."

"Then I don't . . . I mean, not unless . . ."

"Yes. I am Sir James Francis."

Entwhistle's mouth hung open. He tried to speak, but no words would come. Eventually a strangled sound emerged from his throat. "What! You would have to be . . ."

"Over one hundred forty years old."

"But how is that possible? The djinn?"

"Yes, the djinn. She cannot grant immortality, but she helped me live out my natural lifespan. Seems that we, as a race, could live much longer than we typically do. It's all a matter of the mind and being in tune with ourselves, apparently. I would appear to be in my eighties. However, I was not born in the last century, but the one before that. It sounds so very impressive when one says it in that manner." He smiled deprecatingly.

"So you did not die in the desert?"

"It seems not," he replied with a chuckle.

"And everything in the diary is about you and it's all true?"

"Yes and yes."

"And it was never lost. You put it in the telephone."

"Correct. It was, shall we say, by way of a little test. The journal was not simply hidden, you understand. It was *hidden*." He stressed the word, as if that would convey more meaning. "I had Jinny protect it. My sword in the stone, so to speak."

Entwhistle was reeling. He had never even suspected. Once again he had the extraordinary experience of accepting an impossible fact as true.

"Why did the diary suddenly stop then? Why did you not continue writing it?"

"Oh, I did. I did. Over the years I wrote a little more. It is here, in the house. The day after the last entry in my journal, something happened. Then when it was over, I simply did not have the heart to continue writing. I needed a new journal. I felt that phase of my life had ended and I wanted to start afresh."

"But if you did not die, then what the hell am I going to put in my book?"

Francis looked genuinely amused at this. "Why Mr. Entwhistle, the truth of course! Or as much of it as you deem appropriate."

Philip shook his head. Really? The truth? The famed explorer turned spy went to North Africa, married a local tribeswoman, lost her, resurrected her and then lived for almost a century, hiding in the English countryside. That would be something. For a moment he wondered what Sam Evans would make of it if he *did* write that. He chuckled. That would be sure to sink his chances of promotion. And of teaching. And possibly earn him a psychiatric evaluation at a hospital of his choice.

"I have some questions. Do we have, uh, time?"

"Certainly. Just be quick."

"Why did the old Bedouin leave you the bowl? Why did he gift you the djinn?" This had been praying on Philip's mind. It all seemed so random.

"*She* knew I was in the desert. That I was coming. It was not an accident that the old man was there. He was the last of his family too. They had all been killed, mostly by people who wanted to take her from him. You should know, that there are always those that will do anything for the power that a djinn can bestow. That is why you need to be careful not to reveal too much in your book. The truth is a powerful thing."

"I have a feeling," said Philip, "that the world may not be quite ready for the truth. Obviously we have to keep a balance. Certain things are too unbelievable."

"Indeed, and I am sure you are right. But," and Francis raised a finger in warning, "you have a duty to protect Jinny, and exposing a djinn to the world at large is not a good idea. Believe me, it is hard enough when no one knows. This was why I had to disappear. I was a very recognizable figure, in some circles. I contemplated living the life of a Bedouin myself, but there was too much of Taj in the desert. It was simply too painful for me, so I came back to England and decided on a life of obscurity. I invented a nephew and never looked back."

Philip shook his head. He wanted to laugh. He wanted to jump for joy. Here he was, talking with the living, breathing Sir James Francis. A thought occurred to him. All those people that believed they knew him.

"The things that your contemporaries said about you. Were they true? You were something of a rake?"

"Yes, I was a hell-raiser when I was young. I had a few affairs, which mostly ended with me leaving abruptly. All that stopped with Tajeddigt. She was special."

"Alright. But did you really fight duels?"

He nodded. "On a number of occasions. The last one is in the diary. Well, not exactly." He looked thoughtful for a moment. "In a short time you can ask Jinny to help you see that."

Still reeling from the shock, Philip went back to the study. He sat in Sir James' chair, and picked up his journal. He flipped to the final page of the little book. There, in the neat copperplate hand of Sir James, was the final entry. On the opposite page was the calligram he had drawn for the rebel scout. It was as lovely in reality as it was in his dream. A complex form of interweaving lines in the elegant Arabic script. Not for the first time, Philip wished he could read and understand it. But he turned back to the last entry.

*August 1. Ibrahim's men have me. Not looking good. I do not think that I can talk my way out of this. Damn that Egyptian.*

And that was it. Entwhistle checked to see if he had missed something. Was that all? It was the shortest entry in the entire journal. And it was the last? He had expected more. It was a tremendous anticlimax. Yet even so, it begged more questions. Who *was* this Ibrahim. Clearly Sir James was in danger, since he could not talk his way out of whatever predicament he was in. But what did Sir James do to him? Why was Ibrahim chasing him across one of the most hostile environments on the planet? It raised many more questions than it answered.

Philip went back to the kitchen. Sir James was not there. But the back door was open, so he went out into the garden. He found the old man collecting his gardening tools, placing them in the wheelbarrow. For a moment, a wave of sadness hit Entwhistle as he realized that soon there would be no one to care for the beautiful plants and lawn. The old man would be gone and with him a world of living history. For the first time, Philip understood just what Mr. Francis meant to him. He sighed as he watched the strange old man putting away his tools.

"James, who was Ibrahim?"

Sir James Francis, famed explorer, linguist, occasional spy and gardener turned and shook his head sadly.

"He was my friend . . . and I betrayed him." He walked the wheelbarrow to the small shed at the bottom of the garden, put it inside, then shut the door. It was a very final

act. The last time he would tend the garden for Tajeddigt.
He walked back towards the kitchen.

"Come on," he said. "You'd better hear the rest of it."

They entered the kitchen and Francis settled himself
into his chair. Entwhistle checked that there was enough
water in the old copper kettle, then lit the gas and set it to
boil on the stove.

"Ibrahim was Tajeddigt's betrothed. They were to be
married. It was all arranged. I traveled with Ibrahim as I
needed to get out of Cairo after a spot of bother with the
authorities. But when Taj and I met, well . . . sparks flew.
She immediately broke off her engagement with Ibrahim
and her father was forced to make restitution. He was not
best pleased, I can tell you. But she was resolute. She said it
was either *Jam-ez* or death. She always called me Jamez,"
he smiled sadly, his eyes shining. A single tear was caught
in the lines of his face. "She could never pronounce my
name properly. So, that was that. Ibrahim was shamed,
angered. Betrayed. He vowed vengeance on us for the
humiliation he suffered. He left. His last words were a
prophecy of a kind. *You will live just long enough to regret
this, James.* I do not believe that he was responsible for
Taj's death. Deaths. But he was determined to kill me at
any cost. I was his friend and I took from him the one thing
he wanted most in the world."

Francis shook his head and sighed. Entwhistle listened
with rapt attention, even as he continued to prepare the
tea.

"We were living near a village in the Sudan. I learned
that Ibrahim had put a price on my head so we went on the
run. I hired Izem as my dragoman, more to act as a cover
than because I needed him. I was still a Pasha then. You
know most of the story. It is all in the diary. But when
Ibrahim's men caught me, the day after I ran into that
scout, well, that was the when I realized I was not ready to
die. So I killed him. He was my friend and he wanted me
dead. But I killed him."

Philip's mouth was hanging open and he closed it with a slight shake of his head. "What happened? You said his men caught you. How did you kill him?"

"Oh, he was very honorable. He would not just torture and kill me. He gave me a sporting chance. A pistol and a horse. He said that I could either ride for my life and maybe escape, shoot him dead and thereby earn my own life or put the gun to my own head and end things. I chose to ride."

The kettle chose that moment to start whistling, quickly building up to a shrill shriek. It defused the tension in the room, and Philip poured the hot water into the teapot. The metal handle of the copper kettle was too hot and in moments he was blowing on his hand. He looked accusingly at the old man, who chuckled at his obvious discomfort. In all the times he had seen Mr. Francis making tea, he handled the kettle without a glove or cloth and yet had never been burned. Obviously, he was either immune to pain or Jinny simply did not let him feel it.

"Great. That hurt."

"I imagine it did. Sorry, but Jinny cannot help you. Not today. She is not . . . present, shall we say. It is no easy thing for a djinn to transfer to another human, even when all the conditions are right. She needs her strength. I have made some arrangements to ensure a smooth transition. You will know, soon enough."

"Oh, it's fine. I'll live." Philip chuckled to himself. Then stopped abruptly when he realized how callous that sounded, given the circumstances.

"Sorry," he said, shooting the old man a contrite look. "Tell me what happened the day after you met the scout."

Entwhistle sat in his chair and poured tea into the cups on the table. He passed one to his friend.

"Well, let's see. I tried to avoid the village that the scout had mentioned. Jinny had warned me away. But Ibrahim had a number of men out looking for me. Two of them found me some miles west of the village and brought me back. That was when Ibrahim gave me the choice. Fight or flee. Naturally, I chose to flee. He was quite satisfied with that, I can tell you. He was a good horseman. But then, so was I, back in the day. We had a merry chase across the desert. He let me pick any horse and said if I could outrun him I would live. Or I could face him with pistols. His men had recovered many of the things the villagers took, including Taj's flintlock."

Sir James stood. "You should see for yourself. I don't need Jinny for this." He walked around the table and stood over Entwhistle.

"When you live with a djinn for a while, you pick up a thing or two."

Grasping both the younger man's hands, he stared deeply into Entwhistle's eyes, his lined face creasing in concentration.

It was not like the previous times when the djinn had given him a vision. Entwhistle did not feel the same dislocation or momentary dizziness. He was not living Sir James' life, experiencing every tactile sensation as if it were his own. This time it was like a faded shadow of the memory, a pale reflection. He could see, but he did not feel the emotions, or experience the thoughts connected to the images that slid into his mind. There was sand, and canvas. He was in a tent.

A young man, dressed in flowing robes entered and motioned for him to leave. A group of similarly dressed men encircled him as he came into the light. They were hard, desert men, and there was no sign of comfort or clemency in their gaze. Ibrahim was at least ten years older than Sir James, but he had the look of a tough and proven fighter.

They had bound the djinn to prevent her from interfering. One of them held her meta-anchor in his hand. Salt shone brightly within it, the dagger he pressed upon it small, but it was enough. Salt and iron. They were men of the desert and knew how to handle her kind. There would be no relying on the djinn. If Sir James fell, so would she.

Ibrahim looked at his one-time friend with a scorn born from his humiliation. He wanted revenge and he intended to get it, but his men would not follow a man that killed like a coward. He had to face his enemy directly, with the same weapons and risk the same fate. It was their code.

Ibrahim was taller than Sir James. Made taller still by his black turban. He towered over the Englishman, as he did the men that surrounded them both. In his belt a curved dagger and a pistol; a Webley six-shot. He gestured towards the horses.

"Choose," he said, his voice guttural.

Sir James looked to the horses. There was little to distinguish between them but he examined their teeth, looked closely at their hocks. He chose a young mare with good lines. Ibrahim smiled and there was much good-humored discussion from the men. They made bets on how far the Englishman would get. It would be a good chase. Good sport for their leader.

The desert rolled in all directions, an ocean of rippled sand with peaks of golden, knife-edged domes. The brilliantly blue sky stretched endlessly, unmarred by any cloud. A lone hawk, soaring on rising currents of hot air, hovered as if weightless as it scoured the ground far below for the darting shadow that meant prey.

Sir James shifted his stance, still focusing on remembering the events of that day. Entwhistle could see the effort on his face, beads of perspiration on his forehead. Evidently, it was a strain for him to enable Philip to see into his mind, to share his memories. Philip closed his eyes.

The horses raced across the sand, their passengers almost shoulder to shoulder, the straining beasts throwing themselves hard into their stride, hooves barely touching the ground. The turbaned, dark-skinned Ibrahim, a blue scarf across his face, raised a leather crop and slashed at Sir James, forcing him to duck and shift slightly in his saddle, almost causing him to fall. But Sir James recovered and drew the old pistol from the crimson sash around his waist. He pulled back the flint with the hand clutching the horse's reins and thrust the weapon at Ibrahim's head. The gun fired, its pall of gray smoke instantly lost behind them as they thundered on, but the noise and flash caused both horses to shy and swerve, separating them. A narrow miss parted the turban and left a shallow furrow in its owner's temple. Ibrahim dropped the riding crop to press the hand to his head. Blood ran into his eyes and blurred his vision. His horse slowed slightly, as if sensing its master was injured and, with a snarl, Ibrahim drew his own pistol from within his billowing robes. He dug his heels into the horse's flanks.

Sir James was now defenseless. He too spurred his horse harder, his only option to outrun his pursuer. But the horses were well chosen, equal in stamina and speed. Ibrahim, skilled in shooting from a galloping horse, smiled in anticipation as he took aim. He fired, and Sir James fell.

Fern knelt outside the house in the back garden. She had placed wards at cardinal points around the building and now she was completing the ritual that would provide spiritual protection for herself, as well as the other residents.

Of course, it would not stop someone throwing a brick through a window, but a spell or psychic invasion would be blocked. She hoped. It was a habit for her, as it was for most who followed the old ways, to weave elements of the spiritual into her daily life. Not in the way that most religions did, with their prayers for intervention, begging a god to hear them. There were many paths, she thought. But some just went in circles. No, she took a practical approach. The goddess helps those, who help themselves.

With eyes closed, she visualized the wards in her mind, seeing them connected. Golden rays of energy linking each ward to the next, creating a barrier around the house.

Fern was pleased that she could help Philip. He seemed to be a gentle soul that did not understand the world he lived in and she felt a maternal urge to look after him, as if he were a lost little boy. And aren't they all? Plus, there was the card she had drawn from the Tarot; the Lovers. She smiled, knowing that what was fated could not be avoided.

Not that she wanted to avoid this fate. She liked Philip and was eager to know him.

She climbed to her feet and brushed stray grass from her knees. There would be no danger of any spiritual or mental attacks for anyone living there now. Not that they would notice anything different. At least, not unless they knew what to look for. The signs would be there, but few people had the eyes to see. In years to come they might look back at the time they lived in the building and think of it as a lucky period in their lives, or remember how happy they were.

A magical attack on this house would have to be extremely powerful to break the wards, and at the very least, she would then be aware of the danger and could take counter measures. Fern did not fool herself into thinking that she was a match for Sandwell, but she was no novice. One day she would be the representative of the Lady.

Satisfied with her work, she made her way back to her own rooms, humming a tune that her mother had taught her, the words coming to her lips as easily as breathing. It was a simple song, but the old Norsk words were somewhat strange, even to her own ears. She pondered for a moment, then translated them into English, trying them out with the tune.

Lords of the North way
in the land of snow,
watch over this homestead
For the hero is gone.

With a jerk, Entwhistle pulled his hands from the old man's. "What?" He said, the surprise evident in his voice. "You were shot?"

Francis chuckled as he lowered his hands. He had a mischievous glint in his eye. "No. It seemed that the fates had a different plan for me."

"But I saw . . . wait, it was Jinny. She helped you in some way."

"Oh no, Jinny was quite unable to help. She had been restrained in a manner that would have been nigh impossible for her to break. Salt and iron can be very effective. No, I didn't fall. I said I was a good horseman, in my time. I'd ridden with some of the best in the world, even if I was not quite up to their standards."

Entwhistle smiled ruefully. The old man always seemed to have a trick up his sleeve. And why not? He had lived long enough to learn plenty of them.

"I should have known," he said. "So what did you do? Hold on to the mane as you jumped off? Then used your momentum to swing back up onto the horse?"

"I could have done that, if I wanted to break my neck. That sort of thing on a galloping horse would have been very dangerous. No, I did something else. As he aimed, I simply fell back, hanging more or less upside down for just a moment. It is also very dangerous but has the advantage that you do not have to get off the horse. The shot missed. I came back up ready to grab him and pull but I didn't have to. Perhaps distracted by the shot, his horse foundered and he was thrown. They rolled, with him still in the saddle. Broke most of his ribs, I think, and possibly his back. He died in my arms, drowning in his own blood."

He shook his head and sighed. "I did not want that. He was my friend once. But he would not stop. Not until one of us was dead."

"I'm sorry, James. Really."

"I am not a squeamish man, Philip. Some deaths are deserving, but not that one."

Philip nodded. But something Francis said intrigued him.

"You said that salt and iron were effective at constraining the djinn. How so?"

The old man considered for a moment before answering. "There was a time when magic was a common feature of life. Everyone had charms and performed spells."

Philip had read many studies of inscriptions on rocks or clay tablets, mostly curses, apparently.

"Sure, like the Farliegh lead scroll. A defixio."

"Exactly. Did you know those spells would often be buried with salt or pinned with an iron nail to a tree or sacred site?"

"Well, I know some have holes in them consistent with their being nailed."

"Quite so. Both iron and salt are conductors. Magic is simply a method for aligning natural forces. All matter is a complex dance of energy and the purpose of magic is to manipulate that energy in order to affect the material. It is something that scientists are now just beginning to understand. We are finally getting to the point where the relationship between matter and energy is being understood at a quantum level. Something ancient man knew and we are now rediscovering."

"Okay, but what has this to do with the djinn? How is it constrained by salt?"

"A djinn is a creature of pure energy. The salt and iron act as an earth in much the same way that a lightning conductor works. Simply put, it loops the djinn's energy, and therefore its entirety, back on itself, binding it."

"Alright," said Entwhistle slowly. "But how? They couldn't put salt on a djinn. It's not a physical being. The bowl, obviously is the key."

"Indeed. They put it on the object that links it to our world. As you say, the bowl. Just put salt and iron on the object that binds the djinn to our plane and you have it. I shouldn't wonder they were planning all sorts of amusing fates for Jinny. But when I came back with Ibrahim they had to let me go and I took the bowl with me. And the horse, as was my right."

Once again Entwhistle found his mind full of more questions than the old man had time to answer. He shook his head in recognition of the fact that he would never be satisfied with the extent of his understanding. Even this conversation was throwing up more questions. What did

Mr. Francis mean when he said that *ancient man knew, and we are rediscovering?*

"I am going to miss you, James. I wish we could have had more time to talk."

"I know. But when I am gone, you can talk to Jinny. She will have my memories. It will not be exactly the same as me being here, but I will never be truly gone."

"How do I talk to her? You seem to have a telepathic link. I don't feel anything."

"You will, in time. But for now, if you want to communicate with her, just hold the talisman. It will help focus your mind."

Entwhistle's hand went to the chain about his neck and he pulled the pendant from under his shirt.

"So I just hold it and talk?"

"You don't even need to talk. Just think. She'll hear you."

Philip had butterflies in his stomach. Even after all the time he had spent around the djinn, he was nervous trying to talk directly to her.

"Perhaps later," he said.

Francis smiled but he looked tired. For the first time, Entwhistle thought he really did look frail.

"I think that I would like to go outside," he said, and started to make his way to the garden, through the still-open door. "My time is come, Mr. Entwhistle. Help me to the bench, please."

Entwhistle sprang up.

"Should I call an ambulance?"

"No. Not until I am gone, anyway. And then there is hardly any need to rush. I think that I would like to look one last time at the sun. If you could sit with me, Philip, I would like that."

Entwhistle helped Francis to the bench in the garden and sat beside him. One emotion after another washed over him; loss, longing, regret, but strangely, not sadness.

*Death is transformation, not termination.* Philip hoped he was right.

The old man closed his eyes and turned his head up to the sun, its warmth caressing them both. Neither man spoke and for some minutes they sat peacefully, only the droning of a single bumblebee as it flitted from flower to flower encroaching on the perfect silence.

# And if the precious gifts are lost

## 11

"It is not for you to judge me. I have gone beyond this realm of men."

—*Pontius Pilate, The Secret Epistles*

"Hello, Mr. Entwhistle?" The voice on the phone was soft, cultured. A voice with money.

"Yes?" Philip replied, groggily as he awoke.

"My name is Benjamin Rappaport. I am sorry to inform you that Mr. Francis passed away yesterday. You have my sincerest condolences, sir."

The man spoke slowly and with care, as if paying attention to each syllable. The sympathy seemed genuine.

"Thank you. Yes, I know," replied Philip. "I was with him at the end."

Philip sat up in the chair where he had fallen asleep the day before. There was a blanket around his legs. Fern. He smiled at the thought of her.

"Ahh, yes. Did you know Mr. Francis well, sir?"

"Yes, I think I did. Not for very long, but we were . . . close."

"Mr. Francis informed me that you would be cognizant of his intentions regarding his last will and testament."

"He told me. I'm sorry, but who are you again?"

"Apologies, sir. Benjamin Rappaport, of Rappaport and Associates, Attorneys at Law. My firm represented Mr. Francis for almost sixty years. Since my father hung out a shingle, so to speak. A valued client."

Entwhistle knew that Francis had left him his cottage. So this must be the executor of his will.

"What can I do for you, Mr. Rappaport?"

"Well, sir, it's more the case of what I can do for *you*. Mr. Francis left me specific instructions to call you and arrange a time to deliver a package. I would like to do this now, if that is convenient. Mr. Francis was most insistent that this be done with all haste."

The clock over the fireplace said it was only a quarter after seven. It must be important if it could not wait until business hours. "What sort of package? What's in it?"

"As to that sir, I cannot say. But if I may be so bold as to make a suggestion?"

"Please, feel free," replied Philip. Now in the kitchen he put the kettle on. He needed his early morning tea.

"I would very much like to read the will as well. Mr. Francis was most anxious that this be done without delay. Since there are no other beneficiaries it really is just a question of when it is convenient for you. I do apologize for ringing so early but as I said – as quickly as possible."

"I see. Now is fine. You know my address, I presume?"

"Indeed, sir. I can be with you in about thirty minutes."

"That's great. I'll be here."

Philip lowered the phone. Francis had slipped away so quietly that he had not been sure of the actual moment. Basking in the sun with the man he now thought of as a friend, Philip had closed his eyes for a minute, perhaps two. When he opened them again, Francis was gone. He dialed the emergency number and waited, at peace, until the paramedics turned up. A few quick checks, thanks and brief condolences, and that was that. Philip watched them go then went looking for the cat. He tried calling her. Nothing. She was gone. So he closed the back door and made his way home in a state of steadily deepening sorrow. By the time he pulled up outside his apartment he was almost in tears, swamped by a profound sense of loss. Five short weeks. Five years would not have been enough. He would never hear the word gentleman again without thinking of Sir James. A true gentleman, in the old sense of the word. Philip sat in his car until he had recovered some of his composure. When he went inside Fern was standing in the hallway. She seemed to be waiting for him. Before he could speak, she threw her arms around him, stroking his hair, making comforting noises.

Her sudden empathy unleashed something in him, and he was unable to contain his grief. It came out in a sob that would not end. Mrs. Hardy opened her door, caught sight of them and closed it just as quickly. Not everything needed an audience.

"It's okay, Philip," Fern said. "You think you've lost him, but he's not gone. Not really."

"How did you know? About Mr. Francis, I mean?"

"I didn't. But I could feel your grief. I was meditating, and I could feel your pain. I know that feeling myself." She pulled back from him, eyes searching his.

"It was your friend? The one who gave you the talisman?"

Philip nodded. He sighed, and took a steadying breath. "I'm okay. Really. Thank you Fern."

She smiled in reply, then led him by the hand up the stairs. Once inside his apartment she proceeded to make tea while Philip threw himself into a chair. He was quickly asleep. When the ringing of his phone woke him the next morning, he found a blanket from his bedroom around his legs and a mug of cold tea on the table. She must have gone home after that. Part of him wished that she hadn't.

Philip found he was nervous waiting for the attorney to arrive and although it was less than the expected thirty minutes, it felt considerably longer. Eventually there was a buzz from the intercom system. He pressed to open, and a minute later there was a gentle tap at his door. He opened it to find a middle-aged man, dressed in a smart, gray suit with gold-rimmed glasses. He was clutching a briefcase to his chest as if it were precious to him.

"Mr. Entwhistle?"

"Yes. Come in, please."

"Thank you, sir. Before we begin, I will need to see some identification. I have to be certain that you are, in fact, the man that Mr. Francis intended to deed his home to. Amongst other things.

"Will a driver's license do it?"

"That would be most suitable, sir. Most suitable."

Philip went to his jacket and retrieved his wallet. He pulled out his driver's license and the attorney examined it carefully. He passed it back to Entwhistle.

"Thank you, sir. And now with that out of the way, perhaps you would like me to read the will?"

"Yes, okay. Why don't we do this in the kitchen. We can sit at the table."

"Very good, sir."

They both went into the kitchen and sat opposite each other at the small table. Rappaport opened his briefcase and removed a sheaf of documents. Turning from the papers, Rappaport took a wooden box from his bag and put it on the table next to them, before placing the briefcase on the floor.

"I would like to start by informing you, that according to Mr. Francis' instructions, I have power of attorney for all his interests. What this means, is that I control his estate. In due course however, this will be transferred to you. Now, shall we start with the will?"

"By all means," said Philip.

"Very good, sir. The last will and testament of James Francis." He cleared his throat, giving the papers a small shake.

"I, James Francis, being of sound mind, declare this to be my last will and testament. I revoke all previous codicils and wills made by me. Article one. I appoint Benjamin Rappaport, of Rappaport and Associates to be my personal representative and executor of my estate."

The attorney cleared his throat and peered at Philip over his glasses. "Article two. I request that my personal representative ensures that all debts owing are paid out of the estate prior to the remainder being settled on the primary beneficiary. Article three, I bequeath all my worldly goods, properties, shares, trusts and all monies to

Dr. Philip Entwhistle. In particular, I expressly request delivery to Dr. Entwhistle, upon my death, of a box placed in the possession of my executor. Said box to be delivered to Dr. Entwhistle at the earliest possible opportunity. The box must not be opened in the presence of witnesses."

The attorney put down the will, removed his glasses and slipped them inside his inner jacket pocket, then with a solemn expression he picked up the wooden box and holding it in both hands, extended it across the table like an offering.

It was a ceremony, of sorts. Philip knew exactly what was in the box. The gift had to be freely given and freely received. He reached out his hands and took the box, placing it down on the table in front of him. Thank you, James.

He had expected to feel something otherworldly at that moment, but there was nothing. No mystical rush of energy, or any other indication that he was now the guardian of the djinn. He eyed the box and smiled. He would have to find somewhere to keep it. Probably not the sort of thing he should just leave lying around.

Rappaport took a small silver key from his pocket and placed it on the table beside the box, then drew an envelope from the stack of papers. He held it out to Entwhistle, who raised a querying eyebrow.

"I don't know what is in the letter, Mr Entwhistle. But I was instructed to give this to you, along with the box."

Philip nodded and took the envelope. It was addressed to him, saying *P. Entwhistle, to be read in the garden*. He recognized the handwriting as Sir James'. A letter from Mr. Francis.

"Well, Mr. Entwhistle. Now that that is done, I have a number of tasks to complete before I can give you a precise accounting. And of course before it passes to you legally the will must pass through probate. A formality in this case. All it means is that until probated, the contents of the estate are not legally yours. You must not dispose of anything. However, the property, Little Flower Cottage, is yours as it is a transaction outside the inheritance. You must give me a nominal payment in consideration and sign the deed of transfer that Mr. Francis completed some days ago. All you need to do is sign here."

He presented Philip with a document, each location for a signature denoted by a colored sticker. Philip took the proffered pen and carefully signed his name, then initialed in each required location.

Rappaport held out a hand, and Philip, realizing what was required, fished in his pocket. He produced a pound coin. He shrugged. "Will that do?"

Rappaport chuckled. "Certainly, sir. That will do nicely." The attorney pocketed the coin, then removed from his briefcase a set of keys, fixed to a metal ring.

"There. Now the cottage is legally in your name. After probate there is the matter of the vintage car and motorcycle collection, the various shares in numerous companies, the landholdings and of course the balance of Francis' accounts. This last, however, will need to pend until all the sundry expenses are resolved."

Philip was confused. He had expected the cottage, but nothing else. Was there more? Francis had said he would not have to work again, if he chose not to, but Entwhistle had not really considered what that meant.

"I'd really only thought about the cottage," he said.

The attorney's expression did not change in the least and he continued to speak in his calm, reassuring tone.

"Well, without wishing to say too much, there is quite a deal more to it than that. However, it really is not my place to give you information that is not accurate. We should have everything wrapped up with regards to death duties, funeral arrangements and so on, in a couple of days, at which time I will be able to furnish you with an accurate summary of the estate. I will, naturally, contact you once everything is resolved to inform you of the balance of your inheritance. In the meantime, the cottage is yours. In addition, here is a summary breakdown of some of the major assets."

He passed Entwhistle a document containing an itemized list of assets, arranged by type. At the top of the page was the word Landholdings. It seemed that there was quite a parcel of land around the cottage. Next was Vehicles. Under it he spied the words Rolls-Royce. The next was MG TA Roadster. He did not know what that was. There were more cars, of varying ages some of which he knew, others not. Further down the page was an entry that read, *Sundry Motorcycles, numbering eight in total.* Then there were lists of companies he had never heard of with shares and stocks specified.

He did not know what to make of it all.

"Mr. Entwhistle, unless you have some questions for me, that just about concludes our business for now. As I said, I will be in touch once things have been resolved regarding the finalization of all duties. But if you need me for anything," he reached down and extracted a card from his briefcase, placing it on the table, "please call."

"Thank you, Mr. Rappaport. I don't have any questions just now. I guess I'll have to think about things a bit. Let it soak in. This really is quite a shock I can tell you."

The attorney stood and closed the locks on his briefcase. He shook Philip's hand.

"As I said, Mr. Entwhistle, just call if you have any additional questions, or problems. We are a full service firm for our . . . select clients. Whatever you need, just let us know."

"Well, actually, I guess I do have a question. Where are these cars stored? I've been to the cottage many times and never seen them."

"Ahh, no. They are not there. But you may have passed them on your way. Did you ever notice the large red barn in a field, about a mile from the cottage?"

Entwhistle had seen it. He had driven past it almost every day for the last five weeks.

"Yes, of course. That's where they are?"

"Yes. The barn belongs to the cottage. As does the land. Mr. Francis rents . . . rented it out to various farmers in the area. You own quite a sizeable piece of the countryside now, sir. Well, good luck."

And with that the attorney left, leaving a bemused and rather conflicted Philip Entwhistle behind him.

Philip looked at the polished wooden box. The *meta-anchor*. Jinny's magic lantern. He opened the box and there it was. The small bowl, chipped and worn just as he remembered. He took it out, half expecting it to give him a shock. Nothing happened. No sense of magical otherworldliness. He put the bowl back, locked the box.

He looked around, then decided that the top of the bookshelf would do as far as a safe place for it was concerned. The letter lay on the table in the kitchen, and he went back for it, holding it in his hand for a moment as if it would reveal its contents to him through osmosis. *To be read in the garden.* Francis's last request.

Breakfast could wait. He put on his shoes and got his car keys.

Paul Sumpter ground the stub of another cigarette beneath his heavy, booted heel as he watched the front door of his old building. Waiting was hard for him. He was impatient to get on with things. He had a job to do. A special job. From *her*. He felt a surge of pride that she had chosen him.

Earlier he had seen a man ringing Entwhistle's bell. He'd come out about twenty minutes later. But that meant that Entwhistle was still there. Sumpter bided his time and lit another cigarette.

Movement. Mrs. Hardy had opened the front door and was leaving. Sumpter quickly moved back behind a parked van, its bulk hiding him from her sight. He could still see her through the passenger door window. She looked up at the sky, and satisfied, proceeded to march off. She would be on her way to work. He did not know what she did, but he knew she would be gone the whole morning, and that she was usually the last to leave the building.

There were six apartments, two on each floor. Sumpter had made a study of the occupants' habits, and he knew the best time to rob the place was mid-morning. No one would be home then, and he would have the entire place to himself.

Of course, it was not possible to guarantee anything, but he had timed his arrival to coincide with Mrs. Hardy's departure. And with her gone, he was free to just walk in and kick down any door he pleased. But Entwhistle must still be there.

He did not have long to wait. The door opened again some minutes later and Entwhistle emerged. Sumpter moved behind the parked van again and watched as Entwhistle got into his car and drove away. The memory of their last encounter was still fresh in Sumpter's mind, his broken nose still tender. But that little prick would regret it.

He did not know exactly what it was he was supposed to be stealing, but he hoped it was something Entwhistle could not afford to lose. And this time there would be no one to interfere. All he had to do was find it. The only problem was, Sandwell could not tell him what *it* was.

"You need to look for something that does not belong," she had said the night before. They were sitting in his local, a pub that catered to the rougher elements and where he felt at home. He had noticed the envious looks from the other men in the bar. They must have all thought that she's my bird. Of course, he'd had her the one time, but she wouldn't let him touch her since. But they didn't know that. He'd puffed up his chest and tried to make his biceps stand out.

"I don't know what it looks like," she said "but he was given something in the last day or two. An object of some kind. It could be anything, but most likely it will be very old."

And he nodded, all the while thinking about her breasts. She poked him in the shoulder, hard.

"Ouch!"

"Keep your eyes on the prize, Paul."

He resisted the urge to tell her that was exactly what he had been doing. Some of the men in the bar sniggered at the apparent lover's tiff.

"How am I supposed to find something, when you don't even know what it is."

"Just get in there, and take anything that looks out of place. It could be Arabic. That might help. Or it might not be. There's no way to say. But make sure you have your phone with you. You can call me when you are in and tell me what you see. Maybe I can help narrow the field."

"Yeah, alright. No problem." A thought occurred in his sluggish mind. "Hey, why don't you do it? I can kick the door in for you. Keep an eye out, that sorta thing. You can find the thing yourself then."

She shook her head. "No. I tried to *see* him earlier. Something is blocking me. Suffice to say that I cannot go there, but you can."

Paul did not understand what she meant. But then, he rarely did. Their relationship was not built on mutual understanding. If she said jump he did not care why, he just asked how high.

He waited another twenty minutes in case Entwhistle came back, but now it was time. He crossed the road and approached the front door, fingering the phone in his pocket. He would call her as soon as he was inside the apartment. He took the spare key he'd made before being evicted, and let himself into the lobby. Everything looked the same. He almost instinctively went to his old apartment, but then took the stairs, making his way to the third floor. He wondered briefly if anyone had taken over his old place.

He approached Entwhistle's door. Just to be sure, he knocked quietly. There were no sounds from within and he stepped back. A quick look over his shoulder confirmed he was alone. He thrust out his booted foot hard and the door flew open, splinters flying wildly. He grinned. Easy as pie.

He entered the apartment, pulling out his telephone, then kicked the door closed behind him.

Philip sat on the bench in the cottage garden that he had last shared with Mr. Francis. He had the keys on the big iron ring in his pocket, and although the place now belonged to him, he did not feel right just going inside. So he sat and admired the trees and the fields and the garden that Mr. Francis had given years of his life to make beautiful, and where he had finally died.

The old man had loved his garden. It was his Eden. He had used that phrase in his journal. *Tajeddigt* was his Eden. Philip could not let it go wild. He would have to teach himself how to care for it. After all, he was part of the story now. Part of the history that began in the desert almost a hundred years ago.

He took the letter from his jacket pocket and held it, staring at it. Mr. Francis had probably written this just before he died. These would be his last words.

He opened the letter. The neat hand, so like the script in the journal, but less flowery, less ornate. The hand of a much older man. He started to read.

*Dear Philip. I have done everything I can to make the transition easy for you. I could have given you the meta-anchor, but I wanted you to meet Mr. Rappaport. He is a good man and you can trust him. If you prefer to use the services of another attorney that is your right, but I knew him man and boy and put my faith in him for many years. He has never disappointed.*

*Philip, it has been a strange experience sharing my life, my memories with you. But I am profoundly glad of the experience. I learned much from you, even if you do not think so. Certainly about dedication and integrity. You are a rare individual and that is why you were chosen. Or perhaps, why you chose yourself.*

*I did not really know who to turn to, in order to take over the role of guardian. You would think that a man of my age would have had ample time to find a replacement, but the truth is, there were very few that I trusted, and none met Jinny's tests with anything other than abject failure. Until you.*

*So thank you, Philip. You made my last days a pleasure and reminded me of so much. Both good and bad, it is true. And I am sure that your writing has made me look better than I was.*

*I imagine that you will be surprised somewhat by the extent of my estate. If you raise your head and look about you, the land you can see is now yours. All of it. The horses in the field belong to a neighbor's daughter, but I allowed her use of the paddock. It would please me should you continue the tradition. The same goes for my other charitable concerns, which Benjamin can fill you in on.*

*In a few days, Jinny will be attuned to your energy. She is a font of interesting information, much of which, I am sure, you will be hard pressed to accept. But take your time. You have your whole life to get to know her.*

*She is not always easy to live with, but the rewards are great. I wish you well and a long and happy life. Remember, Philip, it is a partnership above all else.*

*Don't feel sorrow for my sake. I lived far longer than I had any right or wish to. And now I go on a grand adventure. Who knows what I may find.*

*Your humble servant,*

*Sir James Francis*

Philip lowered the letter and looked to the sky. Somewhere in whatever dimensions the souls of the dead inhabit, James Francis was having a good time, he was sure. He felt better about things, having read the letter. There were no last-minute revelations after all, which he had half expected.

He got up from the bench and took out the keys to the cottage. There were quite a few, far more than he expected.

Some were clearly modern, while others looked hand-forged. He eyed the lock on the heavy front door, the face of the knocker peering at him with suspicious dead eyes. The lock was heavy duty. He took the biggest key and tried it. It clicked, locking the door. He had felt bad about leaving it unlocked during the night, but there was little other option. Now, he turned the key in the lock again, and heard the smooth click of well-oiled metal on metal. He pushed the door open and went inside his new home for the first time.

He walked down the passageway past the open door of the study and paused at the row of paintings hanging from the wall. He looked at the portrait of Sir James, standing alone with his horse. Except he was not alone. Philip frowned, then his eyes widened with astonishment. What was this? He peered closer. There, standing slightly to one side and behind Sir James was another figure. How had he missed her? In all the times he had looked at the painting, he had never noticed another figure.

She was wearing the flowing robes of the desert, a blue scarf covered her hair, but her face was bare. She had luminous skin, with tiny blue dots tattooed under her lower lip. Her brown eyes seemed to look out at him, amused, challenging.

Somehow she had been hidden from his sight. She was beautiful. Young, but there was such strength and determination in her face. His heart ached knowing that she had been taken from the world. Knowing that Francis had lived nearly a hundred years with the burden of his loss. *Tajeddigt, my little flower.* He reached out a hand and with a finger gently caressed the rough canvas, as if that would connect him to the past.

She had been everything to Sir James. A love so private that he had hidden her from all eyes but his own. Philip smiled and a low chuckle escaped him. So the old man did still have some surprises after all. It made him happy even knowing the old man was gone.

He made his way to the kitchen. On the stovetop was the dented old kettle. Same as always. Even Francis' chair was pulled out from the table as if he has just got up and left.

Philip sat in his usual place and tried to come to terms with everything that had happened. He tried to process the emotions, but he couldn't decide if he was excited, scared or sad. Perhaps all of it. He sat quietly, staring through the window to the beautiful garden when his phone rang, making him jump. He pulled it from his jacket pocket. Fern.

Fern's coven was aware of Sandwell now. Finally, they had a name to put to the sinister energies they had been detecting for so long. However, Fern was certain that no one had any idea of just how powerful that woman was. If half of what Philip said was true, then Sandwell was a very dangerous person indeed. Fern had no reason to doubt Entwhistle. She was gifted at reading people and she saw in him a gentle soul, without duplicity or malice. Perhaps he may have exaggerated something, but he would not lie. No. The woman was dangerous in the extreme, and Fern was in no doubt at all that the coven would have to step in.

Sandwell did not appear to belong to a circle of her own. At least, none any of the covens in the area claimed her. However, she was most certainly a practitioner, and at a very high level. Anyone sensitive to the natural order could feel the ripples she caused. Her influence had been felt by a great many, causing a deal of concern.

What worried Fern and the other members of her circle, Tessa and Alicia, was that if Sandwell was capable of the power that Philip Entwhistle had described, then she must be using the darkest and most secret of arcane knowledge. She was playing a dangerous game. The black arts were a closely guarded secret for a reason, but they were the quickest path to the kind of power that Sandwell appeared to command.

Fern had watched Philip leave the building a few minutes before, glimpsing him through her window as she prepared to meditate. She smiled at the memory of the spreading blush that had colored his face. He was an emotional man. Nothing wrong with that!

A fact he had demonstrated when he cried in her arms. She had expected that he would need to talk, but after making him tea, she had found him asleep in his chair. Nothing else to do but get him a blanket and let herself out. But that was fine. There would be plenty of time to know him.

She settled into the lotus position, quickly calming herself, slowing her heart, preparing to put her mind into a trancelike state. She cleared her mind of all thoughts. Except Philip seemed to intrude. She could see his face, his smile. The way his eyes crinkled when he laughed. And how good it had felt to hold him.

A surge of emotion washed through Fern, surprising her with its strength. She wanted him, there was no point hiding from the fact. Unable to focus, she breathed deeply, slowly. Eventually she managed to shut him out, finally entering a deep meditative state. She was not aware of the outside world or the passing of time. All her attention was on her inner being.

How long she remained in that state was difficult to say. Fern did not concern herself with the hours of the clock. Her body would be roused when it was time.

Returning to the here and now, she became immediately aware of noises in the building. A muffled thump, followed by the unmistakable sound of breaking glass. Oops. Someone has had an accident. She cocked her head to one side while the sound of objects being thrown or dropped continued. That was no accident. Then she felt it, like a sting. Malice in the house!

Frowning, she rose easily to a standing position. The noises continued. Somewhere above her. She stepped into the hallway. The noise was slightly less apparent, but still audible. Upstairs then. From the second floor it was clear the noise was coming from the floor above, from Philip's apartment. Above the crash of breaking china she heard coarse laughter.

She raced up the steps to Philip's door, only to find the doorframe splintered and broken, with a dirty footprint clearly visible on the door itself. Fern shook her head at the stupidity of thinking that the only attack on Philip would be magical.

She stepped through the door, a defensive spell forming in her mind and coming automatically to her lips. Before she could utter a single syllable, a heavyset man sprang at her from inside the kitchen. His fist swung back and connected with her face. She staggered, her head coming into violent contact with the wall. She slid down in a heap as the burly skin-headed man stepped over her, his face contorted by hate.

"Nosy bitch. Well, you got what's coming to you."

The skinhead took a look around the apartment. Apparently satisfied with his work, he walked out. In one hand he held a polished wooden box. Fern tried to grab his leg but he shook himself free with ease, his laugh loud and malignant. He ran down the stairs, his heavy steps felt through the floor.

Fern shook her head and touched her nose. It was clearly broken. Blood poured in a steady stream and her eyes watered. She blinked, trying to clear her vision and took a deep, shuddering breath, muttering a calming mantra while tipping her head back.

This was not a casual break-in. That box, whatever it was, mattered a great deal. To Philip.

She sat up and tugged her phone from her pocket. She had exchanged numbers with Philip the night they had dinner together. *Just in case*, she had said. Her foresight had turned out to be prophetic. She dialed Philip's number and he answered almost at once.

"Fern?" he said. His voice held a note of surprise.

"Philip," she gasped. "You had a break-in. I just caught an intruder in your apartment."

"Oh my god. Are you okay?"

"Yes, I'm fine. He punched me, the little drittsekk. I think he broke my nose. Some skinhead with an ugly face. I'm going to call the police and report the assault."

"I'm so sorry, Fern. Are you sure you're alright? Should I call an ambulance?"

"No, don't worry. I'm fine, really."

"Did you say a skinhead broke in?"

"Yes. Why?"

"It was Sumpter. Paul Sumpter. He used to live there. In your apartment."

"Okay. I'm sure the police will know where to find him. But Philip, he's trashed the place. It's such a mess! He broke everything. All your books are torn and ripped, and he slashed your chairs and sofa. Everything from the kitchen is broken. I'm just sorry that I couldn't stop him from taking whatever it was."

"What do you mean? Fern, what did he take?"

She could hear panic in his voice. Moments before he had sounded concerned for her safety, a fact that pleased her. Now there was something else. Something had given an edge to his fear.

"Just a little wooden box, as far as I could see."

There was a pause, the line quiet. When Philip spoke, his voice was controlled but she could sense real fear now. She started to feel scared too. This *was* more than just a casual robbery.

"Was it polished? Like a jewelry box?"

"Yes, maybe. I don't know."

"Fern, listen. You have to go to the bookshelf. On the top shelf is there a wooden box?"

Fern wiped away some of the stream of blood from her hose and levered herself up. "Hang on, I'll check."

She took a chair, the only one not broken, and stood on it before the book case.

"There's no box, Philip."

She heard a gasp and then his words came out in a rush.

"Fern, call the police. We have to stop him before it's too late."

"What is it, Philip. What was in the box?"

"I can't say, but it's vital I get it back."

"Is it something to do with what you told me? About Sandwell?"

"Yes. Look, I'll be back as fast as I can. Tell the police it was Sumpter, but do not tell them that Elizabeth Sandwell put him up to it."

He ended the call and Fern stared thoughtfully at the mess of broken glass, spilled food and smashed furniture. She got down from the chair and sank into it.

She dialed the emergency services and asked for the police. Almost immediately a woman's voice came on the line. "Detective Hanlon. What can I do for you."

"I want to report a burglary and an assault."

While she gave her name and address, Fern could hear the detective quickly conferring with someone. She distinctly heard Philip's name.

"Sorry," said Fern. "I thought I heard you say the name Entwhistle."

"Yes. We had a report about him last week. Do you know him?"

"He's my neighbor. It was his apartment that got robbed."

"I see. And he assaulted you, did he?"

"No. Of course not. It was someone else. I believe his name may be Paul Sumpter. I caught him breaking into my neighbor's apartment and he punched me in the face when I confronted him."

"Okay, miss. And you're sure it was this Sumpter, not Philip Entwhistle who assaulted you?"

Fern shook her head. This was crazy. She pressed on. "Of course, I'm sure. Look, you have to pick up Sumpter. He stole something valuable from my neighbor."

Again there was a whispered comment which she could not quite hear.

"Okay, miss, we've alerted a patrol car. Someone will be with you in a couple of minutes. Don't go anywhere, just sit tight."

Fern shook her head in disbelief. She closed her phone and tilted her head back. She could call John. Perhaps together they could tackle Sumpter? She already knew where Sandwell lived. The inner circle were now well aware of Dr. Elizabeth Sandwell. One of the circle, either Tessa or Alicia, would already be watching her house. With luck, they could intercept Sumpter before he delivered whatever it was he had taken. She would call Tessa, let her know the thug was on his way. She quickly punched a number into her phone again. The faint wailing of a police siren dimly heard in the distance. She would have to be quick.

Philip broke every speed limit racing back to his apartment, catching the flash of at least three speed cameras. He would probably lose his license as a result, but that was a problem for later. His phone rang. It was Sam.

"Philip, my boy. Congratulations. I had a look at the manuscript. It's good. Very good indeed."

Philip was hardly in the mood for talking about the book. He tried to cut Sam short without being obviously rude.

"Thanks, Sam. I'm in a rush right now, I can't talk."

"Well, that's okay. I just wanted to say that I think you found your Hail Mary after all. Well done."

Philip swerved around a slow-moving car, missing a high-speed frontal collision with a truck by scant seconds. His old car had not been made for this kind of driving.

"Just one more thing, Philip. I have to ask. Did you hear about Sandwell?"

Philip had heard entirely too much about Sandwell. Enough to last a lifetime. But he could not help himself and his curiosity got the better of him.

"No, what about her?"

"She's been suspended. Conduct unbecoming and all that. She had a master key to all the offices! Can you believe it? Seems that you were right all along."

"Okay, Sam. Thanks. Got to go."

He unceremoniously hung up. Sandwell suspended. They believed him now. It hardly mattered now she had taken the one thing he had promised to protect and could not afford to lose.

He put his foot down on the accelerator and the engine groaned its response. A bucket of bolts it might be, but it was hitting ninety. He felt proud of it. Until there was a savage bang and the back wheels locked, skidding the car into a wild fishtail.

Philip fought the wheel, trying to turn into the skid as he had been taught over a decade before. He almost succeeded but then the back end drifted away and he lost control. The car spun, slamming into the embankment at the side of the road with a tremendous thud that left Philip shaken. If the car had turned the other way . . . it did not bear thinking about.

He reached for his phone, but it was lying in the footwell, flung there by the force of the crash. A flash of light in the mirror told him it was too late. A police cruiser had pulled in behind, its lights flashing blue and white erratically.

Philip slumped back in his seat. Perhaps he could persuade the police to take him to Sandwell's house. If he could just figure out a way to explain. But he did not even know where she lived. He slumped into his seat. It was over. He had messed everything up and there was nothing he could do about it.

A heavyset officer emerged, approaching cautiously. His bright Day-Glo jacket in no way reduced the intimidation factor of his size or authority. In fact, the incongruity heightened it. Like seeing a clown; carrying an Uzi.

He rapped on the window and Philip dutifully wound it down. The officer leaned forward. "Do you know how fast you were going then, sir?"

Philip looked up. There was no point denying anything. He had been speeding and he did not care. He shrugged. "It doesn't matter," he said.

The officer scowled, pulling out his ticket book. "I think," he said, "that you will find that it matters very much. License please, sir." He held out a hand expectantly.

Philip sighed, his hand reaching into his jacket pocket. He brushed the silver chain around his neck as he did, and his skin tingled. He paused, then pulled out his wallet and extracted the license, passing it to the officer.

The officer examined it, then looked at Philip, frowning. "Is this license yours, sir?"

"What? Yes, of course."

"It says here that you are five ten, weigh one seventy, and have green eyes. I am not normally one for staring into another man's eyes, but I could not help noting that you, sir, have blue eyes. Very blue. So, whose license is this then?"

Philip was surprised for a moment. Blue eyes. Of course, Jinny was linked to him now. Curious, he grasped the silver chain and the talisman, the presence of the djinn immediately there. He could feel her in his mind. She was in pain.

I have need of you, little man.

The talisman grew so cold it burned. Philip gasped and the officer looked down at him. "What are you do . . ."

The driver's seat was empty. The officer looked around in bemusement.

# Then death will surely be the cost

## 12

Realize this: one day your soul
will depart your body and you will
be drawn beyond the curtain that separates us
from the unknown.

*—Rubaiyat of Omar Khayyam*

Elizabeth Sandwell shrugged off a sheer silk robe as she entered the attic, in one hand a polished wooden box. It was locked, but that was no hindrance. Naked, she padded across the room and gently placed the box on a low table next to the ritual items, her sacred Athame, with the polished bone handle, a vial containing a dark and viscous fluid, and a silver bowl — twin to the one in her office — filled with salt.

Focusing her mind on the lock, it clicked open obediently. She lifted the lid and carefully removed the clay dish. Holding it from her, she raised one hand over the bowl. Small blue sparks flitted between it and her palm.

Ridiculous that Entwhistle had been given this boon. So much power to one who could not wield it. It was a waste and she was right to take it. If not her, then it would just be someone else. Someone undeserving. Besides, he had wronged her and now he was going to pay. They would *all* pay.

With the sacrifice of the djinn, her Master would give what was promised and she would finally be free, unshackled from the limitations of her frail, mortal frame. What she could achieve after that was beyond imagination. She would be like a god. She would *be* God.

Sending Sumpter to get the binding vessel had paid off. Not only did he find it, miracle of miracles, but the timing could not have been better. The djinn had just transferred itself to Entwhistle and it would be days before it recovered its full strength.

She took a moment to admire the design of the pentacle she had created. It was very different from the one she had laid out for the previous spell. This was not going to be a mere summoning. This time there was an offering of great meaning and value. The Master had instructed her carefully on its construction, and she felt a thrill of pleasure. But it was far from complete.

The pattern on the floor followed the semi-traditional methods known to all practitioners of the occult science. A perfect circle, binding the points of a pentagram spanning its diameter. At the heart of the pentagram a smaller circle, the conduit, the channel to the other realms. Sandwell ceremoniously placed the djinn's bowl at the center of the inner circle. Going to the gabled window, she yanked aside the tattered curtains behind which a six-inch railroad spike hung from a piece of cord. She tugged the iron free and hefted its weight in her hand. She would still take precautions. Weak as it was, the djinn was not defenseless. Not yet.

She carefully lay the spike over the meta-anchor then she got the silver bowl from the table. She scooped up a handful of salt and sprinkled it over the vessel. Salt and iron diminished the creature. The djinn would be unable to manifest. Not without her allowing it.

Sandwell scooped more salt into her hand. Getting down on her knees, slowly, painstakingly, she started to stream the tiny crystals in thin lines, creating symbols, sigils of power. She worked assiduously, correcting even the smallest irregularity. In time, the circumference of the inner circle was ringed with the intricate designs. Then she started working on the outer circle. It was slow going and she soon felt shooting pains in her back and knees. But it was a sweet agony, something to relish, knowing what it would gain her. What she accomplished this day would last forever. She smiled, the point of her pink tongue wetting her lips.

Metaphysical geometry was as much a science as the study of physics. It *was* physics, but without the blinkers. Her research into the basic building blocks of magic had led her to rediscover some of the most ancient wisdoms. But it was the Entity, her Master, that had enabled her to progress so far. It was in tune with the higher planes and controlled energies that she still only understood theoretically. After years of supplication, she had come to win its favor and it now accepted her as its disciple.

It had no name, or at least, none it was willing to share. It was demanding, capricious, and just as likely to hurt as help her, but she had persisted in her devotion. And it had paid off. She had become more powerful than any other follower of the old ways. Capable of doing things that would seem miraculous to both the initiated and uninitiated.

Finally done with the salt, she stood, careful not to disturb a single grain. Any small variation in the circuit could have disastrous consequences. What she was calling forth was volatile and balance had to be maintained. Too much energy, or energy of the wrong kind, and it would spoil everything. And that would be bad. Don't cross the streams. She smiled grimly at the thought.

She was ready to begin. She took a deep breath and then another. Try as she might she could not stop her heart pounding. If anything were to go wrong! But she could not think like that. She had worked her whole life to get to this point. She had sacrificed much of herself and nothing was going to stop her achieving her destiny. She was more than ready; she was born for this.

Walking slowly to the table, Sandwell put down the silver bowl and took the small bottle containing the black liquid, pulling the cork that sealed it. She took a deep breath, then put the bottle to her lips. The contents slid down her throat, thick and cloying. Fighting an urge to gag, she swallowed, wiping her mouth on the back of her hand. Now she took the knife, her sacred blade. The Athame - the instrument of her deliverance, and the djinn's demise.

She gasped as she felt the drug enter her system and begin to work. Her pupils expanded until her violet eyes were black, then shrank again until they were little more than dark pinpricks. She laughed, the sound wild and free. A lovely laugh, innocent as a child's, without guile or malice, taking pleasure in something simple and pure. And as she laughed she gently sliced the flesh of her belly with her razor sharp knife. Again and again. Blood welled up from the shallow cuts, plainly marking the outline of a pentagram in her pale flesh. It was time.

Philip did not know where he was. He was not dead. At least, he did not think so. But he was not in his car, that much was for certain. He was not even sure if this was still Earth. Whatever this place was, it was strange; alien.

The light hurt his eyes. Not bright exactly, but sharp and brittle. Everything was gray and formless and out of focus. As if seeing through a thick fog, yet at the same time, there was a brilliance to the light, as if it were refracting off untold diamonds. There were shapes, some moving, but they were indistinct, far away. Still, they frightened him. He closed his eyes but was too anxious to keep them shut.

His head hurt. There had been an accident. Was he in a hospital? He felt like he was being squeezed and stretched simultaneously. Perhaps he had a concussion? He couldn't be sure. He wasn't sure of much anymore. He remembered talking to the police officer, and then . . . this.

As his eyes adjusted, he made out tiny bright points of light in the grayness, glowing gold and yellow and occasionally purple. They hung in the air, suspended like fireflies, yet somehow he knew they were vastly far away. And in that moment he understood. The words of the djinn came back to him. *The lower mortals are many. They glow brightly. They burn. We can see them. We can see them burning . . .*

This was how the djinn saw the world. The lights were people. Their spirits, or aura. This was where the djinn came from. This was *their* world. It occupied the same space, yet was somehow apart. *A different dimension?*

He found it hard to breathe. Everything felt slightly wrong. Even the air hurt his lungs, and every movement was fraught with pain. The hairs on his neck stiffened and he felt a rising fear. A cold sensation that began in his groin and worked its way up to his stomach.

There was a presence nearby. It was getting closer. He could feel it coming. Like the blast of wind from a tunnel when a train roared through, it was upon him. Strong, overwhelming his senses, he cringed mentally before it. A force of malignant energy coursing around him, bludgeoning its way into his mind, cold, hard and angry.

*WRONGNESS. NOT BELONG.*

A djinn had found him and Philip was more frightened than he had ever been. He gasped compulsively, like a fish stranded on a beach. He was sure that it would hurt or even kill him. In its own dimension, the djinn were not ephemeral creatures of formless thought. It was a tidal wave of remorseless strength. His fear tasted sour in his mouth. Again, the djinn brutalized his consciousness.

*LEAVE THIS PLACE.*

Philip wanted to explain. He wanted to say he was not there through choice. He had been brought there, he was not responsible. But he could not speak. He could hardly think. The djinn overpowered him.

All he could manage was a feeble thought. A visceral reaction to the weight of the raging djinn's power. And with all of his own meager strength he called out.

"Jinny, help!"

It was only a moment before he felt another presence; this one familiar. He saw images flashing in his mind. A black cat with blue eyes, a man with long golden hair, a bird of prey, resting on the arm of an armored knight. And Jinny enveloped Philip, her strange energy comforting, fending off the rage of the other Djinn.

*This one is mine. He is protected.*

Philip could feel the other presence withdraw slightly, then it surged back stronger than ever.

*NOT BELONG!*

*I claim him. He is mine.*

*ATLN FAILED. YOU HAVE NOT THE RIGHT!*

And for just a moment Philip saw a shape in the fog. Like a man, but too tall, too slender. Then it was gone. Jinny's presence was subtle where the other's was brutal and Philip found he could think and feel again. And as his fear subsided, the researcher in him resurfaced. He breathed deeply, though the air still hurt his lungs.

"Jinny. Is this your world?"

*Yes. This is our plane. You cannot exist here for long. But I have strength enough for this. I have need of you.*

Philip was no longer frightened. He did not know if he was becoming numb to the environment or if Jinny was doing something. His emotions were muffled, as if this place did not encompass feelings. But Jinny needed him and it seemed he needed her. If only to get back to the safety of his own world.

"Where are you? What do you need?"

*Hold the talisman. It will draw you to me. I am in grave danger.*

Philip clutched the talisman. Where before it had been cold to the touch, now it burned his hand. He grimaced, but held it tight. Immediately he felt a pull on his mind. The gray fog turned to white and then was gone. Shocked, Philip realized he was back in the real world. He glimpsed a table, bare rafters and a rough wooden floor. There was something white on the floor. No, gold. A pattern. He shook his head as he staggered slightly, body overwhelmed by the transition.

He could hear a rhythmic chanting. The words writhed in his mind like snakes. The room darkened then, as suddenly as if a switch had been thrown. He felt a chill wash through his mind and his testicles shriveled in response.

He took a step, then there was a sensation of movement and he was grabbed from behind. The hand in his hair pulling, jerking his head back, forcing him to stand straight. By the time he saw the blade it was too late.

"Not this time, Philip."

Sandwell. He could feel her body pressing against his back. Was she naked? Humming, she pulled again on his hair, jerking viciously. A tiny movement of her other hand and warm blood trickled down his neck. He let out an involuntary groan, in equal parts pain and fear at the realization that the blade was not an empty threat. Sandwell meant him harm. Right here, right now.

Dozens of gnarled tallow candles littered the floor, their feeble glow illuminating nothing. A shiver coursed through Philip, the candles ineffective against the pervasive chill that seemed to suck both heat and light from the room. Shadows moved, growing deeper. He felt certain there were things in them. Bad things. Watching. Waiting.

A dormer window with ragged curtains looked out over the residential street below. It was not just the layer of grime on the glass; the murk in the room was far more than daylight's mere absence.

Was it still daytime? How long had he been in that other place? That other *world*? Perhaps the power that had snatched him from his car and transported him to Sandwell's attic was not as instantaneous as it had felt. One moment he was racing back to London, the next he was ... somewhere ... and then he was here.

Philip inched his head around, starkly conscious of the pressing blade. On his periphery, he could make out a bowl in the center of an ornate circle and star pattern etched on the floor. An honest-to-God pentacle! It glowed, pulsing pale gold, its gentle rhythm like a heartbeat.

Despite himself, Philip marveled at the situation. He was a historian. His only concern lately had been a promotion, and now he was about to be killed by a twenty-first century witch. The absurdity of it all! He made a sound halfway between a nervous snort and a laugh. Sandwell yanked his head back again.

"Is it funny, Philip? Is this?" She pressed the blade harder. Another flash of pain as it sliced into him and the trickle of blood became a stream.

"No!"

Through the gloom, he could see something lying across the bowl. A railroad spike? Of course. Salt and iron to disable the elemental. He pulled away from the blade, pressing himself back against Sandwell's breasts; a parody of an embrace, his empty hands clenched impotently at his sides. She jerked his head savagely. He had never felt so powerless.

Sandwell leaned in close. He could feel her hot breath, then, incredibly, her probing tongue in his ear. He recoiled in disgust. Mistake. A line of fire lanced across his throat as the blade cut another shallow trough in his skin. Now it was Sandwell's turn to laugh. Blood flowed in a hot, steady stream, collecting in the hollow of his collarbone, soaking into his shirt. She was getting off on this, making him squirm. He stopped struggling, denying her the satisfaction. She pulled away.

"You're just in time, Philip," she said. "I've waited a long time for this."

"Liz, I don't know what you're trying to do here" –he tried to sound confident but his voice betrayed him, cracking with fear– "but if it's what I think, then I can't let you."

She laughed again, this time husky and low. He could feel her breath on his ear again. Her voice was seductive, almost a whisper.

"Let me? I don't see how you can stop me. I take what I want, when I want. You should know that by now."

He flinched. What she had done to him that night came back in a rush. He could still feel her nails ripping into his chest, and the memory of what she had made him swallow . . . he almost gagged. She laughed in delight at his reaction.

"Please, Elizabeth," he gasped, lips barely moving. "You don't need to do this."

"No," she said. "No, you're right, of course."

He felt her move away and relief flooded through him. Then the hand in his hair tightened and her body pressed hard against his.

"But I want to."

He could hear the smile in her voice as she drew back the blade. In one sharp movement, the knife bit into his neck. He jerked spastically, knees buckling in shock. His hands clutched at his throat, trying to close the wound, to stem the bright crimson that spurted in time with his wildly beating heart.

Falling to his knees, he looked up at her in mute accusation. She stood over him, triumphant, her eyes wide and shining, pupils mere pin-pricks. The pentacle flared, power coursing brightly throughout the lines and arcane words.

Philip's blood arced across Sandwell's breasts and belly but she did not appear to notice or care, her lips curling into a lascivious smile as she breathed deeply, a smell like hot copper filling the darkness.

Instinct told him the wound was fatal. But instinct, too, drove him on. With one hand clutching his throat, Philip tried to crawl towards the pentacle. Sandwell laughed. Philip reached the edge of the circle, then collapsed. There was no pain. In seconds his brain was starving for oxygen and his eyes began to dim. Only the pentacle held any light and he reached out to it.

One hand touched the salt of the outer ring. Philip pushed forward, brushing aside the arcane sigils and symbols that traced the circumference. He slumped, just inside the pentacle, rolling onto his back. His blood stained the salt pink. It started to dissolve. As the circle broke, the glow faded, leaving only an after-image in his retina. Dimly heard, Sandwell's panicked voice sounded.

"No! No!"

His blood pulsed feebly. Philip reached out for the bowl, but he was too weak. Sandwell moved to stop him, reaching out to pull him away. Out of strength, his hand fell upon the bowl's rim. He fumbled, knocking against the heavy metal spike, causing it to roll slowly to one side before falling with a thud to the wooden floor.

For a moment everything was still, then there was a thunderclap and a blast of wind tore through the attic. The flames on the candles curved over, almost horizontal in the fierce, howling gale. The wind began to turn, to gyre. Swirling around the room, it centered on the pentacle, growing tighter, closer, a twisting maelstrom.

Through dimming eyes, Philip could see Sandwell. She stood above him, staring at something over the pentacle, her face a rictus of fear. Then she shrieked in abject terror, her scream cutting through the raging wind. A shape formed above the supine form of the historian. An utter absence of light. A void, primal and raging. Sandwell turned to run but the void pulled her back. For a moment there was a shape in the black, as if darkness had taken form. Something vast and terrible existed there and for the briefest of moments Philip saw something reaching out. Sandwell resisted, then she was pulled into the darkness. There were no more screams.

Philip closed his eyes. All he could hear was a pulsing roar, like the sound of the sea inside a conch shell, then that too began to fade away. The last thing he heard was the faintest of whispers in his mind. Just the suggestion of a sound. *Not this time.* Then the world turned black.


Philip's leg hurt and his head was pounding. What? He had died. He had felt his life ebbing away, then nothing. Could he have a headache in the afterlife? Would it last forever? How very ironic. Anyway, he didn't even believe in an afterlife. Realization dawned slowly. He experimented with opening an eye. He could see the open rafters of the ceiling clearly, and dust motes circling lazily in the air. The attic was now flooded with light from the window. He was clearly not dead after all, but he was still in Sandwell's house.

For a moment more he lay still, enjoying the fact that he was breathing. Then the horror of the last minutes rushed in on him and he grasped at his throat. There was nothing to feel, the skin unbroken.

He was still inside the ruined circle, almost gagging on the smell. The room reeked of ozone. And something else: blood. *His* blood. The floorboards were covered with the dark substance. He sat up carefully, and looked around. Whatever presence Sandwell had called forth, it was gone now, and apparently she with it.

Jinny's bowl was lying within reach and he grabbed it, mouth curling in distaste at the dark puddle within. Everywhere was a sticky conflation of blood and salt. He stood, trying to avoid touching it as he clambered to his feet.

"Jinny?"

Nothing. No response. No sense of her presence either. He grasped the talisman and directed his thoughts towards the elemental. Jinny, please. What happened here? Talk to me! The absence was palpable, like a piece of himself missing.

He was alone in the room. Looking about he saw the implement of his death, lying discarded on the floor, the white bone handle of the knife contrasting starkly with the crimson puddle beneath. He shuddered. Carefully, he started to pick his way through the blood to the attic door but he stumbled, knocking over a lit candle directly below the loose hanging curtains. They instantly caught and flames quickly climbed towards the ceiling. Philip stood gaping, as if bemused by the spreading conflagration.

A wave of heat washed over him and he was suddenly conscious of the fact that he was standing in a burning building. He backed away from the roaring animal that now spread across the ceiling. He spotted the door, and staggered towards it.

He made his way down the narrow stairs, almost falling several times as his balance fled. By the time he got to the ground-floor, the noise of the burning building was a physical presence. He strode to the front door. A window shattered somewhere and the roaring took on a new urgency as fresh air fanned the flames.

He pulled open the door and ran outside, straight into a petite woman with short brown hair marching determinedly up the path towards him.

"Who are you?" she demanded.

Philip tried to push past her, but she obstructed his path. He looked her in the eye. "My name isn't important. There's a fire. We need to get clear."

She looked him up and down, taking in the state of his blood-soaked clothes. "Are you Entwhistle?"

He did not even try to hide his surprise. He nodded curtly and the woman grabbed his arm.

"Okay, come on then. I'm Alicia."

Philip resisted, pulling his arm away.

"A friend of Fern's."

At the mention of Fern he succumbed, allowing her to propel him towards a battered car parked at an angle in the driveway. She flung open the passenger door, pushed him inside, then raced to get behind the wheel.

"Stay down," she ordered and immediately put the car into gear, pulling into the road and flooring the accelerator. Philip could not resist looking back. The house was engulfed in flames, burning much faster than he would have expected. People were emerging from their houses, pointing and milling about, shielding their eyes from the black smoke coiling into the air. He caught sight of an old woman. He was sure she was looking right at him, then they were past. Catching a flash of blue, Philip ducked out of sight as a police cruiser sped by, in the direction of the fire, its emergency lights frenetically announcing its presence. A uniformed officer was at the wheel but in the passenger seat was none other than Detective Hanlon, the officer who had grilled him with such determination.

If they caught him here, there would be no explaining his way out. He hunkered down lower, looking up at his rescuer. Who *was* she?

Philip poured steaming water into his cup, a cloth around the copper handle protecting his hand.

He sipped the tea as he stared out at the back garden. Francis had dedicated it to his wife, but Philip could only think of it as belonging to the old man. It would always belong to Sir James. He put his cup down on the windowsill next to Jinny's meta-anchor. The small clay bowl had a brown substance within that he could not bring himself to clean. Dried blood. His blood. Philip was not sure what had happened but suspected it was the blood that had undone the pentacle, causing Sandwell's spell to fail.

But he had freed the djinn. Freed it just long enough to save him. Jinny must have given everything she had to bring him back. *Not this time.* And now she was gone. Dead, or back to her own plane of existence, Philip did not know. But one thing was for sure, he had failed. Jinny, the old man, himself.

In the carefully manicured garden the absence of the old man's care was already noticeable. He would have to mow the grass soon. And that tree needed cutting back. He could still see Francis in his mind's eye, pulling weeds, creating the quintessential English Eden. He would never be able to equal the old man in his dedication.

Fern had offered to help. She knew a thing or two about gardens, she said. Thinking of the young Norwegian woman was almost enough to raise a smile on his lips. They had become very friendly. More than that, even. He would have to take her up on the offer. Should he pay her? That would not be a problem. He was making more money now and Francis had left him the cottage and a deal else besides. He no longer had to worry about the rent or a mortgage. He did not really have to worry about anything it seemed. He did not even need to concern himself with Sandwell either. She was gone. Dead most likely, but he could not say for sure. Sandwell's house had burned to the ground but no remains had been recovered. She was officially missing. He alone knew the truth, or at least, some of it. Where she actually was didn't matter. Gone was gone, and good riddance.

The woman who had rescued him was a witch too. One of Fern's *coven*. He marveled that he could say that and not think it a joke. She said her name was Alicia, and he later learned that she was the Mother in their *circle*. Fern was the Maiden. Intellectually he understood that this was a representation of aspects of the Goddess, but there his knowledge ran a bit thin. But there should be three. Three aspects . . . a trilogy. So who was the crone?

It was three days since he had died and been resurrected. He didn't feel any different, no great epiphany.

He had not planned to move into Little Flower Cottage and carry on with his life as if nothing had happened, but that is exactly what he had done. Sumpter had trashed his apartment and Philip simply did not have the heart to clean the place up. There would be time for dealing with the mess later.

Fern had promised to visit. That would help get his mind off things. He felt slightly better at that thought. He liked her. A lot. In spite of her . . . interests?

The strident chirping of his phone startled him. He searched the pockets of the jacket on his chair.

"Hello?"

"Philip, it's me, Sam. How are you doing?"

"Fine, I guess. I moved into the cottage yesterday."

"Super. I have to say I'm still surprised about that. I would write more if there was a chance someone would leave me a house." He laughed. Philip found his gentle chuckle welcome, even if he did not share it.

Philip had explained his windfall by saying that Francis and he had become good friends, and that he appreciated someone taking an interest in his family. And as the last of the Francis clan, he simply decided to leave it to the one person who wanted to tell the true story of his illustrious ancestor.

Sam had thought it odd but did not question it. Philip was half afraid of suggestions that he had acted improperly in some way, perhaps taken advantage of a confused old man. He could hardly tell anyone about the deal he had made.

"What can I do for you, Sam?"

"Well, after that business with Sandwell stealing a master key she was removed from consideration for the Professorship. At that point it was a bit of a forgone conclusion. And now that she's disappeared, done a runner most likely, we only had one viable choice. Still, we had to follow form. We met yesterday and the vote was unanimously in your favor. I would like to be the first to congratulate you, Professor Entwhistle."

Philip supposed he should be pleased. He did not feel much like celebrating but he tried to muster some enthusiasm. His voice came out flat, even so.

"Thank you, Sam. I can't tell you how much this means to me."

If Sam detected anything untoward in Philip's reply, he did not remark upon it. Sam continued in his jovial way.

"You deserve it. If Sandwell hadn't been found with her hand in the cookie jar then perhaps the decision would have gone her way. Still, the end result is what matters. You got it! And your manuscript is good, Philip. Very good indeed. Not too sure of the title though. *Blood in the Sand.* It's a bit, well, melodramatic, isn't it? Raising a lot of eyebrows already, I can tell you. You're keeping it?"

Change the title? No. He would not alter one single word. It was Sir James Francis' story and he had told it as faithfully as he could. He would not betray his memory. Not on top of everything else.

"That's the title. Actually, I had a call from my publisher. They're talking about mainstream distribution."

"Are they, by God! Well, that will put a feather in your cap."

They concluded their talk. Sam's energy was infectious. In spite of himself Philip felt a little better. He looked out to the garden. He would make a start on it. Turning to the back door, heading for the potting shed, he failed to notice the slight stirring in the air, a faint shimmer like a tiny heatwave forming over the old clay bowl in the kitchen window, then it was gone.

# ABOUT THE AUTHOR

MJ Kobernus is an Anglo/American living and working in Norway. He is the founder of Nordland Publishing. He loves his work as an editor and publisher and hopes to continue doing that for many years. He also works in the Environmental arena, doing unspeakable things to bits and bytes.

MJ drives a vintage motorcycle, plays a vintage guitar and has a love of 70s rock music. You can find out more about him on his personal blog, Metaphysical Geometry.

http://metaphysicalgeometry.blogspot.no/

Blood in the Sand, is his first major novel, and is the first installment of the Guardian series. Look out for the next book, Blood in the Snow.

MJ Kobernus

# NORDLAND PUBLISHING
## Follow the North Road.

nordlandpublishing.com
facebook.com/nordlandpublishing
nordlandpublishing.tumblr.com

NORDLAND

www.nordlandpublishing.com